CW01261379

Moscow's Shadows

Kiev's Light

The Story Of A Ukraine Family In Exile

By

Nicholas P Clark

Copyright © 2025 Nicholas P. Clark

All rights reserved.

No part of this book may be used or reproduced, distributed, or transmitted in any form or by any means, including photocopying, recording, or other electronic or mechanical methods, without the proper written permission of the publisher, except in the case of brief quotations apart, embodied in critical reviews and certain other non-commercial uses permitted by copyright law. Use of this publication is permitted solely for personal use and must include full attribution of the material's source.

Table of Contents

A New Beginning 5
   Jack's Quiet Life 6
   Anya's Arrival 14
   Setting Up House 23

Whispers of Danger 33
   Anya's Confession 34
   Echoes of Espionage 42
   Shadows in the Dark 48

The Shadows of the Past 59
   Memories Resurface 60
   The Cost of Secrets 68
   A Call to Action 76

A Mother's Plea 87
   Anya's Desperation 88
   Building Trust 95
   A Dangerous Alliance 102

The Game of Shadows 111
   Unraveling the Threads 112
   Dangerous Liaisons 120
   The Net Tightens 127

Crossing Lines 135
   The Tension Mounts 136
   A Breakthrough—And Setback 144
   The Crossing 154

The Unraveling 167
   Pieces Falling Into Place 168
   The Race Against Time 176
   Shocking Revelations 186

Betrayal and Trust 195
   Unveiling the Enemy 196

    Allies Turned Enemies 205
    A Moment of Decision.. 223
A Light in the Darkness 233
    Finding Strength 234
    A Plan in Motion 243
    A Symbol of Hope 252
The Final Confrontation 261
    The Calm Before the Storm.. 262
    The Showdown... 270
    Aftermath and Reflection.. 280
A New Dawn 289
    Healing Wounds 290
    Jack's Redemption... 299
    A Brighter Future 308
From the Author..317

A New Beginning

Jack's Quiet Life

Jack Malaney stood by the back door of his quaint stone cottage, gazing out at the sprawling English countryside that stretched before him like an unending canvas of green. The soft morning light cast a gentle glow on the rolling hills, and he could hear the quiet hum of nature awakening around him. It was a world untouched by the tumult he had left behind, a sanctuary where he could seek solace from the ghosts that haunted his past.

He inhaled deeply, filling his lungs with the crisp, fresh air, laden with the fragrant scent of blooming flowers and damp earth. It was a far cry from the dank, smoke-filled rooms of intelligence briefings or the hurried exchanges of encrypted messages. Here, there were no codewords or double agents, just the sweet, melodic chirping of birds and the whisper of the wind through the trees. This was the life he had imagined in retirement—a simple, quiet existence where he could tend to his garden and lose himself in the pages of books.

Every day began with a meticulous routine. After a cup of steaming coffee and a light breakfast, Jack would dress in well-worn denim jeans and a plaid shirt, a far cry from the tailored suits he once donned for clandestine meetings. With a pair of sturdy boots, he set out into his garden, a patch of modest size but filled to the brim with life. He nurtured rows of vegetable beds—carrots, tomatoes, and herbs neatly arranged—with a gardener's precision honed through years of careful observation and methodical practice.

His fingers, now calloused from work, buried themselves in the rich, dark soil as he tended to each plant lovingly. The act of nurturing life brought Jack a sense of peace that eluded him during his days at MI6. Yet, even in this pastoral paradise, shadows lurked—a constant reminder of decisions made and people lost.

There were moments, often triggered by the slightest sound or scent, that would whisk him back years to filled hotel rooms in distant countries, flickering shadows cast by the glow of street lamps in enemy territories, and hurried whispers that once meant life or death. The fear and adrenaline were long gone, but the echoes of those days remained lodged deep within his consciousness. He would pause mid-weed, lost in thought, and feel the weight of nights spent wrestling with guilt and responsibility. How many lives had he altered? How many choices had he made that could never be undone?

After a few hours of communing with his plants, Jack would retreat to the comfort of his cozy living room, its worn leather armchair positioned just so that the afternoon sun would spill over him like a warm embrace. Here, he would curl up with the books he had collected over the years—novels infused with the romance of espionage, biographies of spies whose lives unfolded in ways he could relate to, and even some classics that expanded his understanding of the human condition. Engrossed in words, he often found a fleeting sense of adventure, an echo of a life that now felt like a distant memory.

His neighbors, relatively few in number due to the distance between homes in such a rural setting, had learned to appreciate the tranquil presence of their reclusive new resident. Jack would exchange pleasantries at the local market, greeting Mrs. Hargrove as she meticulously arranged her display of jams and preserves. Conversations were polite, punctuated by smiles, but always carried an air of distance—never probing too deeply into one another's lives. In a small village, where everyone knew each other's business, Jack felt both curious and comfortable in remaining a mystery.

He would often visit the little shop run by Mr. Evans, a kind-eyed man with a penchant for storytelling. It was never difficult to find common ground; they swapped tales of the weather and mutual acquaintances, sharing a chuckle over the antics of the village's free-roaming sheep that were known to create chaos at the worst possible moments. Yet, when the laughter faded, Jack would feel the pull of solitude gnawing at him, the realization that despite the warm community around him, he was ultimately alone.

He had purposely chosen this life, yet Jack could not shake the thread of restlessness woven into the fabric of his days. He would lie awake at night, staring at the ceiling of his room, each creak of the old beams surrounding him singing a lullaby of comfort—yet all he felt was a longing for significance. What had he given up for this serene existence? Was it really what he wanted, to blend in with the wallpaper of rural England, living out the rest of his days in quiet obscurity?

Occasionally, the remnants of the past would reach him through letters from old colleagues or murmurs in the news. Jack tried to distance himself from headlines concerning international unrest; the last remnants of his past life tugged at him—reminding him of the inevitable chaos that threaded through the world. Each letter opened like a Pandora's box, filled with tales of treachery and spy games that seemed both thrilling and senselessly destructive. He could not help but feel drawn back to the life it depicted, the intrigue that charged the air, yet he resisted with every fiber of his being, trying to remain focused on the simpler pleasures of planting seedlings and counting the stars on a clear night.

On Mondays, Jack made a point to visit the local pub, The Foxhound, a rustic establishment where oak beams crisscrossed the ceiling, and the scent of roasted meat wafted through the air. It was his only indulgence—an opportunity to engage social circles, if only for a fleeting moment. He would order a pint of bitters and retire to a quiet corner, keenly observing the jovial camaraderie shared by others. He watched as old friends laughed and recounted stories from a time that felt vibrant and full of life. Yet, he found himself in a realm removed from it all, a bystander carefully studying a world he no longer fully belonged to.

Despite the laughter that echoed through the pub, a gnawing sense of detachment crept upon him like an unwelcome fog. He would allow himself to participate in light banter, nodding empathetically at their troubles, but he seldom ventured beyond surface-level conversations. Jack's quiet life had become a series of shallow encounters, lightened only by the occasional nod from those who might sense hidden depths beneath his composed exterior. But the reality was, he wore an impenetrable mask that kept others at arm's length, shielding himself from the vulnerability that inevitably accompanied genuine connection.

The solitude weighed heavy on him, and with each passing day, he wrestled with a growing sense of purposelessness. What good was a life lived merely for quietude when he possessed knowledge that could contribute to something greater? He'd fought hard for his country, sharp intelligence and deduced truths leading him to act for the greater good. But with absence came questions—were those sacrifices now in vain?

In the late afternoons, he strayed from the garden to find solace in a nearby grove, a tranquil patch of trees that stood sentinel over the land, giving him respite from the world. He often sat on a wooden bench, worn smooth by time, contemplating the rolling hills that surrounded him. Here, under the verdant boughs filtering the sunlight, he allowed himself to sift through memories—both precious and painful. A breeze would rustle through the leaves, and he would close his eyes, allowing the fleeting moments of clarity to wash over him, reminding him that beneath the surface of his composed life lay a tempest yearning to be unleashed.

Then there were days when the shadows of the past loomed larger, days filled with explosive recollections of missions gone awry and the faces of those left behind. Jack vividly recalled the night he had made a critical error—an innocent casualty lingering in his mind like an unwanted guest. The weight of that choice pressed on him like a stone, a constant reminder that the world of espionage was unforgiving and blurred with shades of gray.

He had spent years believing he was serving a greater cause, thwarting threats before they wreaked havoc, yet how easy it was for morality to become twisted when faced with the cold calculus required for survival. As he sat in the grove, listening to the gentle rustling of leaves, Jack yearned for a way to atone for those choices while reconciling such a yearning with his decision to pursue a quieter existence.

Moments of introspection were often disrupted by the slightest noise—a squirrel darting between trees or the distant sound of children rejoicing on a warm summer afternoon. Once again, Jack would notice the bittersweet thread of longing stir within him—children's laughter echoing pure and bright, the kind of unfiltered joy that he missed in his own life.

He had never married, nor did he have children of his own. In his line of work, relationships often felt like a distraction, a weakness he could not afford. He frequently reminded himself that his actions were necessary to protect future generations—yet, as he spent time ruminating under the trees, he felt the hollow ache of human connection bubble to the surface, undergoing a metamorphosis from longing into desperation.

Nicholas P. Clark

He found himself reflecting on the vision he had once held—where he would return to the fold as a husband or father, sharing quiet dinners and bedtime stories. Those had been dreams borne from hopes which felt impossibly distant now. Instead, his world had shrunk to the solitary existence he had chosen, and as the years slipped by, the elusive affirmations of companionship slipped further from his grasp.

As the sun dipped lower in the sky, casting elongated shadows across the landscape, Jack would rise from his reflections, brushing dirt off his pants, signaling a transition back into the routine he had crafted. The day would retreat into twilight, and he would find himself preparing a simple meal, steam wafting through the air, enveloping him in the comforting aroma of roasted vegetables and herbs—each slice and stir performed with practiced precision. While he cooked, the loneliness would sneak around the edges of his mind, settling in like a heavy cloak.

In those quiet evenings, as darkness snuffed out the colors of the day, Jack would reflect on the contrast between his past life and the solitude he had chosen. Guilt surfaced frequently, a reminder of the knowledge he carried, the connections he had severed, and the tangled web of espionage he had fled. It was a strange comfort, for in a world where he no longer held secrets, he still carried their weight.

Yet there was a measure of hope simmering beneath the surface. Beneath the initial discomfort of solitude lay a yearning for connection—one that Jack had yet to fully recognize. Perhaps it was the memory of laughter he missed most, the honest presence of another soul shared across a table. As he cast remnants of the day into the compost pile, the promise of new growth surged within him, whispering that maybe this restless yearning for significance was not so far removed from the life he had known.

Then certainty would seep back into his mindset. Maybe it wasn't too late to embrace the uncertainty of new beginnings—a notion robust enough to pull him from the steady chains of monotony and rekindle the flame of possibility. The thought kindled something within him; it ignited a flicker of adventure in his soul that reminded him he could still shape the course of his life, carving out significance from the remnants of his choices.

He took a moment, standing alone in the fading light, and closed his eyes with the wind kissing his face. Despite the heaviness of the past, Jack found a semblance of peace again in the knowledge that change was on the horizon. Little did he know that soon the quiet life he cherished so profoundly would intersect with a story woven with chaos, urgency, and an unanticipated connection that would reignite the heart he thought he had sealed away.

For now, he turned towards the twilight. Wrapped in the tranquility he had found, he would relish the simplicity of this moment. However, in those waning shadows, something new was stirring, a possibility lurking just beyond the edge of the familiar—a promise of adventure ready to push him into the light once more.

Anya's Arrival

Anya clutched her two children close as they stepped off the cramped bus onto the unfamiliar pavement of an English town, a stark contrast to the chaos that had enveloped their lives back in Ukraine. The air was crisp, a fresh breeze that felt foreign against her skin, and she took a moment to breathe deeply, though the ache in her heart made it hard to find solace. The world around her bustled on, seemingly oblivious to the turmoil that had forced her to flee her homeland. She stood frozen, absorbing the sights and sounds of this new place. The towering brick buildings, the neatly trimmed hedges, and the gentle rustle of leaves painted an idyllic picture, but all Anya could feel was the weight of fear coiling tightly in her chest.

"Mama, can we go?" Irina, her eight-year-old daughter, tugged at her hand. Beside her, the toddler, Maksym, clung to Anya's leg, his wide eyes darting around in wonder and confusion. They were safe at last, or so she hoped, but safety felt like a distant concept—one she had long yearned for, yet now struggled to grasp.

"Just a moment, sweethearts," Anya whispered, forcing a smile that didn't quite reach her eyes. She knelt down to meet Irina's gaze, brushing a stray hair from her daughter's forehead. "Let's find our new home, okay?"

Irina nodded, though the worry lines etched across her young brow hinted at the heavy burdens they all carried. Anya's heart ached for her children, for the innocence they had been forced to surrender. War had come so quickly, shattering their lives and leaving them in a whirlwind of fear and uncertainty. They had made the desperate journey from Kyiv, navigating checkpoints and uncertainty, the sounds of sirens and explosions echoing far too vividly in her mind.

With a final deep breath, Anya pushed down her anxiety and led her children through the town. The streets were lined with quaint shops, the scents of fresh bread and coffee wafting through the air, a sharp contrast to the smoke and ash of their past. Yet, every smile exchanged between strangers felt like a reminder of the normalcy they had lost—a normalcy she longed to reclaim for her children.

"How far is it, Mama?" Irina questioned, her curiosity mingling with the fatigue that now marked her small features. Anya glanced at the address written hastily on a crumpled piece of paper in her pocket, the only tether to the hope of finding refuge.

"Just a bit farther, my love. We'll be there soon," she replied, trying to infuse confidence into her voice. Each step felt heavier, the reality of their displacement pressing down upon her. She thought of Alex, her husband, who had stayed behind, fighting not just for their country but for their family. She felt the weight of his absence like a physical blow, the pain of separation coursing through her veins.

Anya recalled their last moments together as they'd hastily packed what little they could carry. Alex had held her close, whispering reassurances that they would reunite, that this was a temporary separation. Yet, deep down, she felt the gnawing fear that the war might steal him away forever.

"Mama, look!" Irina pointed, her spirit momentarily ignited by a colorful mural on the side of a nearby building. The vibrant colors depicted children playing, something Anya had desperately wanted to see more of in her daughter's life. She had always nurtured Irina's imagination, encouraged her to find joy in simple things. In this moment, as her daughter's small face lit up with curiosity, Anya felt a flicker of hope.

"Yes, it's beautiful, isn't it?" Anya agreed, the corners of her mouth lifting slightly as she admired the artwork. A part of her wished they could stay here and create new memories, free from the shadows of war. But as quickly as the thought arrived, it was overshadowed by the burden of reality. A small voice nagged at her, wondering if they could ever truly feel safe again.

After walking for what felt like an eternity, they finally arrived at the address. The modest house stood at the end of a quiet street, modest but sturdy, its facade painted a cheerful yellow that seemed to promise warmth. Anya's heart raced; this was their new home, a refuge from the storm, yet it felt foreign, an empty vessel that needed filling with new memories.

She knocked tentatively, her heart pounding in her chest. Would someone be kind? Would they accept her and her children? The door opened slowly, revealing a middle-aged man with kind eyes and graying hair.

"Jack Malaney," he said, offering a welcoming smile. "You must be Anya. Come in, please."

Anya hesitated, a mixture of hope and fear gripping her tightly. She wanted to trust him, but doubt loomed in the shadows. She glanced down at her children—two precious lives depending on her to make the right choices. Mustering her courage, she stepped inside, her children trailing close behind.

"Welcome," Jack said, stepping aside to let them enter. The interior was warm and inviting, sunlight streaming through the windows, illuminating the modest furnishings. Anya's heart ached at the sight of the warm environment, a stark contrast to the bleakness she had known.

"Please, make yourselves at home." Jack's voice was gentle.

Anya's chest tightened with gratitude, yet uncertainty plagued her heart. The journey had been arduous; she felt like a ship tossed in a storm, desperately seeking a safe harbor. As she looked around the room, she tried to envision what their lives might be like here. Would this be a fresh start or merely a pause in a never-ending battle against despair?

"Mama, can I have some juice?" Maksym whined, shifting his weight from one foot to the other, his cheeks flushed with weariness.

"Of course, sweetheart." Anya quickly moved to the small kitchen area, feeling the warmth of the sunlight on her skin. She was grateful for the kindness Jack had shown, but as she filled the cup, thoughts of Alex invaded her mind. Would he be safe, or would he be caught in the chaos that seemed to follow them like a shadow?

As she handed Maksym the juice, she caught Jack's gaze, and for a moment, the world around them faded. She saw a depth in his eyes, a familiarity that struck her; it reminded her of the times she had looked into Alex's eyes, seeing strength and vulnerability reflected back.

"I—thank you," she stammered, the weight of her gratitude pressing down on her. "For everything."

"Just trying to help," he replied, his voice calm, reassuring. "We'll get through this together."

Anya nodded, although uncertainty curled at the edges of her mind. Together. The word felt fragile when so much seemed out of reach. Each day in this foreign land was an uphill battle she dreaded confronting.

The days slowly unfolded into a blur, each one blending into the next—a cycle of adapting to their new surroundings while navigating the pain of separation from Alex. Anya took solace in moments with her children, the giggles of Maksym providing a flicker of joy, while Irina began to explore her new environment, discovering the local park and making tentative friendships with other children.

Yet, the thought of Alex gnawed at her heart, a constant reminder of what they had left behind. She would stare out the window, watching the children play in the golden light, but her mind would wander back to Ukraine: the warmth of Alex's embrace, the weight of his love, the sound of his laughter that felt like home.

In those quiet moments, Anya felt like a ghost in this foreign land, haunted by memories and tinged with fear—the fear that she might never see him again, the fear that her children might forget the life they once cherished. Would Irina remember their small apartment in Kyiv, the flowers they had planted together on the balcony? Would they continue to hold on to the stories of their life before the darkness descended?

With each passing day, she grappled with the burden of those memories, desperate to shield her children from the pain while simultaneously facing her own. The world was moving forward, and she was left behind, caught between the past and an uncertain future.

As time passed, Jack became a constant presence in their lives, his patience and understanding weaving an unexpected bond between them. He would sit with Anya on the porch in the evenings, sharing stories about his life—though he always stopped short of revealing too much. In those quiet exchanges, she found solace, discovering an ally in her struggle.

Yet, in the back of her mind, doubt lingered. Anya was always aware of the secrets that Jack kept, the shadows of his past that danced around his words. Why had he taken her in? What did he want in return? His kindness was almost overwhelming, yet it raised questions she was too afraid to voice.

As weeks blended into months, Anya sought stability for her children. She enrolled Irina in a local school, hoping to give her a semblance of normalcy, a chance to flourish despite the scars that marked their lives. Yet, as Anya watched her daughter step into the building for the first time, a wave of anxiety washed over her, a fear that the ghosts of war would follow them, haunting her children with memories and nightmares.

That night, as the family gathered for dinner, the atmosphere was heavy with unspoken words. Maksym sat nibbling on his food, his eyes occasionally flitting toward Jack and back to Anya. Irina picked at her plate, a thoughtful frown etched across her brow.

"It's peaceful here, isn't it?" Jack broke the silence, his voice warm, inviting. "You're safe now."

Anya nodded, but inside, a storm churned. Safety felt like a fragile illusion—an illusion she yearned to believe but struggled to embrace.

"Tell me more about Ukraine," Irina suddenly spoke, her voice bright yet tinged with nostalgia. Anya could see her daughter's longing for the life they had left behind.

Anya hesitated, the memories flooding back—the laughter, the celebrations, the pain of parting. "It's beautiful there," she began, her voice softening. "Like a painting, with flowers bursting in the spring, and laughter echoing in the streets."

"Mama, can we go back one day?" Irina asked, her eyes shining with innocence.

The question pierced Anya's heart. "I hope so, my love. One day," she replied, her voice breaking slightly. "But right now, we need to take care of each other."

The evening wore on, and as they finished dinner, the conversation shifted, moving to lighter topics, but Anya felt the melancholy tugging at her heartstrings. Each laugh, each light moment felt like a fragile thread straining against the weight of unspoken fears.

Later that night, as she tucked her children into bed, their small forms cocooned in warmth, Anya sat watching them, tears streaming down her cheeks. She was overwhelmed by a conflicting sense of love and despair. She leaned down, kissing them goodnight, whispering promises of safety and love.

The night stretched on, filled with silence and shadows. Anya lay awake, staring at the ceiling, grappling with the burdens of her thoughts. She thought of Alex, of the life they had built—a life now shattered.

For every moment of solace, there came a wave of fear, echoing louder than the laugh of her children. She felt caught between the desire to protect them from the world's pain and the need to transcribe their past in a way that would keep it alive.

Anya understood that she had to find a way forward, not just for herself but for Irina and Maksym. The freedom they had sought was a dream felt too precarious. But as she closed her eyes, the image of her husband—brave, loving, dedicated to family—anchored her in place. She would carry that love with her, across the miles and through the shadows, forging a path forward through the darkness that surrounded them.

And although the future felt uncertain, Anya held onto the hope that they would find their way, that they would build a life that radiated warmth and love once more, no matter how far they had come from the beautiful chaos of their homeland. She would fight for it, with every breath in her body, for her children, for Alex, and for the life they all deserved.

Setting Up House

The early morning light filtered softly through the lace curtains of Jack Malaney's quaint countryside home, illuminating the humble but inviting space with a gentle glow. It was the kind of light that seemed to hold a promise of warmth and new beginnings. Jack stood at the kitchen counter, cradling a steaming cup of tea as he gazed out at the garden he had tended for years, now free of the weight of espionage and danger. He felt a lingering sense of unease, however, something unidentifiable and nagging.

It was the first morning after Anya and her children had arrived, a single day that had been both exhilarating and overwhelming. The calm solitude he had cherished was now punctuated by the sound of little feet scurrying across the wooden floor, the excited chatter of children transitioning from Ukrainian to English, and the occasional, almost cautious, clatter of kitchenware as Anya tried her best to adjust to the new environment.

The kitchen was cluttered with items: plates stacked precariously in the drying rack, utensils strewn about as if they had been abandoned mid-action. Anya seemed to take one step forward and two steps back in her attempts to help. He caught a glimpse of her across the room, her brow furrowed in concentration as she coaxed her daughter, Sofia, to help with a few simple chores. Her son, Pavel, ran about with a sense of unrestrained glee, unfettered by the weight of their shared trauma.

Jack found solace in watching them. In many ways, the innocence of the children was a balm to his restless spirit. They were living reminders of what was pure and untainted by the complexities of adult life—yet they were also constant reminders of their fragile situation, suspended between past and present.

"Here, let me help with that," Jack offered as he set his cup down and made his way toward Anya, who was kneeling on the floor, trying to root out the small collection of toys that had found their way under the couch.

Anya's head shot up, her expression one of surprise mixed with something deeper—perhaps pride. "No, it's alright. I can manage," she replied, her English tinged with a soft accent that felt like a whisper of her homeland.

Jack hesitated, taken aback by her reticence. He could see that while Anya was determined, the subtle exhaustion etched across her features spoke of burdens too heavy for one woman to bear alone. "I know you can," he said gently, kneeling beside her and beginning to pull out an assortment of colorful toys. "But I'd feel better knowing we're both working together. It'll go faster."

She sighed, a blend of frustration and gratitude clouding her expression. "I want to contribute. I don't want to be a burden," Anya confessed, her voice barely above a whisper.

"Neither of us are burdens here," Jack assured her firmly, his heart aching at the vulnerability she displayed. "You and the children are welcome in my home. Let's make this a place we can all share."

"Thank you," Anya said, a touch of uncertainty lingering as she considered his offer. It wasn't just about the physical help—it was the underlying message of cooperation, acceptance, and the fragile bridge they needed to build between them.

A few feet away, in the living room, little Pavel had found a box of hastily packed crayons. The vibrant colors seemed to pull at the edges of the room, hinting at joy that was sorely needed. "Look, Mama! I can draw!" he shouted, his excitement infectious.

Anya's demeanor softened as her attention was diverted to her son. "Yes, my love, you draw beautifully," she encouraged, her smile illuminating her features momentarily.

Jack observed this interaction with a mix of admiration and nostalgia. He thought of his own children, now grown and living their lives far from him, carrying on with responsibilities and distant pursuits. The memories brought a bittersweet pang to his heart. He remembered the way they would color pictures for him, savoring every brushstroke as if it conveyed their love. Would he ever have that again?

As Anya quickly joined Pavel on the floor, seated cross-legged, it provided a brief moment of levity. Jack took a step back, needing to steady his own emotions as he watched their familial bond unfold.

There was laughter, soft giggles that melted away the tension lingering from their new reality. This was the heart of the family he missed; the warmth of connection he had long yearned for since walking away from his own life.

He returned to the kitchen, focusing on boiling a kettle for more tea. As he waited, his mind drifted. Anya was here, a stranger in circumstance but not in heart, facing trials he could hardly comprehend. His resolve to assist was wavering, compounded by the unique and chaotic feelings they were both experiencing.

Minutes later, Anya entered the kitchen, her hair slightly messy but her spirits visibly lifted by the shared joy with her children. "I hope you don't mind," she said hesitantly, "but the children want to color on the kitchen table. Is that alright?"

Jack chuckled, "Of course! Just be careful with the crayons—I'd like my table to remain unmarked for as long as possible."

Anya nodded and pulled out a few sheets of paper, glancing nervously at the table. "You are very kind, Jack," she murmured, an underlying vulnerability threading her voice.

"Kindness is the least I can offer," he replied. "You've been through so much. It's what neighbors do, right? Take care of each other."

But they weren't neighbors. The more he tried to reach her, the more walls seemed to rise, and he sometimes felt invisible, like the connection they were both hoping to forge vanished at the slightest provocation. That push-and-pull dynamic swung between them; he wanted to help, yet she seemed to clash with the very act of accepting help.

They settled into a rhythm, albeit a strained one. Jack took up the dishes as Anya supervised her children. He filled the sink with hot water and soap, scrubbing at the remnants of the previous day's meals—moments of solitude broken only by the sound of laughter.

"What's your plan for today, Anya?" he asked, hoping to engage her despite the invisible distance that lingered.

"I thought perhaps we could explore the garden. The children love to play outside, and I…" she hesitated, looking down at her hands. "I would like to see what this new place is like."

"It's lovely out there. A few roses blooming and the bees are busy," Jack replied cheerfully. "And also, some vegetables, if the rabbits haven't eaten them all."

At the mention of the garden, Anya's face brightened ever so slightly, a spark reflecting the hope of discovery. "Then let us do that."

The scene shifted as they moved outdoors. Jack had prepared the house with care, making sure the kids had a safe area to play without getting too close to the edge of the garden's fence where the trees grew dense. The sun draped its warmth across their shoulders, and the fragrance of blooming flowers wrapped around them in a comforting embrace.

As the children raced toward the swings, Anya carefully observed their hurried movements, a smile tugging at her mouth. Yet he could see a lingering tension in her posture.

"Why don't you join them?" Jack nudged gently. "You'll find it refreshing. They need you close."

Her reluctance was palpable. "I'm... not familiar with this place. It feels strange."

"You're amongst friends now," he reassured her, his tone earnest. "This can be a new beginning for all of us."

Anya closed her eyes momentarily, as though summoning strength from within. "I suppose you are right," she finally said, walking slowly to the swing set, allowing herself to sink into the role of mother and protector that she so fiercely longed to fulfill.

The sight of her pushing Pavel as he giggled filled Jack with a bittersweet warmth. He admired the way she embraced her children, the tenderness yet tempered by caution.

"Higher, Mama!" Pavel squealed, his joy infectious as the squeaky chains of the swing creaked in rhythm with Anya's steady push.

Sofia soon joined the fun, her light laughter weaving through the air like a melody. It felt like an echo of Jack's past—fragments of his family fluttering in his memory.

"See, they love it," Jack said, leaning back against a wooden post, arms crossed, watching them savor simple moments he feared they might never fully grasp.

Anya turned to him briefly, her expression inscrutable. "Yes, they do," she replied, her voice softening. "I sometimes forget that joy exists after... everything."

He nodded, understanding the weight of her words. In this moment, they shared a profound fragility—two beings dealing with losses too heavy to bear alone. The garden, a sanctuary for sorrow and laughter, became a neutral ground for their coexistence.

As the afternoon wore on, they took turns helping the children with simple games, laughter bubbling between them all. Yet even as the sun began to set, casting a warm golden hue over the garden, the clouds of uncertainty loomed just above—a reminder that the peace they were finding would inevitably be challenged.

"Thank you for today," Anya said later, as they gathered indoors again, small voices retreating upstairs, tired from the excitement. "I… I appreciate your patience."

"It's nothing less than you deserve, Anya." Jack replied, trying to smooth over the tension that still seemed to linger. "But I must confess…I wish you would let me help you more."

Her eyes darted down at the floor, her nervousness creeping back in. "It is difficult to rely on others," she admitted, her vulnerability creeping in. "Back in Kyiv, we learned to depend on no one. It's what kept us safe."

Jack felt a weight in his chest at the honesty buried in her words. "I understand. Painful truths can build walls, but you shouldn't have to carry this burden alone."

They shared an uncomfortable pause, both trying to navigate past the debris of their pasts—a world filled with shadows, deceptions, and fears.

As the evening pressed on and the room dimmed, Jack sensed the unease returning, a reflection embedded deeply within the heart of their makeshift family. They were both trying so desperately to carve out a semblance of normalcy while grappling with the shadows of their lives—each carrying their own invisible burdens.

He took a breath, choosing to emphasize the importance of the moment they were sharing. "Tomorrow, we can tackle the garden together. Perhaps plant something?" he suggested.

"Like what?" Anya asked, curiosity lighting up her eyes.

"Perhaps flowers, some vegetables," he proposed, a smile forming. "Something to symbolize a new beginning."

Anya nodded, though a flicker of doubt passed over her face. "I will do my best," she replied cautiously.

"Your best is plenty." He offered her an encouraging glance.

As they parted for the evening, Jack lingered in the hallway watching Anya tuck her children into bed. His heart swelled as he caught the faint trace of a lullaby escaping her lips—an echo of home.

The quietness of the night settled in, with only the distant sounds of nocturnal life resonating beyond the walls. Jack felt the tenuous thread that connected them sway between anticipation and uncertainty.

In between the laughter and tears, it was clear the journey ahead held challenges neither had anticipated, and they would need every ounce of strength they could muster to face them together. For now, they would set their sights on tomorrow, hoping it would offer a more solid foundation upon which to build their new lives.

But he felt it in his bones; the shadows they'd uncovered had only begun to reveal themselves. And it was this realization that would mark them both—the weight of that knowledge creating an uneasy coexistence, pushing them to confront the fears they carried, both individually and together, as they embarked on a path rife with unpredictability.

Tomorrow would be a new day, but the specters of their pasts would continue to linger, reminding them that safety and solace were often elusive, even in the most welcoming of homes.

Whispers of Danger

Anya's Confession

Anya stood at the kitchen window, her hands gripping the sill as she stared out at the garden Jack had tended so lovingly. The sunlight filtered through the leaves, casting dappled shadows on the ground, but the warmth of the day did little to soothe the chill creeping through her. She could hear the faint sound of the children playing in the living room, their laughter a stark contrast to the storm brewing within her. But despite the apparent normalcy of their surroundings, Anya felt far from safe.

Jack entered the kitchen quietly, his presence gentle and unobtrusive. He had been a careful observer since Anya and her children arrived, allowing her the space to settle into their new home while remaining ready to lend a helping hand. Jack was a man of few words, but his steadfastness provided a comforting anchor in an unfamiliar land. Today, however, she knew she couldn't hide her turmoil any longer.

"Anya?" Jack's voice broke through her thoughts, laced with concern. "Are you alright? You've been quiet."

She turned to him, her heart racing. For so long, she had been the one to keep her fears at bay, to keep her children safe from the harsh realities of their world. But now, standing before Jack, the weight of her fears felt insurmountable. She took a deep breath, her resolve gathering like storm clouds. "Jack, I… I need to talk to you about Alex."

His brows knitted together, and he stepped further into the kitchen, giving her his full attention. "What about him?"

"Things aren't what they seem… back home," Anya began, her voice trembling slightly, betraying her composure. "Alex has been acting differently since the war started… paranoid, suspicious."

"What do you mean?" Jack interjected, his tone shifting from concern to something sharper, more alert.

She hesitated, searching for the right words. "He believes there is a Russian spy within the Ukrainian intelligence. Someone he works with." The confession hung in the air, heavy with implication. Jack's expression shifted, interest piquing in his blue eyes.

"Are you certain?" he asked, his voice steadier than before, each word deliberate.

"It's hard to say," Anya replied, the words spilling out in a rush. "Alex is not the same man I married. The tension… it's suffocating. He often comes home late, whispering to people on the phone, looking over his shoulder." Her voice cracked slightly, tears welling up as she recalled the late-night arguments and sleepless nights filled with worry. "I try to reassure him, but he dismisses my fears. He's convinced that everyone, even me, is a potential threat."

"And you think he's right?" Jack pressed gently, his brow furrowed with concern.

"I don't know what to think anymore," Anya admitted, her heart racing as she weighed her next words. "But Alex… he said something to me last night that scared me. He said he suspects someone in his department is giving information to the Russians. He's deeply unsettled, and he believes this person could be responsible for the deaths of his colleagues."

Jack leaned against the counter, arms crossed, processing her words as the tension in the room thickened like summer air before a storm. "And you came here to escape that? To protect your children?"

"Yes," Anya said, her voice barely above a whisper. "But that fear… it follows me. I can't just ignore it. What if he's right? What if they find him, or worse, find us?"

Jack remained quiet, deep in thought. Anya could see the internal battle playing out on his face: the sharp, analytical mind of a former intelligence officer grappling with the instinct to protect someone who teetered on the edge of a dangerous precipice.

"Did he express this suspicion to anyone else?" Jack finally asked, his tone cautious.

"I don't know," she replied, her voice trembling. "But he's been more distant, like he's isolating himself from me. I think he's trying to protect me and the children. But what if he's wrong? What if in trying to protect us, he puts us in even more danger?"

Jack's eyes softened as he observed the vulnerability etched across Anya's features. Her courage struck him as both admirable and heartbreaking. "You can't carry this burden alone, Anya," he said softly.

"I know," she replied, looking down at her hands. "But who can I trust? I came here to escape that chaos, and now it feels—"

"—like it's following you," Jack finished for her, his voice firm yet understanding. "But you're not alone. You have me now."

Anya's gaze lifted, her heart pounding in her chest. "You don't understand. This isn't just a small worry. This could endanger your life too, Jack. I can't put you at risk."

Jack straightened, a look of resolve in his eyes. "You're already in this, Anya. You and your children. So let's figure out what we're dealing with. If your husband believes there's a spy, maybe we can uncover the truth and ensure your family's safety."

"But how?" she asked, her brows furrowed in uncertainty. "I'm afraid of what that truth might be."

Jack took a deep breath, his mind racing through the implications of her revelations. The world he thought he had left behind was beginning to creep back in, and with it, the shadows of espionage and danger. But his instincts were sharper than ever, honed through years of experience. He could not turn away now—not from Anya, not from the terror threatening to engulf her family.

"We start by being prudent," he said, the calmness in his voice settling like a soothing balm over her fraying nerves. "If Alex has been acting suspiciously, we need to observe him from a distance. Gather information without alarming him. I'll help you."

Tears brimmed in Anya's eyes at his unwavering support. "But what if it's too late by then? What if he gets caught up in something larger?"

Then let's take it step by step, Jack urged internally, acknowledging the frustration bubbling just beneath the surface. "We won't rush into any conclusions. Your primary concern should be your children's safety."

Anya nodded slowly, feeling the weight of Jack's resolve. "You're right. I just... wish I could tell him. I want to believe in his instincts. If he is right, he deserves to know he's not alone in this."

"And if he is wrong?" Jack offered, uncertainty threading through his words. "What happens then? We need to consider that as well."

Anya let out a shuddering breath, her heart heavy with the burden of uncertainty. "I don't know what will happen next," she admitted, her voice barely above a whisper. "All I know is that I am terrified."

Jack's gaze softened as he considered her vulnerability. "Then we navigate this fear together."

She looked into his eyes, searching for assurance. "But you must promise me one thing, Jack," she said, firmness creeping into her voice. "You must not put yourself in harm's way for me or my family."

Jack met her gaze directly, his blue eyes steady and determined. "I promise nothing will happen to you or your children while I'm around. But I can't ignore the potential danger that lies ahead either. We need to be vigilant and prepared."

Anya swallowed hard, the reality of their situation settling over her like a heavy blanket. "What can we do? I don't know how to approach this without putting Alex or the children at risk."

Jack thought carefully, running through strategies that had once been second nature to him. "We'll collect information discreetly. I'll help you assess the environment around Alex, look into his work situation. If there's a Russian spy, we can identify possible suspects."

"Do you really think this is possible?" Anya asked, her tone a mixture of hope and disbelief.

"It's not just possible; it's necessary," Jack replied firmly. "If Alex is in danger, then you are in danger. We have to act."

Anya leaned against the kitchen counter, fighting the wave of emotions threatening to overwhelm her. "And what if Alex completely dismissed my concerns? What if I'm just like one of his paranoid fantasies?"

"Then we deal with that when we get to it," Jack reassured her, his confidence steadying her racing heart. "But you know your husband better than anyone. If he's truly scared, there will be signs to follow."

Anya wiped her eyes, determination surging through her as she straightened her posture. "You're right. I need to be strong for the children, and for Alex."

Jack took a step closer, the gravity of their conversation hanging between them like the weight of an anchor. "It's okay to be afraid, Anya. But fear can't dictate our actions. We can't let it paralyze us."

The fire within her reignited as Anya nodded, feeling emboldened by Jack's conviction. "So, we start looking for clues. But we have to be careful. Alex can't suspect anything."

"Agreed. We will proceed cautiously," Jack said, his voice low, as if they were already in a covert operation. "We'll create a plan to observe him without raising alarm – and I'll support you every step of the way."

In that moment, Anya felt an inexplicable bond forming between them, stitched together by their shared resolve against the impending chaos. "Thank you, Jack," she said, her voice steadying. "You don't have to do this. But I am grateful you are."

Jack offered her a subtle smile, a glimmer of reassurance that somehow illuminated the shadows lurking in the corners of their lives. "You and your children deserve a chance at safety."

With that, Anya felt a surge of hope stir within her, mingling with the fears that threatened to overwhelm her. They had determined their course of action. Now, the challenge lay ahead—one that could unravel everything she loved or pave the way towards a new future.

Jack turned to leave, giving her a moment to gather her thoughts, but she stopped him with a soft call. "Jack?"

He paused, looking back at her expectantly.

"Can I ask you something?" she asked hesitantly.

"Of course."

"Why are you doing this for me? Why not simply keep to your quiet life and let things unfold on their own?"

Jack looked thoughtful for a moment, his expression becoming more serious. "There are moments in our lives that we can't ignore," he said, his voice steady. "Moments that call us to act, even when we think we've left that world behind. You're one of those moments for me."

Anya could feel her heart swell at his honest admission, knowing that in this person, she had found an ally—someone who would stand with her against the shadows of uncertainty. "Then we will face this together," she said, her voice emboldened. "For our children, and for the truth."

With that silent agreement forged between them, the weight of their shared secrets settled into a pact of determination. The path ahead would be fraught with danger, the shadows lurking with menace, but in that moment, Anya found strength in knowing she was not alone.

Together, they would confront the unknown, unearthing the truth about Alex's fears and protecting the fragile future that awaited them. Unbeknownst to them, the whispers of danger were only beginning to unfurl, and the real test of their resilience was yet to come.

Echoes of Espionage

Jack sat in his modest study, glancing out of the window at the rolling hills of the English countryside, their serene beauty almost mocking the turmoil swirling within him. The soft rustle of leaves and distant chirping of birds felt like a world away from the chaotic memories that now demanded his attention. He couldn't shake the feeling that the calm of this pastoral existence only served to accentuate the storms brewing in his mind—troubled recollections of a life lived in shadows and deception.

His gaze drifted to a framed photograph on the wall. It captured a moment frozen in time, one of his last days with MI6 before he hung up his proverbial cloak and dagger. He looked younger then, filled with the fire of youthful ambition and unwavering confidence, ideals that had slowly eroded under the weight of moral ambiguity and betrayal. Beside him stood a group of colleagues—trusted allies, now scattered across the globe, some retired, some lost in the dangerous game they played. The laughter in the picture seemed almost haunting, a reminder of friendships fractured by the inherent mistrust of the espionage world.

With a heavy sigh, Jack closed his eyes and leaned back in his chair. The walls around him closed in, pulling forth vivid memories like an unwelcome tide. He recalled the stark, cold interrogation rooms of MI6, where he had first learned the art of deception—not just of others, but of himself. What did it mean to serve a higher purpose at the expense of personal sacrifice? At first, the answers seemed simple: loyalty to one's country, to one's comrades. But as he delved deeper into the murky waters of espionage, the questions multiplied, fracturing his once steadfast convictions.

One flashback surged forward, distinct and vivid. He remembered his first mission in Eastern Europe, tasked with infiltrating a small but vital political faction suspected of harboring ties to Russian intelligence. The adrenaline had been intoxicating. He recalled the cool precision with which he had drawn on the skills of deception, creating a false identity that blended seamlessly into the shadows of the community's underbelly. In the dim light of the backroom meetings, he felt the thrill of the game, the subtle power of manipulation coursing through him like a drug. But the deeper he dug, the more he realized how easy it was to become lost within his own lies.

Weeks turned into months, and he found himself ensnared in a network of conspiracy that challenged his beliefs about right and wrong. The deception was not limited to political maneuvers; it seeped into personal relationships, altering the course of his life in ways he could have never foreseen. He had grown close to a woman named

Elena, a local activist who was passionate about exposing corruption. She had been so earnest, so full of hope, and Jack had found himself drawn to her spirit like a moth to a flame.

But the darker the shadows became, the more he understood the risks of involvement. Jack pulled away from her, convinced that love within such a dangerous game was a luxury he couldn't afford. The days blurred into one another, filled with secrets and betrayal, and Elena had ultimately fallen victim to the very dangers Jack sought to escape. Her disappearance haunted him, a ghost that followed him even into his retirement. How could he have justified abandoning her when she had trusted him completely? What had it cost him to prioritize duty over affection?

In the years that followed, the weight of such choices had woven a dense fabric of regret that enveloped him tightly. Jack visualized other operations gone awry—missions where the lines between friend and foe became grotesquely blurred. During a critical operation in the Middle East, he had collaborated with a police chief who he later learned was double-crossing him. The whole affair spiraled into chaos, leading to the deaths of informants he had grown to care for, individuals whose lives had been extinguished due to his naivety and trust. Those consequences often replayed in his mind like a broken record, an ever-present reminder that every action he took could unravel more lives than he could count.

Sitting in his study, Jack's fingers tightened around the armrests of his chair as the tension built within him. The moral quandaries that had once plagued him returned with renewed intensity. Did he ever truly know what loyalty meant? He had fought for his country but often found himself questioning whether he fought for the right reasons. The intelligence community operated within a web of loyalty that demanded sacrifices, yet the true meaning of that loyalty remained elusive, tangled within layers of deceit and betrayal.

Now, as he considered Anya's plight, Jack realized that the echoes of his past were far from mere memories. They reverberated through his present, forcing him to confront the uncomfortable reality of his choices. He couldn't afford to let her down, not when her children's lives and her husband's fate hung in the balance of his decisions. The thought of Alex being embroiled in a conspiracy that might lead to conflict with Russians stirred a deep unease within Jack. He envisioned those unmarked cars trailing Anya, the cold eyes of the spies who might be lurking just beyond the shadows.

Anya needed someone she could trust, a steadfast ally in her fight against the darkness looming over her family. In a way, this situation echoed his own experiences, where trust had been both a weapon and a poison. He could almost hear Elena's voice in his mind, reminding him that true courage involved embracing vulnerability, that there was no shame in seeking help instead of running away.

A soft knock at the door snapped him from his thoughts. He opened his eyes, feeling a slight jolt at the intrusion. The memories receded like the tide, but their imprint lingered. Anya stood there, her face a mixture of hope and apprehension. She clearly sensed the mental struggle that had just transpired within him, perhaps because she was entangled in her own web of fear and confusion.

"Jack, can we talk?" Her voice was steady, but he could see the tremor beneath it—a slight quiver that belied her strength. He nodded, motioning for her to enter, and felt an unexpected rush of responsibility settle on his shoulders like a heavy cloak.

They settled into the small sitting area, the silence stretching between them. Jack glanced at Anya, studying the lines of worry on her face, and felt an odd sense of connection. Despite the chasm of danger and uncertainty that separated them from one another, shared experiences had already begun to forge a bond. He sensed her pain, her longing for safety, igniting a determination within him that had long lain dormant.

"Thank you for listening, for being here," she said softly, her vulnerability shining through. "I just can't shake the feeling that something is very wrong, and I am terrified for my children."

Jack's heart ached for her. He understood that helplessness, the gnawing uncertainty that had once consumed him when Elena had vanished. "I'll help you, Anya," he said, his voice resolute. "We'll figure this out together. But we need to proceed carefully. The world we're dealing with is not just dangerous—it's filled with shadows."

He watched her expression shift, a flicker of gratitude mingling with the fear in her eyes. In that moment, a profound sense of clarity washed over him. He would not shy away from the present; he would meet it head-on. He owed it to Anya, to her children, and, perhaps more importantly, to himself. This was his chance for redemption—a chance to confront the ghosts of his past while illuminating the darkness threatening to envelop a family he had come to care for.

As they strategized their next steps, Jack felt the weight of implication settle upon him; the responsibility to protect Anya and her family intertwined with the unresolved burdens of his past. He could no longer linger in the shadows of his memories. It was time to confront the new shadows swirling at the edges of their lives. The stakes were high, and he wasn't prepared to allow fear to dictate their fate.

The resolve crystallized within him as he looked into Anya's eyes—a silent pact forged between them in that shared recognition of struggle and the need for truth. He would uncover the truth behind her fears, not only to protect her family but also as a means to reclaim a sense of purpose that long lay dormant. The echoes of his espionage past were not merely haunting—now they served as a guide. Each decision would reverberate like the echoes of gunfire, reminding him of the delicate balance between loyalty and betrayal as he stepped into the unknown.

Jack stood up, feeling the urgency pulling at him like a tide. "Let's get started," he said decisively. "We have work to do, and I will not rest until we find out what's really going on." The complexity of loyalty hung in the air, but he was ready to navigate its treacherous waters.

Together, they turned towards the future, an uncertain path filled with both danger and the flickering promise of hope.

Shadows in the Dark

The late afternoon sun cast elongated shadows across the quaint English village, painting a picturesque scene that belied the turmoil brewing beneath its tranquil surface. Jack Malaney leaned against his garden fence, his gaze fixated on the flowerbeds bursting with colors. Despite the beauty surrounding him, an unsettling feeling wrenched in his gut—an intuition, perhaps, honed over years of service in the intelligence world. It was a feeling he hadn't experienced in a long time, and it filled him with a sense of foreboding.

Since Anya and her children arrived, Jack had welcomed a fresh energy into his once solitary life, yet that energy brought with it an array of concerns. Anya's tear-streaked face as she spoke of her husband's fears echoed in his mind, becoming a whispering specter he could not shake. Alex's suspicions about a Russian spy infiltrating the very heart of Ukrainian intelligence gnawed at Jack's instincts, awakening his warrior spirit beneath layers of retirement's placid skin.

But the more he considered Anya's dilemma, the more the shadows emerged. It was impossible to ignore the strange occurrences that had begun to punctuate their daily lives—the unmarked cars that frequented the end of the lane, always parked out of sight yet present enough to raise suspicions, and the hushed conversations that seemed to drop suddenly at the sound of footsteps. Jack caught sight of Anya more frequently gazing over her shoulder, anxiety knitting her delicate features into a mask of dread; he sensed her growing conviction that she was being watched.

In the days that followed her emotional confession, he noticed subtle changes in Anya: her smiles appeared less frequent, replaced by a furrowed brow and eyes that darted continuously around her surroundings. She was becoming a ghost in her own life—a beautiful, vibrant spirit tethered to the suffocating weight of fear and uncertainty.

One afternoon, as the sunlight dipped toward the horizon, washing the world in a palette of amber and gold, Anya approached him with a look that spoke tales of nightmares. "Jack," she whispered, pulling him aside into the relative safety of the kitchen, "I think... I think they are looking for Alex."

The tremor in her voice clenched his heart. "What do you mean?" he asked, trying to mask the dread unfurling within him.

"I saw a car... parked outside again. Two men were talking." Her voice trembled, and he could see the flicker of panic in her eyes, the raw vulnerability that a mother wore like armor; she was fierce, but beneath it, she was terrified.

"Did you recognize them? Do you think they're here for you?" Jack asked, seeking to calm the storm brewing behind her eyes.

"No," she shook her head fervently, grasping the countertop as if it were her only anchor, "not me. They were discussing something—someone—whispering about a… a betrayal." The word hung in the air like a dark cloud, rich with implications. Each syllable was weighted with the knowledge that her husband's worst fears were now a looming reality.

Jack offered a steadying hand on her shoulder, allowing a moment for her trembling to subside. "We need to remain cautious, Anya. If there are threats, we must manage them together. We have to figure out what's going on." He felt the heat ebbing from her skin, a mix of concern and determination igniting a spark he had rarely seen since their lives intertwined.

Days passed, each one setting a heavier weight on Jack's shoulders. Their conversations filled with hushed warnings and conspiratorial discussions became a part of their routine. The specter of danger began to fuse with the mundane—the once peaceful sounds of their garden were overshadowed by an eeriness he could not articulate.

Jack's investigative instincts revived as he started looking into Alex's suspicions more seriously. After all, they were like shadows in a dimly lit theater—flickering but nearly undetectable. Every sound, every detail felt loaded; he could feel his past drifting back into his present, the memories of espionage evoking a blend of adrenaline and discomfort. Yet, he recognized that this was no longer the sterile environment of agency operations; these were human lives thrust into chaos through forces he could not control.

That evening, as Anya busied herself preparing a simple yet wholesome meal, Jack stepped outside to gather his thoughts. The sky had darkened considerably, and the stars glimmered faintly, distant and indifferent to the turmoil below. In those quiet moments, the unease roiled fiercely within him, tying his stomach in knots.

He thought back to his last days in MI6—the adrenaline rush of uncovering threats, the chase and stakes that invigorated his spirit. In contrast, this was a different landscape, one where he felt the impending shadow of peril inching closer, and he couldn't shake the feeling that something had begun… something he was unwittingly a part of.

Suddenly, a sound caught his attention: the faintest rustling from the bushes at the edge of his property. Instinctively, he stiffened, his senses heightened. Jack strained to listen, hardening his gaze in the direction of the noise. The world darkened rapidly around him, the shadows deepening as if they were swallowing the light. He took cautious steps toward the sound, heart pounding in his chest.

As he approached, he spotted a distinct figure darting across the edge of his property—a man, tall and cloaked in darkness, with an aura of calculated movements that set Jack's alarm bells ringing. It could have been a mere passerby, but every fiber in his being told him otherwise.

Without breaking his gaze, he reached for his mobile, the urgency palpable as he dialed Anya. "Stay inside, lock the door. I think there's someone on the property," he urged, his voice a low whisper. He could almost hear the heartbeat of fear thrumming on the other end of the line.

"Jack?" Anya's voice trembled, barely above a whisper. "What do you mean someone? Is it... is it a threat?"

"I don't know yet, but I'm going to investigate," he replied, hanging up just as the shadowy figure slipped through the bushes. His pulse raced; he couldn't afford to let this unknown element escape his grasp. Not now.

Carefully, maintaining the distance between him and the figure, Jack followed, his military training kicking in as he moved with the silent purpose of a predator. The night grew colder, the air thick with an unseen tension that coiled around Jack like a vice. Shadows whispered secrets to him as he neared the spot where the figure had disappeared.

He halted beside an old wooden shed, feeling the pulse of night pressing against his chest. And then he heard it—a voice, low and conspiratorial, just on the edge of comprehension. Jack strained to catch the words, his heart racing as he pressed closer, his breath hitching with anticipation.

"...they know too much. We need to silence them."

Silence bloomed as Jack's breath caught in his throat—was it Anya? Was it her children they meant? The ominous quality of the voice twisted something primal within him; he had spent years stepping into shadows for the cold machinations of spies, but never had he felt this urgency, this desperate need to protect.

He edged around the shed, squinting into the darkness, when he spotted them—two men, their forms partially illuminated by the dim glow of a cellphone screen. They were scribbling notes, glancing around nervously, eyes darting back toward the house. Jack's instincts screamed at him; these were players in a game far deeper than he could have anticipated.

"Are you sure they're here?" one asked, his accent thick, slicing through the stillness like a knife.

"They've been moving, but it's just a matter of time before we find them," the second replied, an edge of impatience in his tone. "And when we do… it will be over."

Chilled, Jack fell back against the shed, anchoring himself to its relative safety as the men continued their conversation. The implications of their words weighed heavy on his shoulders, the reality of Alex's fears manifesting before him in living color. They were here for Anya. They were here for him.

He had to warn her. Moving swiftly yet quietly, he flitted back to the house and slammed the door behind him. "Anya!" he called out, urgency lacing his voice, "Get the children—now!"

"What? What happened?" Her startled expression mirrored her fear.

"There are two men, they're here for you and Alex," he breathed, scanning the room for anything that could serve as protection. The children were unusually quiet; he could sense their worry pressing heavily in the air.

Anya's eyes widened. "But… how? Why would they come here?"

"It doesn't matter," he replied, cutting her off. "We need to get out of sight. I don't know how much time we have."

They hurried to gather the essentials, Anya clasping her children close. Jack orchestrated their movements using the knowledge he had gained throughout his career. They would have to evade, outsmart their pursuers, to escape the shadows pressing in from all sides.

As they prepared to leave the house, Jack turned his phone to flashlight mode, illuminating their hasty exit plan. "Follow me, stay close." He led Anya and the children toward the back door, opening it with caution, peering into the oppressive darkness that surrounded them.

His intuition warned him that danger lingered too close for comfort. The shape of the world around him stretched into a menacing silhouette, torn between reality and the unknown.

Just then, a noise shattered the stillness—a crunch of gravel beneath hurried footsteps outside, sharp and deliberate. Jack's heart raced anew. "We're not safe here, we need to move," he insisted, scanning for an escape route.

Anya's eyes brimmed with urgency. "Where do we go? They could be anywhere!" She clutched her children, determination battling with fear.

"There's an old hollow oak at the edge of the woods," he urged. "If we can reach it, we can hide until they pass."

In that moment, Jack's resolve crystallized—their silent connection to each other framed in desperation against the shadows. He beckoned them closer, his mind racing with plans and contingencies. They needed to navigate the terrain with the utmost stealth and precision. He thought back to his training, each lesson a solid thread binding his intuition to action.

With a single glance back at the house, the home that had been a refuge now felt like a cage with every creak and sound amplifying the very real threat looming just outside. They slipped through the back door and into the clammy embrace of the evening air, a bracing chill making them shiver as they began their stealthy retreat.

Jack led the way into the shadowy expanse of the garden, doing his best to absorb every sound and movement around them. The world had become a tapestry woven with uncertainty and fear, each thread twisting into something ominous. Anya's breath quickened beside him as they passed beneath the low-hanging branches of the trees, which obscured them from view.

"Jack, what if they find us?" Anya whispered, her nails digging into her child's arm as they pressed deeper into the thicket.

"They won't," he assured her, casting a reassuring glance back at her. "Keep moving. We'll be okay."

But the clamor of approaching feet hardened into reality, the night swallowing their hurried breaths. Jack's instincts buzzed like a live wire, and he felt the weight of protection mounting upon his shoulders. He had faced dangers before, but never with such personal stakes involved.

They reached the oak, its gnarled roots a sanctuary as they ducked inside, each feeling the sacredness of their escape. Anya's children huddled close, wide eyes brimming with worry. Outside, Jack recognized the faintest sounds of a voice rising like a specter in the shadows.

"He can't have just disappeared," the first man's voice echoed through the quiet night, slicing through the fragile tranquility surrounding them. "He must be hiding close by."

The second man didn't respond; Jack could sense tension mounting thick enough to cut. Instinctively, he held his breath, his body steeling against the pulse of anxiety thrumming through him as he positioned himself to listen intently from within the hollow.

What followed next made his stomach knot. "Let's split up. Check around; if they're out there, they won't get far." The order rang through the air, sharp and lethal.

Panic flared within Anya, a flicker of despair illuminating the fear in her gaze. "Jack, they're coming! They'll find us!"

With gentle resolve, he reached out and clasped her hands, steadfast in their shared conviction. "We won't let that happen. Trust me."

Time stretched thin as they stayed shrouded in the ancient oak, silent and poised like shadows themselves, aware that the darkness concealed both their fear and their hope.

Every breath felt like an eternity, as noises permeated the quiet night—a rustling of leaves, the crisp snap of twigs beneath shifting feet. Jack felt acutely aware of how isolated they truly were in this moment—a cocoon of darkness enveloping them.

It became painfully clear that the shadows weren't merely chasing Anya's family—they were hunting him too. He would have to respond; he would have to confront the threat waiting in the dark.

As the night deepened, Jack felt the tremble of impending decisions pressing against him. Soon the hunter would become the hunted. And if he had any hope of delivering Anya and her children from this web of intrigue, he would have to confront the shadows that loomed over them both.

But as the moments melted into one another, the distinct yet familiar sound of an approaching vehicle resonated from their left, the soft rumble growing louder before the headlights swept across the fields, illuminating trees and bushes in stark relief.

Reflexively, he tightened his grip on Anya, the dread curdling deeper within him; they were about to plunge into the depths of an unknown peril. As darkness converged over them, he steeled himself, knowing that whatever came next would demand every ounce of his resolve.

Their time was running out; the shadows were gathering, and as fate would have it, their confrontation with the looming threat had only just begun.

The Shadows of the Past

Memories Resurface

Jack Malaney stood at the window, staring out at the undulating hills of the English countryside that had become his sanctuary after years in the high-stakes world of espionage. It was a peaceful afternoon, the golden sunlight filtering through the leaves, casting dappled shadows on the well-trimmed lawn. The chirping of birds and the distant sound of a lawnmower should have brought him solace, but instead, he felt a tightening in his chest, an awakening of memories he thought time had buried safely.

As he moved away from the window, he glanced at the small clutter of his lived-in home—books stacked on the coffee table, a half-finished garden project lying abandoned in a corner, and photographs of a life once filled with laughter. In those images were his wife, Margaret, and their two children, laughing on a summer's day, carefree before tragedy had become a shadow in their lives. His hands moved to the mantelpiece, lightly brushing over the frame of a photo from years ago, the three of them beaming against a backdrop of their favorite holiday destination.

That was the family life he had sacrificed on the altar of duty. Jack could still hear the echoes of his children's laughter, but those sounds were now haunting reminders of opportunities lost, moments traded for secrecy and sacrifice. The weight of betrayal pressed heavily on his heart—a betrayal not just towards his family but also towards the very ideals he had sworn to protect.

Suddenly, vivid images began to flood his mind, taking him back to a time when the thrill of the chase and the camaraderie with his colleagues provided a different kind of family—a family bound not by blood, but by shared experiences, whispered secrets, and the adrenaline that coursed through their veins as they danced on the edge of danger.

He closed his eyes, surrendering to the torrent of memories, each image a slice of a life lived under constant scrutiny and pressure. He remembered his first operational assignment in Eastern Europe, where he had navigated a web of intrigue that had felt intoxicating at the time. The dimly lit cafes, the hushed conversations, and the thrill of outsmarting the enemy were all part of the thrilling dance of espionage. The camaraderie with fellow officers, shared over midnight drinks, had forged bonds that felt unbreakable—until they weren't.

Standing in a smoky backroom of a pub in Budapest, he could still hear the laughter ringing in his ears, the clinking of glasses echoing the triumph of a successful extraction. There was Michael, a fellow agent, with sharp wit and an even sharper tongue, who had been Jack's closest ally in that world. Michael had joked about the dangers, laughing off the weariness with bravado that Jack admired. They had shared their fears, their hopes for a life beyond the shadows, and for Jack, a promise that one day he would leave this all behind for the love of his family.

But that promise had slipped through his fingers, leaving behind a gnawing regret. Jack had chosen loyalty to his country over the relationships that mattered most. When the mission in Budapest had taken a perilous turn, it was Michael who had paid the price. An ambush set by a double agent had culminated in chaos—gunfire, screams, and the harsh scent of gunpowder carved into Jack's memory. In the aftermath, Michael lay lifeless on the cold ground, a victim of loyalty tested to its limits. Jack had stood there, frozen, feeling the weight of a thousand unspoken apologies suffocating him.

"Should've seen it coming, mate," he murmured to himself, echoing Michael's last words. Regret tangled with the memories, and he could practically hear his friend chiding him for his misplaced trust. Jack had never quite forgiven himself for the betrayal of that bond, nor for allowing the game of shadows to take one of the few people who had truly understood him.

The weeks that followed were a blur of sorrow and guilt, but duty had insisted that Jack push through—because that was the life he had chosen. He forced himself to compartmentalize, to shove aside the grief and continue. But Michael's death had eaten away at him, carving a chasm within that he came to acknowledge only in the quietest of moments, when he was alone with his thoughts.

Recollections of another colleague bubbled to the surface; Lucy, a brilliant analyst in MI6, had provided Jack with vital intelligence during operations. They had spent hours poring over maps and satellite images, analyzing every nuance of the information they gathered. There had been a bond, too, an unarticulated connection fostered through countless late nights and shared caffeine-fueled frustrations. Yet it had also been a relationship shadowed by unspoken barriers—her fierce loyalty to the agency made it clear that feelings were a luxury they couldn't afford.

When the day came for Jack to push for a promotion that would take him away from frontline operations, he wrestled with the idea of leaving that partnership behind. Lucy's fierce determination to excel had inspired him, yet he had never once shared his intention to step away from the dangers of espionage. He could still remember the way she had looked at him, the brief flicker of disappointment that danced in her eyes when he had informed her of his transfer. It was the knowing glance between comrades, a silent acknowledgment of what could have been, tarnished by the choices they made.

Shoving another memory aside, Jack let the flood continue. He had encountered betrayal everywhere he turned; it appeared part and parcel of the world he inhabited. Trust was a fleeting whisper, a false promise. He had learned that the closer someone came, the greater the risk of betrayal.

That lesson had hit hardest during one operation in the depths of a Russian winter. Jack had been embedded in St. Petersburg, working alongside a charming but duplicitous agent who proved to have ties to the very organization they were working against. Jack had sensed the trouble brewing too late, and when the truth about the agent's intentions surfaced, it left a bitter taste in his mouth. The betrayal had not only endangered their mission but also the lives of countless innocents.

As he recalled the icy streets where fear and vigilance walked hand in hand, he could still feel adrenaline coursing through his veins as he chased the truth. The cold had seeped into his bones, but the camaraderie with his team had kept him warm, even when pretending to crack jokes in their shared danger. He had thought they were intangible, but loyalty had been tested in the worst ways, culminating in another life claimed by deceit—a fellow officer had been lost in the fallout of that double-cross.

Jack remembered standing at his funeral, the weight of his sorrow wrapped around him like a cloak. The hollow expressions on the faces of colleagues around him told a story of loss, but the bitter truth was that they should have seen it coming. They had all witnessed the subtle signs, yet too often, they swept the truth under the rug in a bid to keep moving, to keep surviving.

Now, years later, Jack stood in the light of a kinder sun, reflecting back on those moments when choices dictated the quality of lives. He felt the familiar pull toward guilt and regret as he put together the pieces of his own life—a life that had veered dangerously off course in the pursuit of duty. How many friendships had he sacrificed? How many bonds had he severed in the name of loyalty?

Lost in thought, he returned his gaze to the photographs adorning the mantel. His wife. His children. They were the quiet constants who bore the weight of his decisions without their knowledge, innocent bystanders to a war they had not chosen. He could see it vividly—the moment Margaret had confronted him about his late nights, the missed anniversaries, the hidden phone calls, wearing thin on her heart. How she had listened to his reassurances, storing away the pain, as he continued to retreat further into his clandestine world.

"Work comes first," Jack had muttered during their arguments, dismissive, wrapped in his sense of justification, believing the end would vindicate him. It hadn't. Not when she had finally realized the truth—a bitter conclusion he still replayed in his mind, his heart echoing with regret. It had been the night he had finally come home late, terrified, and hollow, only to find her waiting with a suitcase packed and eyes swollen from tears. She had looked more a stranger than the woman with whom he had vowed to spend his life.

"Are you coming back for us, Jack?" she had asked quietly, desperation laced with hope.

At that moment, he could have chosen honesty, could have taken the path of redemption, but his instinct to protect his secrets overrode his yearning for vulnerability. "I have to run this final job," he hissed, guilt flaring in his chest. "Just one last time, and I promise it'll all change."

And it had—changing in ways that would irreparably fracture their family. The truth of his estrangement settled heavily in his heart; the truth was, Jack was never sure if he could keep that promise, even as he tried to convince her, to convince himself.

He was rushed into calls, briefings, high-stakes maneuvering. Weeks turned into months, and Jack, entrenched in the shadows, lost himself with each undercover mission, wrapping layers of deception around his identity to keep it safe from the prying eyes of a life he had chosen but now felt shackled to.

As he returned to the present moment, the weight of those choices bore down on him, and Jack felt raw, a wound continually re-opened by the memories that resurfaced with painful clarity. He had sacrificed too much for someone who might not have cared, for a world that all but forgot those who fell prey to its relentless demands.

The trauma of that choice gnawed at him; it forged deeper reflections about trust lost and the tenuous relationships he had discarded, for while the glamor of espionage had lured him in, the reality had been drenched in shades of gray. He thought about Anya and her children and the burdens they carried within their fragile lives, much like his own family had once borne his silence.

Now that he had tasted the bitterness of that betrayal in his own life, he felt compelled to do better. For the first time in years, Jack yearned to rebuild, to create instead of destroy. He wished for the bravery to stand up for someone else while he wrestled with his demons. Perhaps redemption lay in understanding the importance of trust—of recognizing that without it, he could lose everything once more.

His last thought before he turned away from the window was of Michael and Lucy, their shadows still lurking in his consciousness as he navigated his forsaken sense of duty. The consequences of his choices reverberated through the present, reminding him that the world of shadows only lived where the light was cast.

Jack took a deep breath, steeling himself, for in Anya's desperation, he glimpsed a chance to redeem a life fueled by darkness. The ghosts of betrayal begged to be faced; they beckoned him to act. His memories floated like phantoms, but the possibility of change ignited a flicker of hope. He would not allow those specters to define his existence. There was a path forward, and perhaps, just perhaps, he could help others find theirs along the way.

The Cost of Secrets

Jack Malaney stood at the window of his modest cottage, gazing out at the rolling hills of the English countryside that stretched endlessly before him. The golden hues of the setting sun cast long shadows across the landscape, much like the secrets that clung to him—faint whispers of a past that he couldn't quite shake. He inhaled deeply, the cool evening air filling his lungs, as the weight of his thoughts pressed heavily on his shoulders.

This tranquil existence, this new beginning that had promised solace, often felt like a façade. Jack had sought refuge in the routines of a retired life after years with MI6, but the shadows of his past loomed large. The thrill of espionage had once pulsed through his veins, alongside the heavy burden of secrets that he had carried like a cross. Now, they threatened to resurface, intertwining with the life he was attempting to build with Anya and her children.

The images from Ukraine haunted him—the chaos, the fear resonating in Anya's voice as she had told him about her husband's suspicions of a mole within the Ukrainian intelligence agency. Every word had pulled Jack deeper into tumultuous waters, pushing memories to the surface like a tide he couldn't control. It was one thing to navigate the treacherous world of espionage as a professional, but a different matter entirely to confront the personal implications of those dark waters.

What had drawn him to help Anya? A sense of duty, perhaps; or was it something deeper, a yearning to reclaim the sense of purpose that had slipped through his fingers in retirement? His instincts had sparked to life once more, igniting a desire to protect, to safeguard the innocent from the shadows that stalked them. Yet in doing so, he was pulling his past forth, dredging up secrets that were meant to stay buried.

The clock on the mantel chimed softly, shaking him from his reverie. Time had a way of slipping by too quickly, especially during moments of introspection. He turned away from the window and moved back into the living room, where Anya sat on the couch, her two children—Mikhail and Katya—playing quietly with a few toys he had managed to procure for them. The soft sound of their laughter brought warmth to his heart, but it also stoked the fire of his internal conflict.

Evenings like this wrapped the small space in a cocoon of normalcy, yet the reality of their situation—a situation steeped in the uncertainty of war and whispers of danger—remained ever present. The children needed stability, and Anya needed support. But what would they think if they discovered the truth about him? And how could he possibly share his past without jeopardizing the fragile trust they had built?

With a heavy sigh, Jack settled into an armchair opposite Anya, catching her eye momentarily. She looked up from her children, her brow furrowed in thought. The muted light from the lamp cast a gentle glow on her features, accentuating the strength and vulnerability that coexisted in her. It was that same strength that had pulled Jack from his self-imposed isolation, but here he was, teetering on the precipice of compassion and caution.

"Jack?" Anya's voice broke the silence, drawing him from his spiral of contemplation. "Are you alright?"

He offered a reassuring smile, although it felt somewhat hollow. "Just thinking," he replied, his gaze flickering to the children, who were now engaged in a friendly disagreement over a toy car. "They seem to be getting along quite well. It's lovely to see."

Anya's expression softened, yet he could see the flicker of concern in her eyes. She had become adept at reading him, and that was both a comfort and a source of anxiety. "You've been distant lately. If there's something bothering you, you can talk to me."

At her invitation, Jack felt a familiar tug of temptation. He could share a sliver of his reality, perhaps paint a picture of why his thoughts often wandered to darker places. But just as quickly, the memory of the secrets he bore pushed him back, telling him to guard himself. "We've both been through a lot, Anya. It's going to take time to adjust."

Anya nodded but didn't press further, her eyes searching his for understanding. It was an unsaid acknowledgment of their respective burdens—hers marked by the trauma of war; his scarred by decisions made in shadows. Therein lay the cost of secrets, the perilous navigation between honesty and safety.

Time crawled by as Jack observed the children playing, their laughter amid the silence wrapping around him, offering a fleeting sense of calm that only further accentuated his unease. He had built walls around his past, perhaps too high, yet with every interaction with Anya, those walls felt as if they were crumbling. She deserved honesty; she deserved to know the man who was helping her. And yet, revealing too much could lead to devastating repercussions—a betrayal of the trust they were still forging.

If he told her he had been part of the very world from which she was fleeing—if he shared the truth of his past dealings, the moral quandaries he had faced—would she pull away? Would her children, in their innocence, look at him differently? Would they see the darkness he had tried so hard to escape? The questions circled in his mind like a swarm of bees, buzzing relentlessly, demanding resolution yet leading him only to fear.

Jack stood up abruptly, cutting the quiet atmosphere like a knife. He needed air. Fleeing the confines of the house, he stepped outside into the cool dusk, the weight of the secrets pressing down more heavily than ever.

The garden was alive with the sounds of the night—a gentle whispering of the wind rustling through the leaves, the distant chirping of crickets, the soft gurgle of the stream that wound its way through the property. Jack paced the narrow path that meandered along the garden, the gravel crunching beneath his feet grounding him amidst the swell of emotion.

He closed his eyes for a brief moment, leaning against the rough bark of an old oak tree, and remembered the late nights spent poring over classified documents and surveillance reports, the thrill of the chase, the adrenaline coursing through his veins. Yet, entwined with those memories was the nagging reality of the choices he had made—the innocent lives affected by his decisions, the families torn apart due to the unseen wars waged in dark corners of the world.

How easy it had been to become lost in the thrill, to rationalize the lies told to protect one's country—even if, in doing so, he had betrayed the very essence of trust that he now sought to build with Anya.

The echo of her voice haunted him: "If there's something bothering you, you can talk to me."

Could he really share his life as an operative? Could he risk further fracturing the trust they had begun to create? Maybe it could help her to understand him better, to see that he wasn't just a retired spy hiding behind a wall of professionalism but a man capable of vulnerability. Yet, the concept of honesty felt nefarious when cloaked in complexity.

As he opened his eyes, the night sky beckoned him above. Stars dotted the vast expanse like diamonds strewn across a dark velvet backdrop, and he felt a stirring of hope. Maybe there was a middle ground—perhaps honesty didn't have to mean revealing everything.

He could introduce a sense of authenticity into their interactions without burdening her with the intricate details of his life before her.

With a sense of determination, Jack turned back toward the house, feeling a shift within him, a stirring of purpose that challenged the resinous feeling of fear that had held him captive. He would find a way to navigate the murky waters of trust, even if it meant revealing fragments of himself—pieces that could lead Anya to understand the urgency behind his desire to protect her family.

As he reentered the house, he found Anya still seated on the couch, her brows knit in concern. Mikhail and Katya had moved on to a new game, but her gaze was fixed on him as if sensing the tumult within him. "Jack?" she asked again, her voice a gentle touch against the chaos of his thoughts. "I was worried."

He took a moment to gather his thoughts. Her concern was genuine, a lifeline thrown out into the sea of his internal storm. He stepped closer, choosing his words carefully, feeling the weight of what he was about to share. "I've been thinking… about trust and secrets. About how we build relationships."

Anya's head tilted slightly, her curiosity piqued as she awaited his next words.

"I haven't always been… honest," he continued, the words spilling out, revealing the first cracks in the wall he'd built, "not just with you, but with myself too. My past is filled with shadows. And it's difficult for me to navigate this new chapter without feeling like I'm holding part of myself back."

A flicker of understanding crossed her face, and Jack felt a weight lift slightly. "I come from a world where secrets are currency," he added, his voice steadier now. "I've spent years lying to protect myself and others. But I want you to know that my intentions here are genuine. I care about you and the children. I want you safe."

Tension rippled through the air between them, each breath tense with unspoken fears and hopes. Anya's face was a blend of caution and curiosity, an open canvas where emotions played out like brush strokes. "And what if those secrets put us in danger?" she asked softly, her vulnerability shining through.

Jack felt his heart clamoring in answer, the truth reverberating within him. "That's what I fear most," he confessed. "I don't want anything to jeopardize what we're building together. You deserve honesty. But I worry that the truth will only bind you to my past."

Tears welled in Anya's eyes, and it shocked him to see her so vulnerable. "We all have our pasts, Jack. I've carried my own burdens, and I've learned that sharing them eases the weight. I may not know everything about you, but I trust you."

Her words hung in the air, powerful in their simplicity, a reminder that honesty didn't have to be an all-or-nothing affair. They could begin to share fragments of their pasts, create a tapestry woven with both light and dark threads.

"Then help me navigate it," he said, a newfound clarity forming within him. "I don't want to be that man anymore—the one who kept shadows in his heart. The past is still a part of me, but I want to build a future where we can protect one another and find healing together."

Anya studied him carefully, her gaze unwavering. "Then share your truth when you're ready. I'll do the same. But promise me you'll try."

Jack nodded, the sincerity of her request settling into his bones. Her empathy was striking, and the potential for a stronger bond seemed to shimmer before him, illuminated by the delicate balance of trust and vulnerability. Perhaps the true cost of secrets lay not in their preservation but in the strength gained through shared burdens.

And so they sat, surrounded by unspoken fears and hopeful possibilities, opening the door to a new understanding. Jack found comfort in knowing that they would face their futures together, navigating the uncertainties with honesty and courage. The night continued to envelop them, but the shadows that had once loomed over Jack began to recede, replaced with the courage to embrace the light of a new dawn.

A Call to Action

Jack sat in his dimly lit study, the only source of light coming from a small desk lamp that cast a warm glow over a collection of dusty books and scattered papers. The walls, adorned with faded photographs of a life once vivid, seemed to close in on him, reminding him of the ghosts of his past—figures frozen in time, each captured moment a reminder of choices made and paths taken. He rubbed his temples, feeling the weight of solitude settle over him like an unwelcome shroud.

The peaceful silence of his rural retreat had become a façade, masking the internal turmoil that churned beneath the surface. Ever since Anya and her children had entered his life, a sense of restlessness had begun to disturb his carefully constructed life of tranquility. He had thought retirement would grant him the peace he craved, but the presence of Anya had reignited feelings he believed he had buried long ago—the instincts of a man trained to observe, to act, to protect.

A sudden blaring of the phone jolted Jack from his thoughts, reverberating against the stillness of the room. He glanced at the screen; it was a number he recognized but rarely called upon. Thomas Blake, a former colleague from MI6. They had worked together during tumultuous times in the field, and Jack had often relied on Blake's strategic mind in moments of crisis. He hesitated for a moment, caught between the desire for connection and the apprehension of old wounds reopening.

With a determined breath, he answered the call. "Blake."

"Jack, it's good to hear your voice," Blake's tone was brisk, the kind that held urgency just beneath the surface. "I hope I'm not interrupting anything important."

"Nothing I can't put aside. What's going on?" Jack's heart quickened; he could sense a storm brewing.

"I'll get straight to the point," Blake said, his words clipped and precise. "There's been a significant uptick in Russian espionage activities within the Ukrainian intelligence community. They've infiltrated deeper than we initially estimated, and it looks like they're positioning themselves to disrupt key operations."

Jack's pulse quickened as Blake's words settled in. The details echoed the suspicions Anya had shared with him—suspicions about her husband Alex's fears regarding a Russian spy lurking within the upper echelons of Ukrainian intelligence. He felt the weight of those revelations congeal in his mind, intertwining with Blake's warning.

"And what's our involvement in this mess?" Jack asked, forcing himself to remain calm, though he felt the familiar tension of the past creeping back into his thoughts.

Blake sighed, a sound heavy with the burden of shared history. "We've been analyzing the intelligence reports, and it's clear the threats extend beyond Ukraine. We're looking at potential breaches that could compromise our operations, even here in the UK. I need someone on the ground who understands the landscape."

Jack clenched his jaw, the implications of Blake's words unfurling like a dangerous map in his mind. He thought of Anya and her children, of how precarious their existence had become since fleeing their war-torn homeland. Could he allow himself to be pulled back into the world he had left behind, knowing that it might put them in greater danger?

"Are you asking me to come back?" Jack's voice was steady, though he felt the doubt creeping in.

"I'm asking you to help." Blake's response was firm. "You know those in Ukrainian intelligence better than most. If there's any chance of uncovering the mole before they act, it's going to require someone with your expertise. But I need to stress that time is of the essence."

A danger lurked in his urgency, Jack realized, and it threatened to pull him into a vortex from which he might never return. Yet, the thought of retaking control, of diving into a labyrinth of intrigue and deception, ignited a flicker of excitement within him—an emotion he thought long extinguished. The code of the spy, the commitment etched into his very being, hummed inside him.

"I'll need more information," he said, knowing that if he accepted this path, it would lead him away from the quiet life he had carved out, bringing Anya and her family along the same treacherous road he had walked for years.

"Meet me at The Carpenters' Arms in an hour," Blake replied without missing a beat. "We'll go over everything. And Jack? Be careful. I can't stress enough how delicate this situation is."

The line went dead, leaving Jack with the weight of the decision before him. He glanced out of the window, where the fading light of day cast shadows across the landscape—there it was again, that dichotomy between light and dark that had followed him, a reminder of how easily the line blurred between safety and threat. He looked away, feeling the stirring drive within him begin to solidify into purpose.

After a moment, Jack grabbed his coat and keys, a decisive movement that left no room for second-guessing. His instincts, honed through years of experience, urged him forward. He couldn't ignore Anya's plea for help; his resolve intertwined with an obligation to protect those who had shown him the humanity he had longed for. It was time to act.

The drive to The Carpenters' Arms felt like a moment suspended in time. Jack navigated the winding roads of the English countryside, the landscape blurring outside the window as thoughts raced through his mind—Anya's fears, Alex's suspicions, and the deep-rooted bond they were forming despite the chaos. How quickly the cobwebs of fear could entwine one's heart, and yet how liberating it felt to break free from them, even for a moment.

Upon arrival, Jack stepped inside the pub, greeted by the familiar scent of hops and wood. The dimly lit interior buzzed with the sound of conversation, laughter spilling from the corners. He spotted Blake seated at a corner table, his expression serious as he scanned the room, as if measuring the risk in every face that passed.

"Jack," Blake greeted him with an appreciative nod. "Glad you could make it."

Jack took a seat, steadying himself as he assessed Blake's demeanor—sharp as ever, yet there was an undercurrent of tension palpable in the air. "What do we have?" he asked.

Blake leaned in slightly, lowering his voice. "There's been chatter among various sources that indicates a security breach. We suspect someone within Ukraine's intelligence might be passing information to the Russians. We've already lost a few operations due to compromised intel."

Jack felt a chill run through him, the implications of betrayal and treachery creeping back into his thoughts. "And Alex? What do you know about him?"

Blake's brow furrowed slightly. "I can't confirm his involvement directly, but he's in a position where he could be vulnerable to manipulation. If the mole targets him, it could put Anya and the children in serious danger."

"Damn it," Jack muttered, the urgency of Anya's situation becoming crystal clear in the thickening atmosphere. One man's paranoia could be another's reality, and if Alex was indeed being undermined, the ripples would reach far and wide.

"Your familiarity with the intelligence community could give us a head start," Blake continued. "But I need to stress that you must tread carefully. We cannot afford to raise alarms prematurely."

Jack nodded, the internal conflict churning within him. He wanted to shield Anya from the darkness encroaching upon them, yet he understood the stakes were higher than mere concern for her family's safety. This was a world where information was a weapon; to stand idly by was to potentially invite disaster.

"Where do we start?" Jack asked, determination solidifying in his voice.

Blake pulled out a folder, spreading it across the table. "We've compiled intel on key players within the Ukrainian intelligence, and I've highlighted a few who show suspicious activity. What we need now is to validate this information without drawing attention to ourselves."

Jack leaned closer, studying the names and faces that flickered across the pages. His mind raced with thoughts of Anya—how she had entrusted him with her fears, how she had stepped into his life with incredible bravery amid uncertainty. He resolved to confront the shadows that threatened to engulf them both.

"Let's get to work," Jack said, the fire of action igniting within him.

As they mapped out the steps of their investigation, the thread connecting him to Anya tightened—a bond forged in the crucible of urgency and responsibility. The mission felt like a dance with shadows, one that required careful choreography. He found himself slipping seamlessly into the role he had once played with skill—strategist, protector, soldier behind enemy lines.

Jack listened closely as Blake detailed potential surveillance targets and discussed methods for discreet investigations. The varied approaches reminded him of his past, the tactics he had employed that had both shielded lives and shattered them. Yet now, this dance held another layer—every decision weighed not only on the balance of national interest but on the fates of innocents caught in the crossfire.

That realization settled within him, heavy yet sustaining. He didn't just owe it to Anya to protect her; he owed it to each child, each family member who relied on the web of trust that had brought them all together. He felt the gravity of their intertwined destinies pull them into the murky waters of espionage—a world where conscience and duty collided.

As they moved through the conversation, the dynamics of trust and betrayal wrapped around them like an intricate tapestry, each revelation adding thread to the pattern. Jack's mind remained alive with the urgency of the task, but his heart was equally consumed by thoughts of Anya—her bravery, her vulnerability, and the strength she unknowingly imparted to him through her resilience.

Jack could see it clearly now—the interconnectedness of their fates, the fine line they now walked together. It promised danger, yes, but also purpose—something he thought he had lost forever.

When they concluded their initial strategy session, Jack felt the weight of resolve settle within him. "I need to see Anya," he said firmly. "I need her to understand the stakes."

Blake regarded him thoughtfully. "You believe she can handle the truth?"

"She already carries truths far heavier than she should," Jack replied. "I have to let her in if we're going to face this together."

"Just remember, Jack. In this game, sometimes ignorance is safety," Blake warned, concern etching its way into his features.

"Some truths are harder than others," Jack countered, determination flaring. The thought of facing another truth without Anya by his side was unacceptable; they would confront the darkness as a unit or not at all.

As Jack stepped back into the cool evening air, he took a deep breath filled with the scents of earth and foliage. He could feel the shift stirring within him again—an awareness that the battle he was drawn into would demand everything he had, from courage to resolve.

With renewed purpose coursing through him, Jack drove back to his home, the terrain once dominated by solitude now layered with an intricate web of relationships. Capacity for connection, for both love and loyalty, pulled him onward into the unknown.

He arrived home to find Anya in the living room, her children nestled on the couch with books spread across the coffee table. The sight brought an unexpected warmth, a flicker of normalcy amid the storm brewing in the shadows.

"Jack!" She looked up with a smile that momentarily dissipated the clouds of urgency brewing within him.

"Can we talk?" he asked, and her expression shifted to one of concern, a crack in the shimmering facade he had come to appreciate and protect.

"Of course," she replied, setting aside the moment of levity. Their eyes locked, and in that exchange, Jack realized just how deeply their fates were intertwined.

Leading her to a quieter corner of the room, Jack took a moment to gather his thoughts, knowing that the revelations before him would change the trajectory of their lives once again. As he explained the situation—the intelligence breach, the dangers involved, and the increasing threats—he watched her reactions carefully.

He saw the shadows of fear flicker in her eyes, replacing any semblance of safety they had built together. Yet amid the trepidation, he was struck by her strength, how she accepted the reality of her situation, ready to navigate the treacherous waters alongside him.

"What do we do now?" she asked, her voice steady yet laced with concern.

Jack's heart raced at the trust she placed in him. "We investigate. Together. And we'll find a way to protect your family. I promise."

As the glow of the evening settled around them, Jack knew there was no turning back now. Their destinies were intertwined, and with each passing moment, he felt the urgency of their mission tightening like a noose, the surrounding darkness beckoning them both toward the unknown.

With purpose renewed and challenges ahead, he felt the shadows pulling him deeper into the game, ready to confront whatever lay hidden in the dark—a dangerous dance he hadn't anticipated but one he would face fiercely, for Anya and her children depended on him.

In that moment, Jack embraced the call to action, prepared to weave his way through the intricate web of espionage once again, not only to protect his past but to forge a future filled with hope against the encroaching shadows.

A Mother's Plea

Anya's Desperation

Anya sat at the small kitchen table, the weight of the world pressing down on her shoulders. Sunlight filtered through the sheer curtains, casting soft patterns across the worn wooden surface, but the beauty of the day felt starkly out of place amid her turmoil. She stared blankly at the remnants of breakfast—a half-eaten piece of toast and a small bowl of oatmeal, its surface cooling and congealing. Her children played in the next room, their laughter and innocent chatter swirling around her, a sweet melody that felt increasingly distant.

"I can't let anything happen to them," she whispered to herself, the words barely escaping her lips. Her heart raced with desperation, and a cold sweat broke out on her brow as thoughts of uncertainty gnawed at her insides. Alex had sent her a text the day before, laced with an anxiety that left her breathless. The fleeting glimpse she had of his familiar, loving face on that screen only reminded her of how far apart they were—a gap that felt insurmountable.

She remembered the last time they had spoken on the phone. Alex's tone had been grave, almost haunting, and her every instinct had screamed at her to reach through the phone line, to pull him back into the safety of her embrace. "I don't know who I can trust anymore," he had said, his voice heavy with concern. The things he worried about—Russian spies infiltrating the Ukrainian intelligence she had once known as home—filled her heart with dread. Who could she turn to in a foreign land with two small children depending on her?

A tear slipped down her cheek, and she wiped it away angrily with the back of her hand. No, she could not afford to break down. Not now. Her children needed her to be strong. They had already lost too much, fleeing from the chaos of their homeland to this tranquil English countryside that felt like a dream and a nightmare all at once. Yet here she was, her facade crumbling under the pressure.

The kids' laughter bubbled through the air like gentle waves, momentarily distracting her from her thoughts. They were so blissfully unaware of the dangers lurking outside their little bubble, of the shadowy figures that might be interested in their father—a figure in the sprawling chess game of geopolitics.

"Mommy!" Yulia came running into the kitchen, her small hands gripping a piece of paper, crumpled and scribbled over. "Look what I drew!" Anya forced a smile, taking the drawing and studying her daughter's creation—a colorful sun shining brightly with stick figures holding hands. A tidal wave of emotion washed over her. How could something so small radiate such light? How could she protect this innocent joy when darkness loomed on the horizon?

"It's beautiful, my love," Anya murmured, fighting back another wave of tears. Her heart swelled with pride, yet it was quickly assailed by the gnawing fear for Alex's safety. "Where's your brother?" she asked, attempting to stabilize her racing thoughts.

"In the garden!" Yulia shouted with glee as she dashed out again, her laughter trailing behind her like a kite soaring into the wind.

"Viktor!" Anya called out, but her voice caught in her throat. It felt pointless to exert herself too far beyond the kitchen door. She needed to center herself first before stepping out into the fresh air, which felt increasingly oppressive.

With a deep breath, Anya forced herself to focus. She had to reach out to someone. There was still Jack—the retired MI6 officer who had opened his home to her. Despite his attempts to remain detached, his kindness had given her a sliver of hope. He had listened to her mundane stories of life before the war, and maybe he could help her navigate the chaos that had enveloped her life. His demeanor stirred a flicker of something she hadn't felt in a while—trust.

"Jack…" she murmured, testing the name on her tongue. She stood up abruptly, practically shaking off the cobwebs of indecision. This was no longer just about her; it was time to consider the future of her children. She had to be brave for them. She had to ask Jack for help.

Taking a deep breath, Anya gathered her composure and wiped her cheeks dry with the sleeve of her sweater. She stepped toward the door, each movement deliberate yet laden with trepidation. She had to make this clear to Jack—the urgency of her situation and her husband's fears.

Bursting into his world felt like thrusting her way into the midst of a raging storm, but she could not continue bearing this burden alone. She needed someone to share the weight—the fears and heartache that suffocated her.

As she crossed the threshold into the garden, the scents of fresh earth and blooming flowers filled the air. For a moment, the tranquility of the setting soothed her racing heart, but reality soon rushed back in as she spotted Jack kneeling by the flower beds, his hands deep in the soil. The soft sounds of nature blended with the earthiness of his presence, calming her turbulent thoughts momentarily.

"Jack?" she called softly, her voice quivering slightly. He looked up, the surprise in his eyes quickly morphing into a look of concern as he straightened.

"Anya?" he replied, brushing his hands off on his trousers, a faint hint of dirt smudging the fabric. "Everything all right?"

She hesitated, a churning knot in her stomach mixing with the resolve to be brave. "No," she admitted, her voice faltering before she steadied herself once more. "I—can we talk?"

Jack scrubbed the back of his neck as he nodded, and Anya led him to the small bench under the oak tree, the perfect sanctuary surrounded by dappled sunlight. As they sat down, she felt the weight of her fears crashing down around her. She took a long breath, steeling herself for the words she needed to say.

"I'm… I'm scared." Her voice came out almost as a whisper. "For Alex. There's something wrong in our intelligence department… I think he might be in danger."

"What do you mean?" Jack's brows furrowed, concern overtaking the calm façade he usually wore.

"Alex texted me," she confessed, her hands trembling slightly as she wrung them in her lap. "He believes there's a Russian spy infiltrating the Ukrainian intelligence system. He said he doesn't know who he can trust anymore. Jack…" Her voice cracked. "What if he's right? What if they find him?"

Jack's expression hardened, his level-headed demeanor slipping just slightly as he processed her words. "And you think… you think he's in immediate danger?"

"Every time he goes to work, I worry it might be the last. I can't— I can't live with this fear any longer. I need your help."

"Anya…" He ran a hand through his hair, a gesture that revealed his own internal conflict. "I'm retired. It's been years since I've worked in intelligence. I'm sure you think I have contacts, but I—"

"Please," she interrupted, her voice rising in desperation. Tears pooled in her eyes, the dam threatening to burst. "You were in MI6. You have the knowledge, the skills. I am just a mother trying to protect my kids. You have to understand how terrifying this is."

Jack fell silent, his piercing gaze studying her, an unspoken understanding passing between them. "If you're sure about Alex's situation…" he began, but Anya could see the hesitation etched on his features.

"He's not just my husband; he's the father of my children. They deserve to feel safe. I need you to help me find out what's happening. If not for me, then for them."

Jack's eyes softened, the weight of her words settling heavily on him. "All right," he finally said, his voice firm yet gentle. "I'll help you."

The relief that flooded Anya felt overwhelming—a mixture of gratitude and an immediate new form of dread mixed in the corners of her heart. She couldn't shake off the uncertainty that lay ahead, but having sought this help felt like a small reprieve from the endless worry that had become her constant companion.

"Thank you," Anya managed to say, her voice cracking with emotion as her heart swelled with gratitude. "Thank you."

As she looked into Jack's eyes, she saw not only understanding but also a flicker of determination. It was more than just an offer to help. In that moment, she recognized the budding connection between them—a connection forged through shared burdens, an alliance built on trust amidst the chaos surrounding them.

"Let's talk about the next steps," Jack said, regaining his composure, his tone shifting to one of pragmatism. "We need to gather as much information as we can without attracting attention. I'll reach out to a few contacts, see what they know. We'll figure this out, but we have to be careful."

Their conversation flowed with a new intensity, the air thick with urgency. Anya began to feel more grounded, as if a new path had opened before her.

"Right," she nodded, her resolve strengthening. "I'll gather everything Alex has told me. I have to be proactive. He may be in danger, but I can still protect my family. We'll keep the kids out of it.

They can't know… they shouldn't have to worry about any of this. I won't let them."

Jack's gaze softened again as he listened, seeing in her the unyielding spirit of a mother desperate to shield her children's innocence. "You're doing the right thing," he assured her. "You're strong, Anya. You'll keep them safe."

As they held each other's gaze, Anya felt the gravity of her plea resonate deeply. In that moment, she understood that saving Alex would mean navigating not only the dangerous waters ahead but also the emotional landscape of her own heart. The fear, the love, and the tenacity intertwined like roots of a sturdy tree, binding them together.

"Thank you," she whispered again, her voice steady yet rife with emotion. "For understanding."

And it dawned on her then—this wasn't just about Alex anymore. It was about finding strength in the darkest of circumstances, about forging a bond that might just give them both the means to fight against the shadows closing in around them. Their lives entwined through this tumultuous journey would illuminate a path forward— one of hope and shared resolve, even amid the impending storm.

Building Trust

Jack sat quietly in the dimly lit room, the warmth of the fireplace casting flickering shadows across the walls. His thoughts were a tumult of memories and remorse. He gazed at Anya, whose tear-streaked face was illuminated by the firelight. She had collapsed onto the chair opposite him, her small frame trembling as she poured out her fears regarding Alex—her husband, who was entangled in a web of danger he never intended to enter.

"Jack," she whispered, her voice hoarse and cracked, "you have to believe me. Alex is not just paranoid. He senses something is wrong. There's something dark at the heart of Ukrainian intelligence. He's felt it for months."

Jack leaned forward, his heart racing. Anya's sincerity pierced through the guarded walls he had built around his emotions. A rush of memories washed over him—years spent in MI6, navigating lives threaded through lies and truths, alliances forged in the shadows. He had grown adept at reading people, yet Anya was both a puzzle and a mirror.

What lay beneath her desperation felt achingly familiar. In his years at MI6, Jack had seen how secrecy gnawed at the fabric of trust. He recalled the faces of colleagues who had betrayed him, the friendships that had crumbled under the weight of deceit. Trust was a currency too easily spent in his former life. With every revelation of betrayal, Jack had retreated further into himself, convinced that the fewer people he allowed into his world, the less damage would be done.

But as he listened to Anya, something shifted within him. He saw a mother fighting for her children's safety, a woman on the brink, desperate to protect the little lives that depended on her. The guarded demeanor he had perfected began to thaw, and he found himself wanting to believe her, wanting to step closer rather than retreat.

"Anya," he said softly, "if there really is a Russian agent within Ukrainian intelligence… that changes everything."

She looked up, her eyes brimming with hope. "I know it sounds crazy, but Alex is worried about his boss. He's convinced that he's been compromised. There are whispers—hushed conversations he overheard. Things that don't add up. He thinks someone is feeding information to the Russians."

With each word, Jack felt the stakes rise. The echoes of his past scoffed at him, reminding him of the tangled web of espionage that had consumed his life. His instinct was to protect, but at what cost? He didn't want to become embroiled in matters he had hoped to leave behind. Yet he couldn't ignore the urgency in Anya's voice, the rawness of her plea.

"Do you have any proof?" he asked, trying to anchor the conversation in practicality. "Something tangible I can look at?"

She shook her head, a look of frustration mingling with her sadness. "No, no, nothing solid. Just a feeling, just… suspicions. But Jack, please. I know Alex. He wouldn't come to me with something this serious unless he was sure. He trusts me, he loves me."

Her declaration struck Jack with unexpected force. Love. It was a word he had withheld from everyone since leaving MI6. Love was a weakness, a vulnerability that could be exploited. It was the kind of bond that could unravel under the strain of conspiracy and betrayal. Yet here was Anya, exhibiting a fierce devotion that transcended fear—a testament to her strength and resolve as a mother.

As those thoughts wrestled with his own apprehensions, Jack felt a surge of empathy towards Anya. She had been thrust into a world that she was ill-prepared to navigate, yet she stood before him, steadfast in her resolve. The narrative he had crafted around his own solitude began to wane in her presence.

His voice softened. "If what you're saying is true, then we need to tread carefully. This isn't just about Alex anymore—it's about the safety of your entire family."

Anya nodded, her eyes flashing with determination. "I understand, and I don't want to put my children in danger. But I can't turn my back on Alex; he needs me. We need to figure this out."

The weight of her words settled heavily on Jack's chest. "And me," he added, knowing that as much as he wished to escape, he had unwittingly decided to step into the fray.

Anya met his gaze, and for a brief moment, something unspoken passed between them—an unbreakable thread of understanding. In that shared silence, what began as a plea transformed into a pact. Both were wrestling with their own demons and searching for a way forward amidst a gathering storm.

"Do you really think someone could be working against Alex?" Jack asked, seeking clarity even as uncertainty gnawed at him.

"Yes," she replied, her voice firm despite the quiver in her hands. "He's mentioned names before, but I can't recall them … Jack, I just know. He's always had a sixth sense for these things. I can feel it, too. There's a shadow hanging over our family, and it feels like it's closing in."

For the first time since Anya had arrived in his life, Jack felt a flicker of purpose igniting within him. The struggle for trust loomed large—not just between Anya and him, but within himself. He had spent years doubting every smile, every verbal agreement, and every gesture of vulnerability. He had learned that in his world, secrets were currency, but now these secrets were intertwined with a woman who had nothing left to protect but hope.

"What do you need from me?" he asked, the resolve in his voice steadying his wavering heart.

"Help," she whispered, her eyes pleading. "Help me dig deeper. Help me find the truth about Alex's suspicions… and about his boss."

Her words echoed in his mind, reigniting a sense of duty he thought he had buried forever. Jack realized he was standing at a crossroads—a choice between the safety of anonymity and the threat of danger that came with trust and connection. Each path posed risks, but this time, he felt a strange compulsion toward the unknown mystery of Anya's plea.

"I will help you," he replied, his statement firm and unwavering. "But we do this cautiously. Trust will take time—it's built in layers, not overnight. We need to share everything we know, keep communication open."

Anya nodded again, a hint of relief flickering across her weary features. "I promise. I will hold nothing back. I need you to trust me, too. This is as much about protecting your world as it is about mine. If we fail… it's more than just our lives at stake."

Jack contemplated her words, recognizing the depth of her understanding. Each was entwined in a daunting web of uncertainty. He had been trained to trust no one, but now here was Anya, extending a fallible yet genuine hand of partnership. The irony struck him; at his core, he had been a protector; in this moment, that role was being reciprocated.

They both shared their vulnerabilities, speaking of Alex's fears and Jack's past. As they navigated their fears about the potential threats, it became clear that honesty was imperative. Jack saw Anya's unwavering commitment to her family reflected in her eyes—the same steadfast loyalty he once sought, now standing before him.

"I will do the best I can, Anya. We'll have a plan. We'll be cautious," he reassured her, feeling the weight of their alliance begin to crystallize. "Starting today, we are partners in this."

"Partners," she echoed, a small smile breaking through the sadness. The bond they formed in that moment fostered a flicker of hope, a fragile light in the gloom of uncertainty.

As they discussed their next steps, Jack's mind raced with the practicalities of espionage. He envisioned gathering information, connecting dots, and perhaps discovering allies along the way while also keeping Anya and her children safe. It was risky to step back into this world, but for Anya's family, he felt a renewed sense of urgency.

Their exchange created an undercurrent of shared responsibility; Anya was no longer a stranger, but a woman whose life and heart were irretrievably intertwined with his. They shared laughter and seriousness, with an understanding that this partnership would both strengthen and challenge them. The stakes were undeniably high, but Jack recognized the quiet power of what they had begun: a collaboration built from vulnerability and determination.

In the flickering embers of the fire, Jack caught himself envisioning a future that curled around them like the warmth emanating from the flames. They could protect one another, perhaps even shield Anya's children from the escalating storm. While fear crept along the edges of his mind, it was replaced by a growing sense of solidarity. This connection was something he had long forgotten—a chance to be part of something greater than himself, more significant than burying old ghosts in his memories.

"I want to know everything you recall," he said gently, nodding toward her. "Everything about Alex's fears, those conversations he's had—no matter how small you think they are. Information is our strongest weapon."

"I will," Anya promised, the commitment clear and unwavering on her face. "I won't let despair cloud our judgment. We'll move forward together."

In that instant, Jack realized that perhaps this was the foundation of trust—offering and receiving without reservation. It was a dance of vulnerability entwined with strength. Outside, the chill of dusk deepened, but inside him, a flame ignited. Together, they would navigate this trial. If there was one lesson Jack had learned throughout his tumultuous life, it was that trust could be built brick by brick, even from the ruins of past betrayals.

As the evening wore on and their plans emerged from the shadows, Jack felt a sense of camaraderie sparking between them—a cautious yet hopeful alliance. He knew the road ahead would be fraught with danger; still, he drew hope from the fervency of Anya's plea and the earnestness with which they stepped into the unknown together.

Their partnership had begun amid chaos, but as they exchanged thoughts and ideas, Jack knew they were laying the groundwork for something profound. In that humble home nestled in the English countryside, two lives—previously strangers—were knitting together a tapestry of hope, anchored in the trust they dared to build, one tentative thread at a time. And for the first time in years, Jack felt the stirrings of something he had long buried: a belief that perhaps he could find redemption in this new path, forged through the light of another's determination and love.

A Dangerous Alliance

The rain pattered softly against the window, a rhythmic reminder of the chaotic world outside as Jack and Anya sat across from each other in the warm glow of the kitchen. In this moment, the air was thick with anticipation—an unspoken acknowledgment of the weight that had shifted between them. Anya's eyes, usually clouded with worry, now shone with a fierce determination, a flame fueled by desperation and love for her husband. Jack watched her intently, feeling the shared gravity of their circumstances.

"Jack," Anya began, her voice steady but tinged with urgency, "I need to understand what to do next. If Alex is right about his boss, then this threat… it's not just about him. It extends to us— to me and the children." She looked down, her fingers gripping the edge of the table as if seeking stability in their fragile alliance.

Jack took a deep breath, words swirling in his mind like the storm beyond the walls. He had long resigned himself to a life of quietude, far from the tumult of espionage. Yet here he was, pulled back into a world that had defined much of his past—now infused with fresh stakes and a sense of purpose. "We need to gather information about Alex's claims and the structure of his department," he replied finally, his voice calm but resolute. "If there's even a possibility that a spy is embedded in Ukrainian intelligence, we have to find out who it is. The safety of your family, Anya, depends on it."

Anya met his gaze, the corners of her mouth lifting slightly in a tentative smile. "Thank you." The words were simple but carried the weight of her gratitude and reliance on him. The irony was not lost on Jack—how someone like him, with a tarnished past in intelligence, had now become a beacon of hope for her.

Jack leaned back in his chair, allowing the momentary warmth of connection to linger before re-engaging with the issues at hand. "I think we should start by discreetly exploring Alex's colleagues. We need to identify anyone who might be contacted by or have ties to Russian operatives."

Anya nodded, her brow furrowing in concentration. "But we must be careful. The last thing we need is to alert anyone."

"I know," Jack replied, his mind racing with strategies. "We could use the children as a distraction. While I look into Alex's department, you can keep an eye on the neighborhood. If anyone begins to act suspiciously, we'll need to know immediately."

The thoughtful silence that enveloped the room was palpable as they both contemplated the notion of surveillance, a word that felt foreign yet dangerously familiar. "What if—what if someone recognizes us?" Anya's voice quavered slightly, casting a shadow over the resolute plan.

"It's a risk we'll have to take," Jack said firmly. "But we can reduce it. We have to operate under the radar. I'll do the legwork, while you can blend in. Watching your children in the park can be just a normal outing."

Desperation ignited a spark of confidence in Anya's eyes. "Yes… yes, that's good. I can do that," she asserted, finding strength in her maternal instincts. "But what if I hear something? Something crucial about Alex?"

"Then we'll meet at this same table every night to share what we find," he said. "We have to commit to full honesty. If any detail is overlooked, it could put everyone at risk."

Their gazes locked, and in that instant, Jack sensed an understanding—one forged from shared anxiety and a desire for protection. Anya was not merely a victim anymore; she was a partner, a woman ready to fight for what she loved. It was a dangerous alliance, filled with uncertainty. But he felt the warmth of urgency enveloping him, spurring him into action.

"We should each have a fallback plan," Jack continued, tapping his fingers lightly on the table to emphasize the importance of precaution. "If there's ever a moment where you feel threatened or in danger, you need to know how to escape. I can stash supplies to help you get to safety."

Anya nodded slowly, mentally mapping out the exits of the house, the quickest routes to safety, and constant movement. "What about you? If things go south…"

Jack waved her concern away. "I'll figure mine out as I go. My role is to keep you and the children safe. That is my priority."

A silence again fell between them, punctuated by the soft beats of rain against the window. Anya's resolve was tested by another wave of vulnerability, yet beneath that fear was an unyielding depth of strength. "Jack," she began softly, staring at his unyielding expression, "you're risking everything—your past, your own safety… for us. Why?"

The question hung heavily in the air, and Jack took a moment to reflect. "When I left MI6, I thought I could sever ties—the world of espionage was one that I wanted to forget." He paused, collecting his thoughts before continuing. "But the truth is, I can't just sit idly by while someone else's life hangs in the balance. It's not about just Alex. It's about you, too. You and your children deserve to know safety."

Anya's eyes softened, and the flicker of hope intertwined with her fears illuminated a flicker of understanding between them. Perhaps there was a shared humanity that reconnected them in this post-war life, bound together by the common goal of protection and trust.

"Alright, then," she said, her voice firmer now, echoing newfound resolve. "We do this together. There are safety routes I know from my life back in Ukraine, ways to move under the radar. But you have to promise me something."

Jack raised an eyebrow, intrigued. "What?"

"Promise me you won't go off on your own," she insisted, her voice breaking slightly, desperation edging her words. "I can't bear the thought of losing you too. We're in this together."

"I promise," Jack said, a twinge of sincerity punctuating his words. "I won't take unnecessary risks. I'm not the same man I used to be. I have something to fight for now."

As they fortified their resolve, they began discussing the finer points of their plan. Jack, with his keen analytical mind, mapped out various strategies they could employ to gather intelligence without drawing attention. He was aware of the intricate danger they were walking into—territory filled with shadows from his past, overlapping dangerously with Anya's uncertain present.

Over the next hour, they transformed the tension in the room into a workshop of strategy, outlining names of contacts and possible scenarios that could arise. Each scenario felt like a tightrope walk between safety and danger, but the act of forming a plan brought them closer together and solidified their alliance.

"What about Alex's boss?" Anya asked, her brow creased with worry as she added a new layer to their discussion. "If he is the one we need to be cautious of, how can we find out more about him?"

"Understanding his connections is key," Jack replied. "I'll need to leverage some old contacts. There might be whispers in the intelligence currents about his relationship with the Russian operatives. I'll be cautious, but I'll see what I can find."

Anya leaned in, her eyes shining with urgency. "Is it possible that there could be someone we can trust in Alex's department? A friend? Anyone who might know about this threat?"

Jack pondered for a moment. "It's plausible, but vetting such individuals may take time. We must tread lightly here; if there's a mole or double agent, they'll be watching everything closely. We can't risk exposing ourselves too soon."

They spent the next hour crafting lists, exchanging every detail they could muster, thoughts spilling out as quickly as their minds raced. As they compared notes and her family history, the gravity of the situation became increasingly clear. The danger loomed larger than any of them could truly grasp, and with it, the notion of trust shifted from a luxury to an absolute necessity.

The conversation drifted into their personal stories—Anya recounting memories of life in Ukraine, her skill at nurturing relationships, and the distrust that sometimes haunted those around her. Each revelation bridged the gaps in their alliance, pulling Jack deeper into her world, and he found himself sharing stories of his own experiences: of betrayal, of camaraderie, and the disillusionment that made him step away from the life he had once known so well.

Eventually, the clock on the wall chimed softly, its subtle toll bringing them back to the reality of their circumstances. The weight of time pressed upon them, and Jack knew they needed a plan of action sooner rather than later. He glanced at Anya, whose face was painted with a mix of courage and trepidation.

"Tonight, we take our first steps," Jack declared, feeling an unexpected surge of certainty. "Tomorrow morning, I'll reach out to some contacts. We can't waste any time. But I need you to promise me something—stay cautious. If the atmosphere feels off, prioritize the safety of yourself and your children."

The sincerity in his voice ignited a spark of determination within Anya. "You have my word," she affirmed, eyes steady and unwavering.

A pause settled over them, as if they were daring the universe to intervene before the ink was dry on their pact. The kitchen, now adorned with sketches of hope mixed with the chilling responsibilities ahead, became a refuge—a space where two lives converged amidst the turmoil of espionage.

Jack felt the bond between them solidify, tension radiating into something sharper—a blade forged from challenge and necessity. His internal reflections danced between anxiety and anticipation, losing himself in thoughts about the road ahead. Could they unearth the truth without becoming prey to the shadows? There was a flicker of doubt, but beneath it all, a rush of conviction washed over him.

The rain continued to drum against the window, a turbulent lullaby heralding the tempest outside. Together, packed with a mix of fear and purpose, they stood at the precipice of uncertainty, ready to embark on a journey that promised to challenge their every resolve. As they prepared to step forward, the tightening web of danger enveloped them, leaving an unmistakable sense of impending peril hanging in the air.

Together, against the shadows of their past and the emerging darkness of a broken world, Jack and Anya prepared for the fight ahead. They were ready, allies formed not just by circumstance, but by choice—their purpose now intertwined. In the face of adversity, their bond would be tested and their resolve would be the light illuminating the path forward.

The Game of Shadows

Unraveling the Threads

J ack stared at the laptop screen in the dim light of his study, the glow illuminating the lines of worry etched into his forehead. The weight of Anya's revelation pressed on his chest like a stone; the notion that her husband, Alex—a man he had never met but whose reputation was one of honor—might be ensnared in a web of espionage fueled by a Russian spy sent shivers down his spine. He had lived through the maze of deceit that characterized the world of intelligence, and now he was poised to walk its treacherous paths once more.

He opened a secure communication app, a relic of his MI6 days, knowing that this was just one of many tools he would employ in piecing together the puzzle that could endanger Anya's family. Each keystroke felt heavy with purpose; he was no longer the retired operative tending to his garden in the English countryside—he was drawn back into a life he had thought he left behind.

The Ukrainian intelligence community was not just a network of men and women wearing sharp suits and powerful expressions; it was a living, breathing organism, pulsating with the rhythm of armchair strategists and lurking shadows. Jack's mind raced back to his training days, where he had learned the importance of understanding the terrain—the physical and the psychological alike. With a mental map of Ukraine and its convoluted political landscape laid out before him, Jack initiated a search for anything related to Alex and the allegations Anya had hinted at.

His fingers danced across the keyboard, selecting keywords that would unlock the secrets held within the vast databases of intelligence. "Ukrainian intelligence adversaries," "suspected Russian infiltration," and "Operation Thaw" were just a few phrases he jotted down as a plan began to take shape in the back of his mind. He would need allies, tools, and information—pieces to assemble the jigsaw that could either confirm Anya's fears or expose a misunderstanding borne from the tensions of war.

As the screen pulled up a series of reports, Jack's heart raced at the sight of familiar terminology and denoted signatories. Each document contained details about recent operations and the tense standoff between Western nations and Russian espionage tactics. He knew these documents; they'd been part of his life for years, despite their stark realities. But now, they had a different significance—lives were at stake, and the stakes had never been more personal.

He read meticulously, absorbing every detail. There were whispers of a branching subnetwork—agents operating deep within the Ukrainian intelligence service, laying the groundwork for potential sabotage and espionage. Reports of missing agents, mysterious deaths, and unexplained delays in critical operations blurred the lines between competence and betrayal. The agency he had once trusted was now riddled with threads of deceit, all potentially leading back to the very heart of Ukraine's defense against Russian aggression.

Jack paused, staring at the wall for a moment as reflection gripped him. What lay before him now was an echo of his own past—a reminder of moments when the stakes had been impossibly high, and trust had become as fragile as glass. How many times had he gambled lives in the name of national security? How many regrets haunted him because of decisions made in the shadows?

These thoughts clashed with the pressing urgency of Anya's situation. He couldn't afford a moment of existential doubt. Instead, he had to focus; he had to protect her and her children. He shifted his gaze back to the screen, diving deeper into the digital undercurrents of the intelligence community.

Jack navigated through layers of encrypted files until finally, he stumbled upon a confidential communication that made his heart race—a correspondence between two high-ranking officials discussing an operation titled "Ivory Needle." The specifics were vague but suggestive, detailing ways to siphon information from Ukrainian intelligence. The deeper he read, the more he understood the implications: there were factions inside the agency that he could no longer view as allies.

As he analyzed the message's composition and header, his mind began to draw connections that made the hair on the back of his neck stand up. The timestamps indicated a meeting soon to be held, piecing together the fragmented puzzle of Anya's fears. Someone was orchestrating a game, controlling key players from both sides of the conflict. The significance gripped him—was Alex caught in the crossfire, or was he somehow a part of this dangerous web?

He knew he needed eyes and ears on the ground, someone who could infiltrate this opaque world without raising alarm. His contact book, filled with former colleagues and trusted agents, felt inadequate. Anya's predicament was sensitive; her children depended on their family's well-being. He needed to tread carefully.

Jack pulled a dusty notebook from the shelf, flipping to a page filled with names forgotten but not erased from memory. He noted down Agatha, a fellow officer who had transitioned into a private intel contractor after their time at MI6. Her insights into Eastern Europe were invaluable, especially regarding sensitive political climates. He picked up the phone, dialing her number with a steady resolve, thanking the universe for the connections forged in the past.

"Jack Malaney," he said when she answered, the warmth of her voice reminiscent of long-lost camaraderie. "I need your help."

Hours passed, each minute filled with anticipation that felt heavy in the air. He meticulously reviewed the data gathered, repeating facts in his mind like mantras, determined to find clarity amidst the chaos. As darkness blanketed the countryside, the weight of his task took shape—he was uncovering threads of a conspiracy that could bring ruin to innocents.

His phone vibrated abruptly, pulling him from his contemplative haze. Agatha's voice crackled through, bringing immediate images of bustling Kyiv where hidden threats operated within shadows. "We need to talk, Jack," she urged, the tension palpable even over the line. "I have information regarding the Ivory Needle operation."

Jack's pulse quickened, skepticism stirred beneath the urgency. "Can we meet? It's about Alex's situation—the timing can't be a coincidence."

"There's more at stake than you realize, Jack," she replied, voice calm and steady. "Meet me at the safe house tomorrow, noon. I'll explain everything. Bring your contact with you."

He agreed, hanging up before the weight of those words fully registered. A safe house. It had been years since he had entered one, and now the thought felt unsettling. The notion conjured images of hasty decisions and frantic escapes. It echoed layered realities within a game he had meticulously played for decades—a game he now wished to escape.

As dawn broke, Jack prepared himself for the day ahead, dawn filtering through the windows, casting gentle light against the shadows of his study. He dressed carefully, donning a sensible coat and sturdy shoes, mindful of the need to blend in and remain inconspicuous. Soon, he set out toward the meeting point, his heart racing with the anticipation of uncovering the truth.

The safe house—a nondescript building in a sleepy part of town—was a stark contrast to the intensity of the situation. Inside, Agatha awaited, her demeanor showing both resolve and caution. They exchanged perfunctory pleasantries before she stepped into serious discussion, painting an overview of the factions within Ukrainian intelligence that were festering like a wound.

"The operation doesn't just threaten Alex. It threatens the integrity of the entire agency. Someone is playing both sides," she warned, her expression grave. "I suspect the head of internal operations. We've seen irregularities, but they're often overlooked in the complexity of bureaucratic surveillance."

Jack listened intently, piecing together her insights with his own knowledge. "This Ivanov character—are you sure he's the one making moves?"

Agatha nodded, shuffling through notes. "All signs lead back to him. He has always had a knack for navigating murky waters and has known since the beginning how to play this game. But there are others involved—men with thick histories in espionage stretching back, well... it gets messy."

Jack rested his elbow on the table, asserting focus. "What's our play?"

"We monitor their communications and look for anything that indicates a foothold in the agency. Only then can we propose active measures to bring this to the above board before it gets out of control," she said, her eyes glancing towards the window, scanning for potential threats outside.

The plan solidified in Jack's mind as they exchanged methods and insights on intelligence gathering, peppering each other's ideas with caution and excitement. Together, they mapped out their course of action—connecting threads that could unravel the entire conspiracy.

However, in the midst of strategizing, Jack's mind remained restless, its gears turning continuously. The fog of suspicion enveloped him, sparking memories of situations gone awry, decisions made in moments of desperation. The haunting specter of past mistakes lingered at the edges of his thoughts. Would his pursuit put Alex in further danger? Would he risk Anya's family becoming collateral damage in a game far beyond his control?

As they plotted their next move, Jack took a moment to reflect on the fragility of trust—he had placed his faith in allies before, only to be betrayed in an instant. The thought compelled him to step back, to recalibrate his strategy. Every action held consequences; every choice had unseen repercussions.

He focused on Anya, recalling her tears as she had confided her fears. The image of her and her children bound him in a way much stronger than mere duty; it was personal. He could not let their lives become pawns in a dangerous game. He needed to ensure their safety first and foremost.

"Agatha," he said, steeling his voice with resolve. "We'll start the intel gathering, but we have to limit exposure. I want you to monitor Ivanov closely. If he's indeed behind this, it's only a matter of time before something surfaces. In the meantime, I'll keep an open line with Alex through my contacts."

Understanding crossed her face; she was well aware of the dangers inherent in trusting the instincts of any agent still wrapped up within the chaos. "Very well, but be careful, Jack. This isn't just another operation. There are lives hanging in the balance, including your own."

As the day unfolded, Jack nestled back into familiar routines, only now fueled by an intensity he hadn't felt in years. He needed to stay vigilant in a landscape riddled with deception and betrayal. He immersed himself in information, combing through data long into the night.

Hours stretched into days as he delved deeper. Calls were made, connections revitalized, and amidst the noise, clarity began to emerge. Each piece of information—every thread he pulled—slowly unraveled the tightly bound knot of suspicion surrounding Alex's circumstances.

The ghostly remnants of his previous life as an intelligence officer were no longer burdens; they had morphed into a sharpened tool, sharpened by his sense of purpose. He maneuvered through the shadows, navigating his way toward the deeper truths that waited to be uncovered.

As Jack continued to pull at the threads of Alex's life and the uncertain machinations of the Ukrainian intelligence service, the pervasive feeling of urgency intensified. It was not just about saving Anya's family; it was about uncovering a conspiracy that, if allowed to grow, could destabilize everything he had fought for in his career. The urgency of action hummed louder with each passing moment, intertwining strands of hope and fear into a complex tapestry that was only just beginning to reveal its true form.

Dangerous Liaisons

Jack stood in the dimly lit café, a sense of impatience thrumming through him as he waited for his contact to arrive. The walls, adorned with peeling wallpaper and memories of better days, offered a comfort that belied the frosty atmosphere outside. He rubbed his hands together, feeling the chill of the early autumn air gripping the London streets. He shouldn't have come here, he thought to himself, recalling Anya's worried expression when he first mentioned the meeting. But he needed answers, and with every day that passed, the urgency grew. Alex's fears became increasingly tangible, and Jack felt the kinks in the safety net they had formed growing precarious.

The bell above the door chimed, breaking Jack from his thoughts. A figure stepped inside, shaking off the dampness of the evening. The man moved with a confidence that was both familiar and unsettling. It was Philip Hargreaves, a former MI6 colleague whose path Jack had hoped to avoid after retirement. Yet, here they were, bound by the same shadows they used to navigate side by side.

"Jack," Philip greeted, a thin smile forming on his lips. He looked older than Jack remembered, with streaks of gray dominating his dark hair and lines etched around his eyes. But there was a sharpness in his glance that spoke of a vibrant mind still thriving beneath the wear of years gone by.

"Philip," Jack replied, nodding curtly. "Thanks for coming."

"Let's sit," Philip gestured to a corner table that offered a semblance of privacy. Jack followed him, his instincts on high alert. As they settled in, Jack scrutinized Philip's demeanor, deciphering every twitch, every shift in expression. Once a trusted ally, now he felt like a ghost from the past, pulling Jack deeper into a world he thought he had left behind.

Jack glanced around, ensuring they wouldn't attract unwanted attention. "You said you had information?" he prompted, eager to cut through the pleasantries. "I need to know what's going on with the Ukrainian intelligence community."

Philip leaned forward, lowering his voice. "It's more complicated than you realize. There are whispers of a mole, a Russian agent embedded within the inner circles of Ukrainian intelligence. We've got individuals who may be compromised—men and women, some of whom I was colleagues with."

Jack's pulse quickened. "What do you mean 'compromised'? Are we talking about loyalty or outright betrayal?"

"Both," Philip replied, his tone serious. "There are factions, Jack. Old grudges and new allegiances, blurred lines that make it hard to know who's actually loyal to whom. We're in a game of shadows, and it's escalating."

Jack rubbed his jaw thoughtfully, recalling Anya's fears about Alex. "What about Alex? Do you have anything on him?"

Philip hesitated, and Jack caught the slight flinch, the way Philip's eyes darted momentarily away. "You're getting too close, Jack. Alex got wind that we're looking into this. He's been cautious, and that might make him a target."

"Target for who?" Jack pressed, feeling frustration boiling beneath the surface.

"For anyone looking to take advantage of the chaos," Philip replied. "Just understand that the agency is stretched thin right now, and going deeper could endanger you—both politically and physically."

Jack's thoughts raced, calculation intertwining with concern. Anya entrusted him with her fears; he couldn't let her down now. "I can handle myself," Jack asserted, leaning closer. "What do you propose I do?"

Philip's expression hardened, shifting into something more guarded. "Trust me, Jack. You can't go in guns blazing without backup. There are lines you don't want to cross, and people you don't want to make enemies of. If you push too hard, you'll find yourself neck-deep in a mess."

Jack considered Philip's caution, but the sentiment felt hollow to him. Trust was dangerous in their field, and Philip's warnings sounded less like concern and more like protective self-interest. "I need to know who I can rely on," Jack said, narrowing his gaze. "Tell me who I should be talking to, who I can trust."

"Right now," Philip began, "you'must tread lightly. I know a couple of analysts who can give you more information. If you approach them with caution, you might glean some truths."

"Who?" Jack demanded.

Philip hesitated. "There's Amelia Graves—a sharp analyst. If you want the real scoop on the intelligence situation, she's your best bet. But keep your wits about you. Trust is a currency in this line of work."

They fell silent, both men weighing the gravity of their circumstances. Jack's instincts were on high alert; the thrill of the chase was coming back to him, but so was the fear. Bringing Anya into this was a risk, but if Alex was indeed in danger of being exposed or worse, Jack's protective instincts overrode his fear of slipping back into old habits.

"Listen, Philip," Jack finally broke the silence. "If any of this leads back to Anya or her children, I swear—"

"I know," Philip interrupted sharply. "You're not the same man you were back in the field. I respect that, but be aware of the stakes—we're in a complex web of alliances here, and it can shift beneath our feet in an instant."

The warning was heavy, lingering like a specter between them, but Jack couldn't shake the feeling that Philip had information still hidden beneath layers of guardedness. "What aren't you telling me?" Jack pressed. "If I get caught in this, we all pay the price. Just be straight with me."

After a beat, Philip finally relented. "Someone is pulling strings behind the scenes. There's chatter that links back to some senior figures who have access to both MI6 and Ukrainian intel. If you're too loud, you might end up drawing the wrong kind of attention. This isn't just local; it's geopolitical."

Jack's mind raced. He felt the weight of the world pressing down on him. He was stepping back into a domain rife with danger, one he wasn't sure he was ready for. Yet, he had to do it—for Anya, for her children, and for Alex.

"Fine," Jack said, steadying his resolve. "What's the next move?"

Philip leaned back, crossing his arms. "You should meet Amelia. I'll set it up, but be mindful. She's got ties in the agency, and there are people who wouldn't hesitate to cast suspicion on you based on your past."

"Understood," Jack replied, feeling a knot of tension in his stomach. "How soon can we meet?"

"Soon," Philip replied. "In this game, timing is everything. You need to be ready—this isn't a small operation anymore. You're playing with fire, and every player has their own agenda."

Jack stood and nodded, a sense of determination rushing through him. "I'll take what you said seriously. When can I expect to hear from you?"

"Within a week. Just keep your head down," Philip advised, pushing himself to stand. "And remember, Jack: the line between ally and enemy is thinner than it appears."

As Philip turned to leave, Jack felt a wave of nostalgia wash over him. Years ago, they used to stand side by side, facing threats together. Now it seemed they could very well be on opposing sides of a labyrinthine chess game. He watched Philip slip out into the fading light, the weight of their shared past clinging to the air like smoke from a fire long died down.

Jack lingered a moment longer, sinking back into his memories of the service—the camaraderie, the adrenaline, the sacrifices. But as he stood in that café alone, reality struck him hard. This was about more than just him; it was about Anya and her future, his own need for redemption colliding with the potential for disaster.

With determination coursing through his veins, Jack stepped back into the cool night, the shadows lengthening around him. He needed to understand the landscape ahead, and in that murky world, trust felt even more elusive than before. The stakes were high, and he realized he was walking a tightrope of allegiances, supported by a web that could unravel with a single wrong move.

As Jack made his way through the winding London streets, thoughts of Anya's worry hung in the air, urging him on. He had to forge ahead, to gather allies and decode the labyrinthine path laid before him. He had come too far to turn back now. And with every day that passed, he felt the darkness closing in around them. He had to find the light—whatever that meant in a world where shadows ruled.

Jack clenched his jaw, squaring his shoulders as he charted his course. He would protect Anya and her children, even if it meant wading deeper into a game filled with dangerous liaisons and shifting loyalties. And with every step he took, the gravity of his choices loomed larger—echoes of the past merging with the promise of an uncertain but desperate future.

The Net Tightens

The rain drummed against the window, a ceaseless rhythm that mirrored the turmoil in Jack's mind. He sat at his kitchen table, strewn with papers, files, and photographs, remnants of a life once steeped in shadows and whispers. The solace of the English countryside felt like a distant memory as the specter of danger crept closer with every passing moment. The familiar scent of damp earth wafted through the air, grounding him in the present while his thoughts spiraled into the depths of his investigation.

Jack's eyes flicked over the notes containing Alex's accounts of suspicions regarding potential Russian infiltration within Ukrainian intelligence. Each scrawled word felt weighted with urgency. He had initially pushed the thoughts aside, attributing them to the paranoia that often plagued those entangled in the world of espionage. Yet now, as he pieced together the fragmented clues, an undeniable pattern began to emerge.

He leaned forward, scanning the faces of Ukrainian officials captured in candid photographs, their expressions revealing more than a lifetime of service. Were they allies, or were they double agents? The question gnawed at him, tightening a noose around his resolve. Jack's heart raced—not from fear, but from the palpable sense of impending danger that lingered in the air.

The gravity of Anya's plight weighed heavily on his shoulders. He had made a promise to protect her and her children, yet with each new revelation, he felt the ground shifting beneath them both. If he dove deeper into this web of deceit, what would it cost him? What dangers lay in wait, and could he trust anyone in the labyrinthine world of intelligence he thought he had left behind? The specter of betrayal danced in the corners of his mind, and he could not shake the feeling that he was no longer in control.

His thoughts were interrupted by the harsh trill of his phone, ripping through the quietude like a shot fired in the night. Jack hesitated before reaching for it, a fleeting moment of introspection passing through him. could it be the call that would serve as either a lifeline or a death knell? He answered, only to be greeted by the resolute voice of Timothy, a former MI6 colleague who had once been an irreplaceable ally.

"Jack, we need to talk," Timothy said, his tone grave. "I've heard some troubling things. It's about the situation in Ukraine."

Jack felt a shiver run down his spine. "What do you mean?"

"There are whispers—about a Russian mole. It's deeper than anyone anticipated. You need to be careful."

Timothy's warning echoed in Jack's mind as he contemplated the implications of the words. The network of betrayal was not just confined to Alex's claims; it spiraled into a much larger conspiratorial framework, one that could endanger everything Jack sought to protect.

"What do you know?" Jack pressed, urgency creeping into his voice.

"More than I can say over the line. Meet me at the usual place. And bring a backup. Trust no one," Timothy instructed, his voice a low whisper before the connection cut off, leaving Jack alone once more with the rain's relentless drumming against the window.

He stared at the blank screen for a moment, contemplating the implications of Timothy's words. A backup. In his experience, that usually meant trouble. In his past, it had often meant bloodshed. Would Anya understand? Could she comprehend the risks involved if he plunged deeper into these murky waters?

Decision made, Jack grabbed his jacket and slipped out the door, the cold air biting at his skin. He pushed aside the shadows of doubt that threatened to engulf him. His resolve sharpened with each step. He would face whatever danger lay ahead—not just for Anya and her children but also to reclaim a sense of purpose that had eluded him since retirement.

The pub they had chosen to meet at sat on the outskirts of town, its dim lights flickering like fireflies on the horizon. Jack arrived early, scoping the area for potential threats. His MI6 training kicked into high gear, analyzing the interior and positioning himself out of direct sight. But the creaking floorboards and muffled conversations only reminded him of how exposed they truly were.

Timothy arrived a half-hour later, sporting a thick scarf and an expression that hinted at the gravity of their discussion. He found Jack seated in a secluded booth, the shadows cloaking them in anonymity.

"You should have stayed away from this, Jack," Timothy said, taking a seat across from him.

Jack gave a curt nod. "I didn't have much of a choice. Anya is involved now."

Timothy leaned in, his voice low. "That complicates things. The information I have—there are forces at play that run deeper than anything you've encountered before. You're putting her and her children at risk just by being here."

"I need to know the truth. For their sake. For Alex's sake." Jack's words hung in the air, weighted with uncertainty. He had never intended to become embroiled in such a chaotic mess again, but he could not abandon Anya when she had already fought so hard for her family.

"Listen to me," Timothy urged, glancing around the pub to ensure they weren't being overheard. "You've got eyes on you. People are watching. The longer you dig, the more entangled you will become. If this mole is as dangerous as suspected, it could lead back to higher-ups in the Ukrainian intelligence community."

Jack clenched his fists. "I have to figure this out, Tim. The stakes are too high to walk away now."

Timothy sighed. "You're getting in over your head. You need to be strategic—find your evidence, make sure it's solid before taking any action. Whoever is behind this won't hesitate to cut you down if they sense you're a threat."

"What about Anya? What if she finds out?" Jack felt his stomach twist at the thought.

"She's either a pawn or part of this game, Jack. You can't take chances. Look, if you want to help her, you need to be smart about it. Right now, you're a wounded beast, and you'll only attract more predators."

Jack processed Timothy's words, watching the patrons move about the pub, unaware of the danger lurking just beneath the surface. Loyalty, he realized, was a fragile thread in this world—a thread easily severed if one wasn't careful.

"Let's be clear. I'm going to protect Anya. I don't care what it costs me," Jack stated, resolve hardening in his tone.

"Then you need to play this game like a chess player, not a knight charging into battle," Timothy advised. "You gather the pieces at your disposal, watch carefully, and make your moves accordingly. Then only then can you protect those you care about."

Jack nodded reluctantly. He appreciated Timothy's perspective, yet he was unwilling to accept a passive role any longer. The risk of remaining idle felt heavier than diving deeper into the morass of espionage.

"What's next?" Jack asked, his heart racing with the magnitude of choices ahead.

Timothy leaned back, his eyes narrowing thoughtfully. "I'll look into the intelligence database for more info on the personnel Alex has worked with. In the meantime, stay sharp. And whatever you do, keep Anya in the dark for now. It's for her own safety. Trust me."

As they concluded their meeting and exchanged cautious parting words, Jack left the pub with a tangle of thoughts dancing in his mind. The rain had subsided, leaving a slick sheen across the cobblestone streets that mirrored the uncertainty ahead. The anonymity of the night comforted him as he made his way back home—where Anya and her children waited unaware of the storm swirling just outside their doors.

Upon returning, he found Anya in the kitchen, preparing a simple meal. The aroma reminded him of home, of normality—a stark contrast to the chaos he was embroiled in.

"Hey," she greeted him with a soft smile, her warmth striking him like a lifeline thrown in turbulent waters. "How was your day?"

"Just a run-of-the-mill day," he replied, forcing a casual smile. "How about you?"

She set the pot down and wiped her hands on a towel. "The children have been restless, but we played some games. We're learning new words in English." The light in her eyes made Jack's heart ache with the weight of the truth he bore.

"Sounds fun," he said, watching her with admiration. She was so strong, so resilient, yet he knew the gravity of the peril surrounding them.

"Jack, I wanted to ask you something." The hesitance in her voice sent an unsettling chill down his spine. "Are you okay? I feel like something is bothering you."

He was taken aback by her perceptiveness. It was as though she could sense the tempest brewing beneath the surface. "I'm fine, Anya. Just… things from the past catching up to me. You know how it is."

"Your past?" she echoed, her brow furrowing. "You don't have to hide anything from me."

He met her gaze, searching for an inkling of hope among the shadows. "I know I don't, but it's complicated. Just trust that I'm doing everything I can to keep you safe. That's all that matters."

Her face fell slightly, the worry creeping back in. "I just want to help. If you're fighting something, I want to know about it."

Jack couldn't bear to lie to her, yet honesty could very well endanger them both. "You are helping, Anya. Your strength is what's keeping us all going."

"Promise me you'll let me in if it gets too heavy."

"I promise," he replied, the words tasting bitter on his tongue.

After dinner, he sat in solitude, immersed in the papers spread out on the table. But now, beneath the patter of silence, he felt Anya's unresolved worry haunting the air around him, rendering him restless.

The unease gnawed at him as he flicked through the names on the list. With Timothy's warning echoing in his mind, Jack contemplated his next move carefully. Each syllable, every name invoked memories of loyalty and betrayal.

He resolved to take the next step cautiously. An investigation with multiple avenues to explore, leads to confirm or deny, while simultaneously preparing for the confrontation he sensed looming just ahead.

The clock ticked on, the rhythmic sound blending with the distant muzzle of rain falling against the windowpanes. His heart raced with apprehension, the tension coming to a head as he prepared to delve deeper into a perilous unknown. Each decision cradled the weight of uncertainty; each movement was a step further into the shadows.

With a deep breath, Jack grabbed his jacket and pocketed his phone. Any lingering doubt vanished, replaced by an unwavering resolve. The net was tightening with each clue uncovered, but whatever dangers lay ahead, he would wage war on the shadows. For Anya, for Alex, he would find the truth.

As he stepped into the night, Jack's heart pounded—a furious rhythm threading through the darkness. There was no turning back now.

Crossing Lines

The Tension Mounts

Jack stood in his study, a cluttered room filled with remnants of a past life. The walls, lined with books on espionage, strategy, and intelligence, felt like a fortress that confined his thoughts as much as it inspired them. He had always liked the dark, brooding atmosphere of the place; it allowed him to burrow deeply into the complexities of his mind. However, today, the very air felt heavy, palpable with a foreboding tension he could not shake off.

At his desk, a map sprawled open, featuring doodles and scribbled possibilities born from his thoughts. Each marked location represented not just a place, but a connection to the threat looming over Anya and her children. The more Jack delved into Alex's claims, the more unsettling truths emerged, turning what was initially a simple investigation into an intricate web of danger.

"Jack?" Anya's voice cut through the silence, drawing him from his thoughts. He turned to see her standing at the doorway, her figure framed by the fading light of the setting sun. There was an apprehension in her posture, a slight weight that suggested she sensed the unease in him. Her presence in his home had introduced an unexpected warmth, but it was now overshadowed by the reality of their situation.

"Come in, Anya." He gestured towards the chair across from him. "I was just going over some things."

She crossed the room, the quiet scuff of her shoes against the wooden floor the only sound as she took her seat. The children were already tucked away for the night, blissfully unaware of the dark clouds gathering around them. Jack marveled at how Anya had fallen into a rhythm with life here, yet he could see the underlying fear simmering just beneath her composed exterior.

"What have you found?" Anya asked, her gaze intent yet tinged with hesitation. It was a question Jack had come to dread, one that carried the weight of her hopes and fears.

He hesitated, contemplating the best way to frame his discoveries—how to lay bare the truths without shattering her fragile calm. "I've been tracing Alex's situation based on the information he provided about his suspicions. It's... complicated."

Anya leaned forward, her elbows resting on her knees as if bracing herself for impact. "What does that mean?"

"The more I look into it, the more I find connections that lead back to the very core of the intelligence community in Ukraine. There are individuals here who may have their allegiances compromised, but..." He paused, searching her face for signs of how much she could bear. "There are threats emerging from angles we hadn't considered, ones that could endanger your family more than we thought."

The silence that followed was heavy, laden with the unsaid fears that lurked in the corners of both their minds. "You mean... it's not just Alex? They could be after us too?" Anya's voice quivered, each syllable laced with a vulnerability that struck Jack deeply.

"I'm afraid so," he replied, his heart heavy in his chest. "The more I uncover, the more I realize how intertwined our fates are."

Anya looked down, fingers fiddling with the hem of her sweater—a nervous habit he had come to recognize. "I thought we were safe here. I thought I was doing the right thing by bringing the children here."

Jack's chest tightened. He felt the weight of his own past decisions bearing down on him, the knowledge that moving away from one danger sometimes led straight into another. "I know, Anya. But we need to stay vigilant. The danger is closer than it seems—I can feel it."

Her eyes met his, dark pools of worry reflecting the storm brewing within her. "What do we do now?" Her question was quiet, yet pulsed with urgency. Jack could feel the shift in their dynamic, the transition from mere acquaintances bonded by misfortune to partners entrenched in a treacherous path of truth and survival.

"We keep investigating," he said gravely, willing conflict from his voice. "We keep finding the threads that connect everything, and we prepare ourselves for what lies ahead. I won't let anything happen to you or the kids."

Anya nodded slowly, yet he could see the flicker of fear in her eyes as she considered their reality. Jack understood the weight of the commitment he was making—not just to uncover the truth, but more importantly, to protect her and her children from the looming shadows of danger.

In the ensuing silence, they shared an understanding—a meeting of minds framed by their distinct, entwined struggles. Each of them carried burdens that felt heavier than the other could see, yet, together, they were learning to lean towards one another for support, to forge strength from shared vulnerability.

As night deepened outside, an unsettling thought burrowed into Jack's mind. What if they were too late? What if he couldn't figure out the strands connecting Alex's fears before something catastrophic happened? He had played his part in the world of espionage before, often dancing on the edges of danger, but this felt different. The stakes had grown unbearably personal.

"There's something else," he began, drawing Anya's attention back to him. "I think I might have caught wind of communication that suggests we've been flagged. Someone could be aware of our investigation."

Anya's breath hitched, and Jack could see the realization wash over her. "You mean… we could be in danger right now?"

"Possibly." Jack's heart sank at the deep lines of fear now etched across her brow. "But we have to stay focused. We can't let this dictate our actions. I need you to trust me, Anya."

A small expression of resolve flickered in her eyes. "I do trust you, Jack. I just—it's so hard to keep my fear at bay when I think about my children…"

"I know," he replied softly, crossing to the desk to offer her a comforting hand. "Every step we take from now on needs to be calculated. We've come too far to reverse course."

Anya took a deep breath, visibly steadying herself. "Then what's the next step?"

He paused, brainstorming their options. "I need to vet the intel I have about Alex's circle—identify who's involved, who we can trust." He continued, recalling earlier pieces of information. "We can set up a meeting with one or two of his colleagues under the guise of a routine check-in. Nothing too suspicious, just enough to gauge the environment."

Anya nodded, though uneasiness lingered in her eyes. "And if these people are involved?"

He grimaced. "Then we play our cards carefully. I'll gather more information before we escalate anything too overtly. Discretion is our friend right now."

As they mapped out their next moves, Jack's mind spiraled with intricate webs of connections—faces and names he'd known from his past mingling with the intelligence reports butchered and dissected before him now. Nothing was ever simple in the world of espionage; he had known that all too well. Yet, something about this new reality struck him—there was an urgency to protect not just secrets, but lives.

Anya's voice broke through his turbulent thoughts. "Jack… thank you for doing this. I can't—" Her words faltered as the sudden weight of her emotions filled the room.

"No, thank you," he replied, lifting her chin gently. "You've shown a strength I admire. That alone drives me to do everything I can."

The genuine connection between them felt transforming. It was as if their shared vulnerabilities rewrote the very fabric of their relationship. Suddenly, they were no longer just neighbors or acquaintances caught in circumstances beyond their control. They were allies, facing the looming shadows together.

As the night progressed, Jack once again plunged into research, evaluating connections within the Ukrainian intelligence community. Anya, too restless to sleep, joined him, the weight of their shared purpose cementing their growing bond. Hours passed unnoticed as they unearthed troubling patterns, red flags rising higher than ever before.

Jack couldn't shake off the uncertainty that loomed over them. Each discovery felt like a tightening vice—a reminder of how intricately entwined their fates had become. Time stretched and warped, their conversation morphing into a sinister play of strategy and caution.

As they worked late into the night, it felt inevitable that Jack would find himself leaning into Anya more. She filled parts of him he didn't realize had remained hollow since his retirement. In fighting against an invisible danger, he felt himself drawn closer to her, and in her presence, he found the flicker of hope despite the pervasive threat they faced.

The first light of dawn crept over the horizon, an ethereal glow illuminating the chaos within the room. Jack rubbed his eyes, fatigue pooling beneath them. Anya sat across from him, her brow furrowed in thought, an expression etched with resolve.

"We can't let them take this from us," she suddenly declared, her defiance igniting a spark in the air. Jack felt a renewed sense of hope pulse between them, a reminder that they were not merely passive players in this fast-approaching whirlwind.

Anya stood to pace restlessly. "We have the drive to uncover this. We just need to be smart about it."

Jack nodded, a sense of urgency flooding his veins as they discussed different strategies. They outlined a plan, mapping out every potential move, every possible risk, all while leaning on their newfound connection, deepening their trust.

At one point, Jack could feel the rush of adrenaline surging within him, the creeping danger taking the shape of urgency, compelling him to act decisively. They were in this together, and the thought instilled a sense of strength he hadn't anticipated.

As they worked, a glimmer of determination sparked in Anya's eyes, one that mirrored Jack's own restless spirits and courage battering against the wall of hesitation that had surrounded them. In those moments, amidst the chaos and uncertainty, they became a force of their own, blending intellect with emotion, steadfast against the tide of uncertainty and fear.

Yet, the reality was never far from their minds. Each moment spent poring over documents, pouring over intelligence reports and discussing strategies was followed by a fingerprint of fear running down their spines. With each passing day, the shadows grew longer, and dangers loomed larger, and uncertainty clung to them like a mantle.

Jack looked out through the window into the early morning light, his thoughts swirling with remnants of adrenaline and fear. Deep down, he knew that they were still teetering on the precipice of danger. The pieces of their lives had converged, intertwining them into a story woven with tension, fragmented with dread yet vibrant with a sense of loyalty and bond forged amidst peril.

Together, they would face the shadows. Together, they would fight to defend each other and protect the future they now sought to claim, because in a world steeped in menace and uncertainty, it was the belief in each other that offered the faintest glimmer of light.

A Breakthrough—And Setback

Jack sat at the small, cluttered kitchen table, his laptop open in front of him. The morning sun streamed through the window, but he barely registered its warmth. His mind was a tangled web of information and theories, each strand pulling him deeper into the darkened corners of the Ukrainian intelligence community. The breakthrough he'd been waiting for had finally arrived—a leak of information that could potentially expose the Russian spy Anya feared could infiltrate her husband Alex's operations. But as he reviewed the evidence he had gathered, a sinking feeling gnawed at his stomach.

His phone buzzed on the table, cutting through the thick silence. It was a message from MI6, his contact, a man named Simon Kent, whose once-frank communications had recently turned fraught with tension. A sense of dread settled over him as he picked up the device, glancing at the brief text that read: "We need to talk. This is too hot to handle. Abandon your investigation."

Jack's heart raced, his pulse quickening as he processed the implications. The urgency in Simon's words echoed in his mind, a stark reminder of the risks involved. He had been reinforced by the hope that Anya's fears were not unfounded, and now the mere idea of retreat felt like betrayal—not only to her but to everything he had stood for during his years at MI6. He leaned back in his chair, closing his eyes, the burden of his predicament weighing heavily on his shoulders.

A soft knock broke his reverie. Anya entered the kitchen with a tray, her two children in tow. They carried an assortment of brightly colored pastries that had been baked earlier that morning. Yet, today, even their sweetness felt dull to Jack. He forced a smile, attempting to mask his unease.

"Good morning, Jack!" Anya said brightly, placing the tray on the table and flashing a hopeful smile. "I thought we could celebrate your progress with some of these."

Jack nodded, his focus shifting momentarily to the children, who chirped excitedly about their favorite treats. But even their laughter felt muted against the cacophony of conflicted thoughts in his mind. He forced himself to engage, picking up one of the pastries, but his appetite had vanished. Instead, he glanced at Anya, whose face glowed with optimism, blissfully unaware of the storm brewing inside him.

"Um, my contact at MI6 just...." He stopped, considering how to break the news. Anya's eyes sparkled with encouragement. "What is it, Jack?"

He hesitated, the weight of the world resting on his words. "They're saying it's too dangerous to continue. They want me to abandon the investigation."

Anya's expression shifted, her face paling slightly as shock registered. "But you only just found something! You can't stop now, not when we're so close!"

Jack looked away, the internal battle overwhelming him. "I know, but—"

"No 'buts,'" she interjected, her voice rising slightly in urgency. "This is our family's safety at stake, Jack! You've come this far, and you can't just…give up."

He looked into her eyes, meeting the fierce determination in her gaze and feeling an echo of his own resolve. Yet, a stubborn voice persisted within him. "This isn't just a game, Anya! If MI6 thinks it's too dangerous, then it is! They know the risks better than we do."

"Do they?" Anya's voice trembled slightly, revealing cracks beneath her composed exterior. "Do they understand what it's like to live in fear every day? To worry if you will ever see your husband again? Jack, this isn't just intelligence work. This is about lives—my children's lives!"

Her passion ignited something within him, a flicker of conviction fighting against the shadows of doubt. Jack leaned forward, resting his elbows on the table and steepling his fingers. "Listen, Anya. I want to help you; but if I lose my job—or worse—the information could become compromised. I can't put you in further danger. You need to understand that."

Anya's frustration morphed into desperation, her voice softening as she implored him. "What if Alex is right? What if there truly is a spy in his unit, posing a threat not only to him but to so many others? You can't just turn away now, not like this. I need you."

Her words hit Jack like a physical blow, resonating deep within him. He had grown attached to Anya and her children, their lives interwoven with his own in unexpected ways. They had become more than mere casualties of a distant conflict; they were real, breathing people with stories and futures that depended on their next choices. The stakes were uncomfortably high, but was he prepared to walk away?

"Anya…" he began, but she shook her head in frustration.

"Please, Jack," she whispered, tears pooling in her eyes. "If there is even the slightest hint that something may be wrong, we have to dig deeper. For Alex, for our children… I can't let fear run my life anymore."

He paused, weighing her words. The raw emotional weight hung thickly between them, and Jack felt the resolve begin to harden once more within him. "You're right. I—"

Before he could finish, the children interrupted with bright laughter, oblivious to the heavy tension in the room. Their innocence was a balm, pulling him further away from his anxious thoughts. When their laughter faded, Jack leaned closer to Anya, their faces inches apart.

"Okay. We'll at least look into it together. Maybe we can find something concrete."

Anya searched his eyes, as if trying to gauge the sincerity of his words. "Thank you, Jack," she said softly, relief washing over her features. They held the moment in silence, the bond between them transforming from partners in this tumultuous journey into something deeper.

But before he could bask in the warmth of their connection, vulnerability wrapped around him once more. A fresh wave of anxiety washed over Jack, rallying forth reminders of the implications of their decisions.

"Just—promise me that we'll be cautious," he said, half a plea. "If anyone gets wind of this, everything we've worked for could be jeopardized."

"Of course. But we're in this together, right?" Anya's eyes sparkled with determination.

"Together," he echoed, though the word felt heavy as it left his lips.

As the day wore on, Jack returned to his investigation, pouring over the documents he had gathered—connections, movements, even the whispered rumors that had come his way. The dots were still scattered through the chaotic framework of intelligence that rattled around in his mind, and he needed to pull them together into some semblance of clarity.

Anya stayed in the kitchen, helping the children with their homework as they defended their spaces from growing stacks of papers and folders. Jack worked methodically, combing through each lead, assigning importance to some and discarding others. Hours blended into one another, and just as he felt progress emerging, his phone rang again.

It was Simon, his voice clipped and urgent. "Jack, listen. I know you think you're onto something, but you need to stop. The higher-ups are getting anxious about you digging into this. There are forces at play here that you don't understand."

Jack clenched his fists, irritation flaring underneath. "You don't have to remind me of the risks, Simon. I'm already aware. But it's not just about my investigation anymore. It's about Anya's family—her children. What am I supposed to do? Just sit back and let this potential threat become a reality?"

"Right now, that's exactly what I'm suggesting. Back away before it's too late. You don't want to turn this into a witch hunt. You may not be the only one in jeopardy should you push too hard."

"Jeopardy?" Jack spat, fury spreading through him. "You mean like the jeopardy Alex is in? Or Anya's children?"

A tense silence hung heavily in the air, too thick with unspoken truths. Jack braced himself for Simon's response. "There are bigger games being played, Jack. I can't stress enough how dangerous this situation is."

Jack's heart raced. "What exactly are you implying? Are you trying to warn me away from what should be lifted to the light?"

Simon sighed heavily, the crackle of static in the connection amplifying the silence that followed, leaving Jack feeling exposed and vulnerable. "I'm saying what you're doing isn't just risky. You know how MI6 operates. If we have a mole in our ranks, then it's a far-reaching web, and you don't want to start tugging at any loose threads. Things could spiral out of control."

Jack felt a sharp pang of frustration. "And what about Anya? What about her children—that they could be in danger? What price are we willing to pay for safety? I cannot just fold when there's a possibility we could be saving lives!"

"When does your sense of loyalty turn into blind foolishness?"

"Simon, I'm done doing what I think is expected of me. I'm doing what is right." He hung up, the finality of the gesture sending a shiver down his spine. Shaking with adrenaline, he leaned back in his chair, breathing hard.

A soft knock at the door broke through the fog that had settled around him, and Anya slipped into the room, her expression shifting from concern to sympathy as she approached.

"What was that about?" she inquired gently.

"It's nothing," he said too quickly, a tinge of guilt lacing the words.

"Jack…" she pressed, catching the tension in his features.

"They want me to stop," he said, swallowing the bitterness rising in his throat.

Her brow furrowed. "What do you mean? They're trying to pull you away from us?"

"It's not that simple."

"What's going on, Jack? I can feel the tension in the air."

Jack let out a heavy breath, the frustrations spilling over in a torrent of thoughts. "Simon thinks that this investigation could blow up in everyone's face. He says that there are more dangerous forces involved, but of course, he won't say what they are."

"What does that mean for us? Are we just supposed to sit here and wait?"

A thousand conflicting sentiments bubbled beneath the surface as he grappling with the gravity of their situation. "I don't want to involve you in this," he admitted quietly.

"Jack, I've already chosen to be involved. You don't get to make that decision for me," Anya insisted, an edge creeping into her voice. "You can't ignore my voice in this. I won't let you."

"And I won't let you put yourself and your children in danger," he shot back, frustration coloring his tone.

"But you're willing to risk yourself! How is that fair?" Her words stung, each syllable a reflection of the fear that haunted her.

"It's different, Anya! I signed up for this!"

"But you also signed up to protect people, Jack. Not just the lives of faceless individuals but people with families and futures."

Silence enveloped them, neither willing to back down. The tension between them spiraled, twisting emotions that had begun to forge a partnership now morphing into something brittle, like glass teetering on the edge.

Anya took a step back, closing her eyes as if gathering herself. "Maybe you need to reflect on what you're doing here and who is at risk."

"I am reflecting!" Jack shot back, the desperation in his voice echoing in defiance. "I need to find the truth, and baring that, I have to care about honesty and safety. What else would I be doing?"

Her voice softened, but the resolve within remained unyielding. "You were once part of a system that could help—MI6 could protect you. But now? You're digging deep into a dangerous mess, Jack. I can't turn a blind eye to that."

"We're too close to turn back now," he said, his voice weary.

"I know," she whispered, "but please promise me you will think of the others involved instead of this strange mix of vengeance and redemption for your past. Remember, we have children here who rely on us."

Jack swallowed hard, grappling with the reality of her words. "I promise I will think of them."

"Good, because if I can't trust you, then who can I trust?"

The weight of that statement hung heavily, forcing Jack to confront the crux of their lives in this moment. He had ventured into the shadows of intelligence with a resolute belief in purpose. But in that shifting cloud of uncertainty lay a new understanding of the choices made for families, not just himself.

They took a moment, the air around them thick with tension, and Jack recognized he had stumbled into darker territory than he had anticipated. No longer was this solely about unraveling a potential conspiracy; it was about loyalty, trust, finding a new light amidst the shadows that crossed their lives.

The weight of the conversation broke them apart as Anya stepped out of the room, leaving Jack to wrestle with his turmoil. With every fault line exposed, clarity and uncertainty coiled tightly within him. He looked once again at the evidence sprawled across the table, knowing that his choices were impossible to unpick from the possibilities of conflict and the unknown.

As the sun set, they fell into an uneasy silence that punctuated a tentative truce between them. Whatever choices lay ahead would shape their journey—one that would traverse the shadows of danger and the light of hope as they sought a balance in their lives defined by trust.

The night deepened around them, but the resonance of unresolved tension remained, laying the road ahead as uncertainty spread its fingers wide, hanging like a promise in the stillness of the air.

The Crossing

The muted glow of his desk lamp cast elongated shadows on the walls, the soft hum of the evening outside barely penetrating the serenity of Jack Malaney's secluded office. The air hung thick with tension; he could almost feel it, a living thing swirling around him. He had poured over countless documents, scouring the labyrinth of intelligence he had unearthed over the past few weeks. Each line he read heightened his anxiety as he discerned the increasingly dangerous landscape surrounding Anya and her children.

Jack stared down at the pile of files spread out before him, each page stained with the urgency of truth. Anya's husband, Alex, had been adamant about his suspicions—there was a mole deep within the Ukrainian intelligence community, someone feeding crucial information to their adversaries. It was a chilling prospect and one that had not only jeopardized Alex's career but, more disturbingly, endangered the lives of his family. As Jack wrestled with this revelation, he felt the weight of responsibility settle onto his shoulders.

Anya, with her haunted eyes and trembling voice, had opened up to him in a moment of vulnerability. She had relayed Alex's fears with a desperation that struck deeply and stirred up memories within Jack—memories of loyalty tours alongside comrades he trusted completely, only to discover betrayal lying quietly beneath their camaraderie. Now, confronted with Anya's plea for help, Jack was forced to navigate a maze of moral dilemmas.

What if Alex was right? What if this Russian mole could be the key to dismantling their world, ripping apart the fragile peace they fought to maintain? Jack's heart raced at the implications. But who could he trust? Could he even trust Alex? He was darkly aware that in espionage, appearances were notoriously deceiving.

As the clock ticked on, the hours melted away. Jack's mind flashed back to a mission he had conducted in Eastern Europe years ago, amid a web of deceit that mirrored the present situation. He remembered the quiet terror that gnawed at him day in and day out, the sharp jolt of adrenaline he felt whenever his cover seemed compromised. The stakes felt just as high now, yet his heart was not that of a field agent anymore—it was the heart of a man who had retired from that life, drawn to tranquility and a sense of normalcy he thought he had achieved.

But peace was a fickle master. It had brought Anya and her children into his life, and he could no longer turn his back on them. It was as if by taking them in, he had unwittingly opened the door to a war he thought he had left behind.

He was acutely aware of the risk he faced. He knew enough about the protocols of MI6 to understand that betraying any governmental operation—even one fraught with integrity issues—was treachery of the highest order. Yet, how could he stand idly by when innocent lives hung in the balance? Anya's children needed a safe future. They had already suffered too much.

Despite the swirling chaos in his mind, his decision began to crystallize. He would reach out to his contacts—those few who still dwelled in the shadows of international intelligence. Somewhere, there had to be proof of Alex's claims. He would gather evidence, weigh the truth against the consequences, and then determine a path forward. But then another thought flared to life: there was no guarantee that what he might unearth wouldn't plunge everyone deeper into danger.

Jack leaned back in his chair, raking a hand through his thinning hair. He closed his eyes, allowing himself a moment of clarity amidst the storm. In that silence, he envisioned Anya—her gentle strength amidst chaos, her fierce love for her children. The tears that streamed down her cheeks when she first confided in him were still raw, the echo of her voice pleading for help still ringing in his ears. The weight of his own choices had never felt so tangible.

He knew what he had to do, yet the enormity of it settled heavily on him. He could no longer be the solitary figure standing at the crossroads of decision. Jack had to share the burden with Anya. They would face this uncertainty together. She needed to know that he was on her side, that she wouldn't have to fight this battle alone. A surge of determination filled him. He picked up his phone and dialed.

The line rang, each beep a countdown to a decision that would shift the trajectory of their lives. When the call connected, Jack cleared his throat, forcing his voice to steady itself in the wake of nervousness. "It's me. I need you to meet."

"Where?" The voice on the other end was businesslike, but he sensed the undercurrent of worry.

Jack hesitated. "At my place. I have something important to discuss."

"Give me ten minutes."

As he hung up, Jack's heart thudded against his ribcage. He flicked his gaze toward the window, the bleakness of the night seemingly amplifying the weight of his situation. Outside, the world continued its course, oblivious to the glamour of espionage and the secrets at play. To them, it was just an ordinary evening, but for Jack, every second counted.

Minutes later, the door creaked open, his MI6 contact—a wiry man named Oliver Chase—stepped inside. "You said you had something." His skepticism barely masked his concern.

Jack gestured him to a seat. He took a deep breath and dove into his findings, revealing the intricate intelligence network he had begun to uncover. He detailed everything—Anya's fears, Alex's suspicions, and what he had discovered about potential agents lurking in the shadows.

Oliver listened intently, his brow furrowing in concentration. "You realize that if this is true… if there's a mole, we have a serious problem on our hands," he said slowly, weighing each word. "What's your plan?"

"I'd like to run a background check on every key player within the agency," Jack replied, his voice steady but laced with urgency. "See if we can find anything that connects them to Moscow."

Oliver's jaw tightened. "You're treading on dangerous ground. If you're wrong—"

"I have to do something," Jack cut him off, the desperation in his voice rising. "Anya's family is at risk. She deserves to know the truth—however grim it may be."

There was a beat of silence, punctuated only by the distant sound of a car radio playing slightly off-key in the street outside. Oliver's eyes searched Jack's, gauging sincerity, and somewhere between them lay an unspoken understanding of what was at stake.

"The agency's reputation is fragile," Oliver cautioned. "If you're caught…"

"I'm aware of the risks," Jack interjected firmly, unaware of the unsettling tremor in his own voice. "But I cannot allow Anya to endure that fear alone. If I let her down now, I will never forgive myself."

A long moment stretched between them, a shared acknowledgment unfurling like the wings of an approaching storm. Jack sensed Oliver's resolve waver, but no matter the risks, Jack's mind was made up. His loyalty was not a choice between institutions; it was grounded in the flesh and blood of the innocents he had come to care for.

"Fine," Oliver finally relented, breaking the tension with resolution. "I'll run the checks discreetly. But I want to remind you: if we uncover a mole, there will be repercussions for all involved."

"I understand," Jack said quietly, knowing well the implications of his actions.

Oliver gathered his things, preparing to leave, but Jack seized the moment. "What if they come for me? For Anya?"

"Stay vigilant, Jack. Trust no one but those closest to you. If you sense something is off—"

"—I'll contact you," he finished, a nod of understanding shared between them.

As Oliver departed, both men knew the gravity of the crossing they had just made; there was no turning back now. Jack felt as though he had stepped onto a tightrope, the abyss yawning below him. He returned to his desk and took a deep breath, desperately trying to center himself amid the whirlpool of emotions threatening to swallow him whole.

It wasn't long before he found himself seated at the table in his modest kitchen, waiting for Anya to arrive. He poured a cup of tea, hoping the warm beverage would soothe his roiling stomach and keep the waves of uncertainty at bay. The kettle creaked, echoing the anxiety thrumming in his veins.

When the doorbell rang, it sent a jolt through Jack, the sound slicing through the silence like a knife. He stood abruptly and padded to the door, opening it to find Anya standing there, her dark eyes searching his face for answers. She looked weary; the shadows under her eyes hinted at sleepless nights spent worrying about Alex and their future.

"Jack?" Her voice was barely a whisper, and he could feel her apprehension hanging in the air.

"Come in," he urged, stepping aside to allow her entry. The moment she crossed the threshold, the tension between them felt palpable, electrifying the air.

"Is everything okay?" she asked, her brow knitting together in concern.

He motioned for her to take a seat at the table. There was a moment's pause as Anya settled into the chair, her fingers clasping each other tightly as if holding onto a lifeline.

"Anya," Jack began, his tone serious but gentle. "There's something we need to discuss."

He drew in a deep breath, swallowing down the uncertainty. He owed it to her to be straightforward about the risk they faced. He laid out everything he had uncovered—Alex's suspicions, the potential of a mole in the intelligence community, and his plans to investigate further. Her brow furrowed deeper with each detail he shared, a mix of fear and determination flickering across her face.

"I can't just let this go," she stated, her voice trembling but resolute. "What if Alex is right? What if there's someone inside working against him?"

"I want to find out the truth," Jack confirmed, watching as the realization settled over Anya, their fates crashing together in a storm of shared purpose.

"But what if we uncover something dangerous?" she whispered, her voice thick with anxiety.

"It's a risk I'm willing to take," Jack replied firmly. "For you, for your children. We have to act."

Anya's gaze dropped to the table, her fingers fidgeting as thoughts raced through her mind. "And what does that mean for us? For Alex?"

Jack met her gaze, understanding the weight of her question. Their lives had become intertwined in ways neither of them had anticipated. The stakes were now higher than they had ever been—far beyond a simple investigation.

"We face this together," he said, allowing his resolve to bolster his words. "You will not fight this battle alone. I will help you as long as you're willing to trust me."

The conflict mirrored in Anya's eyes was palpable; hope flickered beneath her worry, but the fear had not yet subsided. "And if it leads to more danger?" she asked, doubt mixing with desperation.

"There's no easy path, Anya. But choosing ignorance isn't the answer either. We have to act before it's too late. The moment you walked into my life, I made a promise, whether I vocalized it or not. I'm here to protect you."

Tears brimmed in her eyes, and he could see the inner turmoil she struggled against, that fine balance between hope and despair. "What if Alex gets hurt because of this? I can't lose him, Jack. I can't lose my family."

Jack reached across the table, his hand covering hers. The warmth of his touch anchored her, providing a momentary refuge amidst her dread. "We will do everything we can to keep your family safe. I promise."

Their fingers remained locked together, an unspoken agreement solidifying between them as they steeled themselves for the unknown. Jack couldn't shake the premonition of impending doom that loomed, a darkness hovering over their decisions—a reflection of the world they had now entered together.

In that charged moment, an electric disappointment flickered in the air. The weight of their circumstances bore down heavily, knowledge intermingling with aching vulnerability. Jack had forged this connection with Anya amid their struggle, and now, as they prepared to confront a shifting world, there was no going back.

They exchanged hesitant smiles, the shadows of doubt only temporarily illuminated by a shared determination. But just as the flicker of hope seemed to take root, an ominous sound resonated outside—a sharp crack that shattered the tenuous calmness in their vicinity.

Jack's senses snapped to alertness, instincts honed from years of training kicking in. The tension in the room thickened with unspoken fears. Anya's breath caught in her throat, eyes wide as she glanced toward the window.

"What was that?" she whispered, each word heavy with apprehension.

"Stay here," Jack commanded softly, rising from the table. He moved quietly toward the window, his heart pounding a frantic rhythm against his chest. The street was eerily still, shadows cast by the streetlights creeping along the pavement. But something felt off, a ripple in the calm that set his nerve endings ablaze.

He leaned closer, pressing his forehead against the cool glass, peering outside as he tried to discern what lay beyond the edge of visibility. Seconds turned to agonizing minutes, the silence stretching as he felt Anya's presence behind him, her unease palpable.

Then he saw it—a figure in the distance, lurking in the shadows, a silhouette that seemed to watch him. Jack's heart dropped, adrenaline surging through him as he recognized the stance, the stillness hinting at danger approaching.

"Anya!" he shouted, a mixture of urgency and fear flooding his voice. "Get down!"

Instinct took over as he spun to face her, just as the sound of chaos erupted outside—shouting voices, a growl of engines, shattering the quiet of the evening. The tension that had already coiled around them became an iron grip as panic seized Anya's face.

"Jack!" she cried, horror suffusing her voice as he hurriedly motioned for her to hide.

"Go to the back!" he commanded, pointing toward the hallway. His mind raced through the possibilities, calculations spiraling with each thought—who was coming for them? What had Alex's suspicions unearthed?

"Jack, please!" she begged, the terror pulsing through her words tugging at his heart, but Jack's focus had sharpened, all thoughts redirecting towards survival.

"Now!" he urged, the fierce command undeterred. As she fled down the hallway, Jack's instincts nudged him toward the door, the tension in the air snapping like a taut wire.

He remembered their conversation not moments ago, the stakes they'd both agreed to. Jack opened the door and stepped outside, knowing that if danger had come to their doorsteps like this, he had to confront it head-on—whatever it might be.

In the distance, engine growls roared closer, tires screeching against asphalt. His heart raced as he focused, observing the approaching figure who had been waiting, tense and shrouded by night. It struck him then: one of those players he had feared lurked in the shadows, a pawn in the sinister game he had unwittingly entered.

And then the world exploded with sound—a loud bang that coursed through the air, the pattern of light illuminating the night sky like a flash of fireworks, only this time accompanied by the stark realization of impending pain.

The dramatic twist tilted the course of Jack's resolve as he stepped forward, ready to face the impending danger. He thrust forward with urgency, a fierce energy coursing through him, the loyalty he had sworn to Anya and her family fueling a fire deep within. He could not let fear dictate his actions, could not let shadows conceal the truth.

In that moment, Jack crossed a line from which there would be no return. But in that leap of faith lay hope—the hope that he could find the strength to combat the darkness that threatened to engulf them all.

He clenched his fists, preparing himself for the storm, ready to confront whatever lay ahead—and he would do it alongside Anya, however perilous their future might be. The choice had been made, and as they spiraled deeper into the maelstrom of conspiracy and danger, Jack resolved to protect the light they had ignited together.

What lay ahead was uncertain, but together they would face the shadows—together, they would fight.

The Unraveling

Pieces Falling Into Place

Jack and Anya sat across from each other at the cramped kitchen table. The sun filtered weakly through the grimy window, casting a soft glow on the scattered papers strewn about like the well-worn pieces of a jigsaw puzzle. Each document represented a fragment of the conspiracy that had engulfed their lives, and together they were beginning to see the outlines of a bigger picture. The air was thick with tension, yet there was an unspoken understanding that had grown between them, binding them in their joint pursuit of the truth.

"Look at this," Anya said, her finger tracing a name on one of the files: Ivan Petrov. "Alex mentioned him a few times. He's supposed to be a key player in the Ukrainian Intelligence service. But now I'm starting to wonder if that's just a façade."

Jack leaned in closer, studying the document with a furrowed brow. "Petrov. I know the name. It's possible he has connections beyond what we see. But we need more than just a name; we need evidence." He paused, allowing the weight of his words to settle in the room. "Information without context can be dangerous."

Anya nodded, gripping the edge of the table as if holding onto a lifeline. The fear flickering in her eyes mirrored Jack's own concerns about what they were delving into. "I can call Alex," she suggested hesitantly. "Perhaps he has more insight."

Jack shifted uncomfortably in his seat. "I understand the urge," he began, choosing his words meticulously. "But if we alert him, we risk the possibility of tipping off whoever is watching. We must tread carefully."

"Then what do we do?" Anya's frustration bubbled to the surface. "We can't just sit here with snippets of information, Jack! I need to know if Alex is safe. If he's in danger, I need to act." Her voice was tinged with desperation, reminding Jack of the fury and vulnerability she carried with her like heavy armor.

"We gather what we can without bringing attention to ourselves," he replied, solidifying his resolve. "We'll need to expand our sources. Verify Petrov's affiliations and his interactions with Alex."

Anya studied him, sensing the unyielding determination behind his stoic facade. In their brief time working together, she had come to appreciate Jack's strategic mindset. His years at MI6 had endowed him with a penetrating intellect—a skill that she sorely lacked in this realm of shadows and deception. But even as she leaned on his expertise, a sliver of doubt crept into her thoughts. Did she truly know him? Despite his calm demeanor, what secrets was he still holding?

"I have connections in Kiev," Anya offered tentatively. "Some of my friends amongst the expatriates could—"

"No," Jack interjected firmly, but not unkindly. "We can't risk anyone else getting involved. The fewer people who know, the better."

"Then what's our next move?" she challenged, a hint of steel in her voice.

Jack contemplated the question, flicking through the documents before him. Each piece of paper laid bare the conspiracy's intricate layers, a mosaic of lies that twisted into a labyrinth of danger. "We'll need to conduct our own surveillance," he said. "Gather confirmation of Petrov's activities without arousing suspicion."

Anya regarded him, intrigued yet skeptical. "Surveillance? That sounds… risky."

"Exactly." Jack leaned back and crossed his arms, his posture both defensive and reflective. "Our safety is paramount. But we're on the brink of uncovering something significant. It'll require balancing the risks, Anya. Trust is going to be integral as we move forward. We can't let fear drown us."

Anya's gaze softened at his words, feeling the current of shared tension envelop her. Despite their difference in outlook—a cautious veteran versus a desperate mother—she was willing to adapt. "What do we know about his whereabouts?"

Jack rifled through the stack of files and extracted a sheet filled with dates and locations. "We know he's been affiliated with the Ministry of Defense. Several meetings recorded in the past few months, arriving at obscure locations, often at odd hours." He turned the paper toward Anya. "This might be our best lead. If we can track him…"

Anya squinted at the details, absorbing the information with a concentrated intensity. "If we follow him, we might catch an interaction that will confirm if he's involved with the Russians."

"Exactly." A hint of pride flickered in Jack's chest as he watched Anya engage with the plan, a determination ignited within her that he had not anticipated. "But we'll need to be careful. We could use a tactical approach—disguises, a safe distance. We want to blend in," he mused, slowly pacing the kitchen, piecing together the ground they needed to cover.

"What about Alex's contacts?" Anya asked, anxiousness swirling in her expression. "If we can turn to some of them, maybe they can help us confirm Petrov's involvement. They could…"

"Anya!" Jack interrupted, frustration boiling underneath his controlled exterior. "You need to realize that your husband's contacts could be compromised. We don't have the luxury of assuming anyone is who they claim to be in this line of work."

Anya recoiled slightly from his outburst, but instead of retreating, her emotional defenses sharpened. "I understand your instincts, Jack. But I also know that Alex wouldn't let me down. If there are people he trusts—"

"And how can you be sure those people won't lead us into a trap?" Jack shot back. "We don't know how deep this conspiracy goes or who is pulling the strings."

Realizing their conversation was escalating, she softened her voice. "I just want to know if he's safe, Jack. I want to trust the people he trusted."

Jack let out a long breath, moving back to a calm demeanor. "I understand, and I want to help you find that peace of mind. But trust takes time, and right now, we have to work with the information available. We can't afford miscalculations."

He paused, searching for the right words to connect with her. "You've shown remarkable strength, Anya. I've witnessed how fiercely you care about Alex and your children. But we must ground ourselves in caution."

Anya's heart ached at his acknowledgment. In a world where her family was prey to vicious games, words of confidence from Jack grounded her. "You're right," she conceded slowly. "Let's focus on Petrov, then. What's our next step?"

Jack felt a swell of relief at her willingness to collaborate, his internal conflict easing just slightly. "We track his movements over the next few days and blend into the crowds. We observe, listen, and learn. The more we know about Petrov, the better equipped we are to deal with him."

As their discussion unfolded, each layer of their respective fears began to unravel. Jack's thoughts flashed back to his own past—an internal landscape laden with perilous choices that had cost lives. He recognized in Anya a fierce loyalty that resonated with his own moral code, something he hadn't fully valued until she had arrived in his life. But with that loyalty came an emotional toll—an understanding of what it meant to risk everything for those you loved.

Anya could sense Jack's shifting emotions. In this moment, they were no longer just a retired intelligence officer and a scared mother;

they were two souls fighting against an encroaching malevolence. She pondered how their destinies had intertwined, how their disparate tapestries had woven a new fabric of shared struggle.

"Jack," she said softly, breaking the silence that had settled around them, "are you scared?"

He looked up, surprised by her vulnerability. "I'd be lying if I said I wasn't. I've faced dangers before, but the stakes are different this time. I'm not just protecting a government; I'm trying to keep you and your children safe."

Her gaze bore into him, unflinching. "I feel it too. I'm terrified of losing everything. But there's a strange comfort in facing this together. You're not just an ally to me—you're something more than that."

Jack's breath caught in his throat. He wasn't ready to let disaster cloud the burgeoning connection they shared, but he couldn't deny the bond forming between them. "Anya, being with you and your family has awakened something in me. I've been dormant for too long, and now…" He paused, struggling to articulate his feelings. "Now I care about what happens to you all."

Anya's heart drummed in her chest, rekindling a flicker of hope as she processed his sentiment. Despite the tempest swirling around them, perhaps there was light in the darkness they faced. "We'll find the truth together," she said resolutely. "We'll save Alex and each other."

"Together," Jack echoed, and the weight of their shared responsibility settled over them like a protective cocoon.

As the plan solidified, the two of them worked late into the night, pouring over photographs and reports, carefully crafting an outline of Petrov's possible movements. Each piece they put together illuminated shadows that had previously haunted their minds, much like the way one slowly adapts to the dark after being blinded by light.

Around three in the morning, Anya leaned back in her chair, rubbing her tired eyes. Jack looked at her—her features were framed by strands of hair that had come loose from her messy bun, and the fatigue etched on her face was evident. "Get some sleep," he urged, rising to clear the table of the chaotic remnants of their investigation.

"I can't," she replied, the tremor of anxiety flickering in her voice. "Not until we've planned everything."

"We'll need you sharp if we're going to act on this." Jack regarded her with an intensity that left no room for argument. "Trust me, I'll keep watch. You've been through enough."

Anya opened her mouth to reply but then felt the tides of exhaustion wash over her. Jack's composure anchored her in a way that made her realize how much she needed his strength. With a sudden resolve, she nodded. "Okay. Just... wake me if anything changes."

He offered a faint smile that crinkled the corners of his eyes. "I will. And I'll save you a cup of that horrendous tea."

Anya chuckled lightly—a rare moment of levity in their tumultuous reality. She made her way to the small bedroom, the distant hum of the world outside a testament to the danger lurking just beyond the walls of Jack's cottage.

As sleep took her, the peace was temporary. Visions of Alex permeated her mind—his laughter echoed, mingling with the tender moments they had shared. But then shadows took shape, and she felt the tightness in her chest build as she dreamed of dark figures lurking in alleyways and deceitful smiles. The weight of her situation pressed down on her, a constant reminder of the stakes involved.

Meanwhile, Jack remained at the table, the dim light of a single lamp illuminating the documents before him. He couldn't help but reflect on the obstacles that lay ahead. The remnants of a life once lived in shadows clung to him, whispering dangers he thought he'd buried. But as he sat there, piecing together evidence and imagining danger around every corner, he felt renewed purpose.

Anya had ignited a fire within him—a yearning to protect, to reclaim the lost threads of his life. The two of them, partners forged in an alliance of necessity and hope, had begun to understand that together, they could face whatever darkness awaited them.

As exhaustion crept into his bones, he knew that danger was still looming, but he had no intention of succumbing to fear. He closed his eyes for a brief moment, a silent promise swelling in his heart—to be her shield, to unravel the conspiracy, and to ensure that they emerged from the darkness into the dawn of a new day, together.

The Race Against Time

Jack squinted against the sun filtering through the leaves of the ancient oaks lining the path to his modest home, the soft rustle of the tree branches belied the urgency gnawing at his insides. The quiet of the English countryside had been both a balm to his soul and, in many ways, a deception. The serenity outside stood in stark contrast to the storm brewing within. The past days had felt like an avalanche, slowly gaining momentum, threatening to bury everything he had worked so hard to build—a safe, solitary existence far removed from the world of espionage.

The moment Anya had confided in him about her husband Alex's fears, Jack had found himself pulled back into a world he thought he had left behind. Now, as he walked, each step felt heavier than the last. He had always known he would be drawn back, but never in this manner, never in his twilight years as he had cared for his garden and vegetables like a man nursing his wounds. Yet here he was, a reluctant knight again, donning an armor of duty, propelled by an unyielding commitment to help Anya and her children.

Inside his study, the scent of aged paper and ink wrapped around him, a familiar embrace he hoped would provide clarity. The desk was cluttered with files, photographs, and notes jotted in his precise script, all documenting Anya's husband, Alex, and the unsettling claims of espionage swirling around him. Jack had spent countless hours tracing the threads of the Ukrainian intelligence community, and now the intricate web of danger seemed closer than ever.

He flipped through the notes one more time, the details spilling out like grains of sand through his fingers. The urgency was palpable—Alex had gone dark for almost two days. His regular communications had ceased, and each heartbeat felt like a countdown, echoing in his mind, reminding him that every second could be the difference between life and death. Jack bit down on his frustration; he needed to find Alex, and swiftly.

Jack's phone buzzed in his pocket, cutting through the stillness. He fished it out and saw a message from Michael, his old MI6 contact. The nearness of a friend, albeit one from his murky past, sent a jolt of adrenaline through him. He opened the message: "We have leads on Spetsnaz move in Kyiv. Get ready for action."

Jack's heart raced. The Spetsnaz—Russian special forces—were notorious for their ruthlessness. If Alex had stumbled into their eyesight, time was indeed running short. He shot a quick response: "Meet me at the usual place. We need to talk about Alex."

He grabbed his jacket and headed for his car. Each turn of the ignition felt like destiny reasserting itself, pulling him back into the fray. The old instincts kicked in: keep a low profile, don't be seen, and above all, avoid drawing attention. The car sped through the lanes, adrenaline pumping through his veins, each mile pulling him deeper into his former life.

The café where Jack had arranged to meet Michael was small and unassuming, thrumming with an energy that belied its cozy exterior. Inside, he spotted Michael immediately, his frame large and imposing, a contrast to the environment. Jack waved him over, and Michael rose to embrace him, their interaction brief yet loaded with unspoken words.

"Things are escalating, Jack," Michael said, the gravity in his voice unmistakable. "The intel isn't promising. We've had reports of a Russian cell looking to eliminate assets in Ukrainian intelligence. Your boy, Alex? He's become a target."

Jack felt his stomach drop. "What do we have? Any leads on where he might be?"

Michael glanced around the café, ensuring they weren't being overheard. "Not much. Two nights ago, he was spotted near the old military base outside Kyiv, but then he vanished. We picked up chatter about an operation aimed at intercepting contacts—Ukrainian officials suspected of leaking information. Alex was right in the thick of it."

Silence descended as Jack absorbed the information, the implications heavy. The thought of Anya's children waiting for their father, caught in the chaos of war while their mother leaned on him in desperation, made Jack's resolve harden. "What's our next move?"

"We need to get you to Kyiv. If he's still alive, we have to act fast. I can get you a safe passage; we'll orchestrate a diversion. You have to find him, Jack."

Every instinct honed over his years at MI6 screamed at him. He glanced at Michael, the man who had seen him through many dark days, knowing they weren't merely attending to a job but launching themselves into the fire. "Let's move."

The urgency of their mission ignited a racing pulse within Jack as they exited the café, a sharp reminder of the sleight of hand that defined their lives in espionage. They drove in silence, Michael deftly maneuvering through the streets until they reached a dimly lit alley where a discreet vehicle awaited them.

"Are you ready for this?" Michael asked, eyeing Jack closely.

Jack squared his shoulders, feeling the weight of Anya's trust resting on his. "I've faced worse. Let's just make sure we both come back in one piece."

As they traveled towards the Channel, Jack's mind buzzed with plans and scenarios. He knew he had to work quickly; time was bleeding away and Alex's life hung in a precarious balance. The flight was swift and disorienting, and he felt every minute stretching into an eternity, leaving their fate uncertain.

Upon landing, an oppressive sense of urgency settled over him. Kyiv was a city on edge, scarred and crumbling under the weight of war. Jack hunched low under the collar of his jacket, blending into the shadows that enveloped him. The streets echoed with the remnants of life, but he could feel the well of despair clinging to the air like smoke—whispers of fear thrumming beneath the surface.

Tapping into his MI6 contacts in the city proved invaluable. He reached out to trusted informants, those still operating on the fringes of the intelligence community. They paint a chilling picture: Alex's struggles against a rising tide, the incursion of Russian influences creeping dangerously close to the Ukrainian government.

As he immersed himself deeper into the underbelly of Kyiv's dangers, the information trickling in was both troubling and illuminating. Each meeting with operatives granted him a fleeting glimpse of Alex's movements while also deepening Jack's resolve. A thick file handed off to him revealed detailed accounts of former allies who had turned traitor, each name striking a chord of loss and betrayal echoing Jack's own past.

"Meet at the old railway station tonight. That's where they plan to make the exchange," an informant said, shifting nervously as he glanced over his shoulder. "You'll need to make your move then, but there may already be trouble brewing. It's crawling with Spetsnaz."

Jack's heart raced. The clock was ticking, and for every shade of darkness, he felt the burden of responsibility pressing down harder. He ducked into an abandoned doorway to gather his thoughts, his mind racing to map out possible routes and contingencies. The labyrinthine tunnels underneath Kyiv could be his salvation, providing a way to navigate the chaos without detection.

At nightfall, Jack made his way to the dilapidated railway station, the air heavy with menace and uncertainty. He moved through shadows, the whispers of conflict rising around him, a constant reminder of the stakes they were playing for. Adrenaline surged through him, but recently unearthed memories of Anya and her children anchored him, pulling him from the abyss of fear creeping into his heart.

He crouched behind an old steel column, eyes scanning the dark expanse of the old platform. The cacophony of distant gunfire punctuated the calm, a terrifying reminder of the brewing storm outside. Jack's breath quickened as he spied a hulking shadow time and time again—Russian soldiers roamed the perimeter. The sight of them pulled at his instincts, reminding him of the familiar patterns he had seen replay throughout the years.

As he observed, two men stepped forward, exchanging hushed whispers and occasionally casting glances toward the shadows. Jack strained to listen, catching fragments of their conversation. Armed with this grim intel, he clutched the file tight. They were discussing routes for a potential extraction of the assets, possibly those connected to Alex. Jack's mind raced as he processed the information. He had to get to Alex first; he wouldn't let this moment slip through his fingers.

As if on cue, the platform erupted in chaos. Jack felt the ground shift beneath him as the men shouted orders; he was incensed with urgency. His heart slammed against his chest, each pulse screaming for action. Jack, drawing on instinct, began to weave through the shadows, mastering the art of stealth, he became a ghost within the folds of the night. He edged closer to the heart of the upheaval, uncertainty gnawing at his gut.

He emerged from the shadows, slipping past guards with the finesse of his years in MI6. The voices grew clearer, the stakes intensifying; he had to act. Suddenly, he saw a familiar figure—a man bound to a chair, disheveled yet determined, Alex looked up just as Jack broke through the final barrier.

"Jack!" Alex gasped, his voice dripping with disbelief.

"Stay quiet," Jack whispered, fear wrapping tighter around them. He quickly scanned the room, looking for a way to free him. The soldiers had turned their attention towards something ominous—perhaps the uprising he sensed earlier.

Jack knew he had to be quick. "We need to get you out now," he urged, pulling at the ropes binding Alex, glancing over his shoulder every second as he worked. Anticipating the inevitable clash, Jack prepared for confrontation; adrenaline surged as the ropes frayed under his grasp.

Just as he freed Alex, a deafening shout pierced the atmosphere. "Intruder!"

Instinct kicked in; Jack pushed Alex forward. "Run!" He ducked instinctively, a volley of bullets ricocheting off the walls around them. The chaos erupted as guards sprang into action, the frightening adrenaline of survival forcing Jack into the fray. He pulled Alex close, guiding him through the spray of gunfire, heart pulsing with a mix of fear and the surging instinct to protect.

The two men barreled through the railway station, ducking and dodging as soldiers pursued behind them. Jack's military training blurred time and panic, every second feeling like an eternity as they plunged deep into the veils of darkness. The labyrinth of tunnels loomed ahead, a path leading them into the underground's cold grip—but freedom lay ahead.

The chaos of gunfire faded, replaced by the hollow echoes of their racing hearts as they dashed through the dim passages. "This way," Jack shouted, adrenaline coursing, turning Alex toward an exit. "We can find cover and regroup."

They burst out onto a hidden street, veering into the protective shadows of abandoned buildings. Jack glanced over at Alex, breathing heavily yet seeming to awaken from a long nightmare. There was a fierce determination emanating from him, something Jack recognized—a soldier's instinct. They felt invincible for a fleeting moment, clutching victory in their grasp.

Yet that victory was fleeting. Just as they collected themselves, the roar of approaching vehicles echoed in the night, and Jack's heart sank.

"They've found us!" Alex gasped.

"Move!" Jack barked, feeling the weight of impending danger close in. Their time was running thin as they skirted around the corners of the cold cobbled street, desperately seeking shelter; Jack scanned the area for a place to hide, a momentary reprieve from the impending storm bearing down on them.

"Over there!" Jack pointed toward an overgrown, dilapidated building. "We can take cover inside!"

They rushed toward the entrance, ducking low as bullets ricocheted off the walls. Jack pushed Alex through the threshold, following close behind before barricading the door with a fallen beam, the light flickering from shattered windows illuminating their tense faces.

They stood together, breathing heavily, the terror of pursuit darkening the air. Jack could feel their connection tightening, but the reality sank in—one miscalculation could unravel everything they worked so hard to build, and every second felt borrowed.

"The Spetsnaz won't give up easily." Jack caught his breath, awareness sharpening his focus. "We have to keep moving, no matter what."

"What about Anya?" Alex looked at him, desperation etched across his features. "She has the kids. We can't leave them like this."

"I know," Jack said, that familiar weight of loyalty flickering painfully in his chest. "But right now, staying alive is the first step."

With that, they committed themselves to the chaos, for urgency was their only ally. The pursuit had transformed from a quiet whisper to a menacing reality; their lives hung by a thread woven through risk and courage.

Jack led Alex cautiously through the chaotic streets, driven by necessity and purpose. The air was thick with tension, each footfall echoing with the weight of their fates. They avoided patrols, slipping unnoticed through alleyways and sidestreets, navigating the chaos of war as shadows in the night.

Their senses heightened, every sound—the scuffle of boots, the hushed exchanges of soldiers—felt insistent, leading them toward what lay ahead. Freedom was worth pursuing, yet so too was the love of a family awaiting their return.

Finally, after an eternity that led them through winding paths and narrow escapes, they emerged into a secluded area for safe passage. Jack's heart quickened as he saw a familiar face up ahead—Michael stood by a nondescript van, worry etched on his brow.

"Get in!" Michael yelled urgently, glancing over his shoulder. Jack wasted no time ushering Alex into the waiting vehicle, their breaths mingling with relief, yet the danger was far from over.

As they sped away, Jack's resolve burned sturdily within him. They had escaped the jaws of chaos, but the journey was only just beginning. Time may have weighed heavily on their shoulders, but together they now shared a thread of resilience entwined through their trials. Jack's heart surged with a singular belief, tempered by the fires of crisis—the race against time wasn't about running from the past, but rather carving a way toward the future, no matter how daunting the road ahead.

Shocking Revelations

J ack and Anya sat across from each other at the dimly lit table in Jack's kitchen, their faces illuminated by the glow of the single, flickering bulb that hung overhead. A stack of documents lay between them, each sheet heavy with implications that weighed on their shoulders like a leaden shroud. Jack's heart raced as he scanned the latest intelligence report Anya had unearthed, her husband Alex's initial fears seeming to spiral into an incomprehensible web of deception.

"They're not just watching him, Jack. They're watching us," Anya's voice trembled as she adjusted the pile of papers in front of her, her hands shaking slightly. "Alex's warnings are more than just paranoia. We've stumbled onto something much bigger."

Jack leaned back in his chair, feeling the familiar nausea of potential betrayal curl in his stomach. "What do you mean? What have you found?" The question hung in the air, heavy and charged with tension. Anya's eyes glistened with a mixture of fear and determination as she pointed to a series of names scribbled across the top of one page.

"Look here. These are senior members of the Ukrainian intelligence community. People Alex used to trust implicitly. They've all had meetings with high-ranking Russian officials. And not just casual chats—these are formal discussions about strategy. About operations," she said, her voice barely a whisper as if afraid that merely speaking the truth would attract unwanted attention.

Jack's mind raced. The truth was stark and punishing. The implications of Anya's words crashed over him like an icy wave, freezing him in place. He quickly flipped through the documents, absorbing the damning evidence, each detail augmenting the sense of dread amplifying within him. The investigation they had begun, the one rooted in Anya's fears for Alex, had morphed into a monstrous revelation extending far beyond their immediate concerns. It was a tidal wave threatening to sweep them both under.

"Are you sure these connections are legitimate?" Jack asked, his tone edged with skepticism, yet ominous understanding crept in—the very essence of betrayal lurked deeper than either of them could have imagined. He felt the familiar pang of conflict between the operative he once was and the man desperate for a quiet life. In the espionage world, trust was a commodity traded with caution, and the gnawing fear that he might be facing a conspiracy from within his own ranks was a chilling notion.

Anya nodded vehemently, her eyes blazing. "I spent weeks digging through everything. The patterns are there, Jack. People in positions of power are playing games, and Alex knew it. That's why he started to worry; it's not just fear. It's intuition, the instincts of a man who has seen too much."

Jack swallowed hard, turning his gaze out the window, as if the answers to the storm brewing within could be glimpsed beyond the glass. He thought back to his past—the complexity of human nature he had observed while embedded in a world that often blurred the lines between right and wrong. "You know this could change everything. If what you're saying is true, we're not just talking about some rogue soldier on the fringe—we're exposing the very systems that should protect us."

Anya leaned forward, her elbows resting on the table, her expression a mixture of fervor and fear. "And if we don't act, what does that mean for Alex? For us? We can't hide anymore. They'll come for him, for us—if they haven't already. I need you to help me get him out."

Jack took a moment to absorb her plea, wrestling with the rise of old instincts. Duty and a keen sense of protection battled against the tantalizing comfort of his seclusion. But Anya's desperation pierced through the kaleidoscope of emotions swirling in him. She needed him now more than ever. "Alright. We need to think carefully about our next steps."

As Jack's gaze shifted back to the documents, a name jumped out at him like a shot in the darkness, sending a shiver through his spine. "Mikhail Volkov," he muttered, recognition washing over him. Volkov was a notorious figure in the intelligence community, known for his ruthlessness and cunning. He had orchestrated covert operations that left no trace, a ghost haunting the shadows. "He's implicated in arms deals," Jack murmured. "If he's involved, the stakes are even higher."

Anya's breath caught in her throat. "Then we're not just dealing with a Russian spy—we're looking at a network, Jack. A serious infiltration that reaches deep into our own intelligence. If Alex was right, and if Volkov is at the center…" She let the sentence hang, the implications heavy and unspoken between them.

Jack's mind instinctively worked to compartmentalize the emotions that threatened to engulf him—fear, betrayal, doubt. The ghosts of his past surged, faces of colleagues and friends lost to the dark games played in the clandestine world, choices that haunted him still. He drew a shaky breath, his heart racing as he envisioned the potential for disaster.

"Anya, we need a plan," he stated, sharpening his focus. "If we're to confront this, we can't rely solely on what we know. We need verification, and we need allies we can trust—though the prospect of that seems limited now. We'll need to reach out to my contacts."

Anya's expression darkened, her brow furrowing. "What if they're the ones we can't trust? What if you dive back in, and they reel you in deeper than before? Nobody is safe in this game."

Jack's hope for reassurance wavered as he met her eyes, aware of the trepidation lacing her words. But there was no turning back—he could feel it in his bones. "I can't just watch from the sidelines, Anya. If you're right—and I believe you are—then doing nothing is a death sentence for Alex and for us."

The dread enveloped him, an unshakable sense of doom as Jack mentally prepared for the chaos ahead. He had thought he left the world of shadows and betrayal behind, but now it seemed fate had cast him back, flinging him into the turbulent waters once more. The emotional weight of betrayal hovered palpably, an omnipresent specter they would have to confront.

"Then what's our first move?" Anya asked, her voice tinged with both despair and resolve.

Jack inhaled deeply, steeling himself for the onslaught. "We take this information and find proof. We dig in deeper and figure out where Volkov is currently operating. We expose the web, but we must be strategic."

"The truth could unravel everything, Jack," Anya said, her voice trembling slightly. "What if we're wrong? What if this leads to Alex being targeted even more? They'll know someone is onto them, and that could mean collateral damage. We're risking so much."

"I know," Jack replied, feeling the weight of conviction settle on his shoulders. "The hardest decisions are often the ones that bring about change. But if we don't act, we're sealing Alex's fate, not to mention ours. We can't let fear dictate our choices."

A silence thick with tension spread over the room as Anya processed his words, her expression shifting from despair to determination. "Alright. If we're doing this, then we're doing it together. I can help with the groundwork, further digging—I've skills that can assist," she stated, her voice firm now.

Jack nodded, appreciating her resilience but also feeling the gravity of their situation. "I'll reach out to my contacts, gather intel. I'll need to prepare for the worst. So, we'll move quickly and silently."

The essence of their lives began to shift, their alliance forging deeper amidst the encroaching darkness. But with each passing moment, the realization of what they were about to embark upon settled heavily upon them—the tenacious loyalty of espionage was a fragile thing, built on doubt and deception.

Jack stood abruptly, a sense of urgency fueling him. "Let's reconvene tonight. I'll have things set up by then. We'll finalize our plan of action. But more importantly, we need to ensure we're secure. They'll be watching, Anya. We need to stay one step ahead."

Anya nodded, steeling herself. "Let's do this."

As she left the room, Jack's thoughts swirled with memories of the life he had chosen years before. He chided himself silently for letting nostalgia creep in, recalling the exhilaration of the chases, the energy of missions shrouded in secrecy. But now, those memories served only as bitter reminders of the stakes, the consequences of courses taken long ago.

Jack spent the next few hours ensconced in research, poring over files, looking for cracks within the conspiracy that would shed light on his path forward. Names and dates scrawled across documents began to morph into connections, a labyrinthine structure of deceit unfolding before his eyes. His past decisions loomed large in the shadows of his mind—every choice and outcome converging into a single, unwavering truth: the most dangerous threats often came from those masked in familiarity.

He found a brief mention of Volkov's recent dealings connected to an undisclosed meeting taking place in London. His gut twisted—this was their in, the portal to a confrontation that could either shatter their lives or break the chains of conspiracy binding them. If Volkov was here, then everything Alex feared might be in reach. Yet the image of him wading into a confrontation sent a jolt of anxiety through his bones, the metal taste of unease lingering on his tongue.

Just as he was about to put the file away, a familiar name caught his eye once more—a former colleague of his at MI6, Maria Karsten. She had once been a trusted ally, their paths often crossing during covert operations. But years in the shadows had marred her reputation; she now walked a thin line between loyalty and self-preservation. Jack had not spoken to her in years.

As doubts and concern enveloped him, he rubbed the bridge of his nose. The prospect of calling on Maria meant revisiting a history fraught with entangled judgments. Yet there was little choice left—the stakes were now too high to ignore, and he needed the intel she could provide. After many years of staying clear from that world, it was time to step back into the abyss.

As he picked up his phone, the weight of his decision bore down on him, the specter of consequence looming large. He dialed the number and waited, a mix of anticipation and dread tightening his chest as the ringing echoed in the silence.

"Jack?" Maria's voice was laden with surprise, tinged with skepticism. "I didn't expect to hear from you. Last I heard, you were enjoying a quiet life, gardening or something."

"Maria," he exhaled, quick to bypass pleasantries. "I need information, and I need it fast. It's about Volkov."

A pause resonated through the line before she spoke again, her tone shifting from surprise to concern. "You're treading dangerous waters, Jack. Volkov's name isn't one to toss around lightly. You know what happens when you poke the bear."

"I'm aware," he replied, determination rising. "But this is bigger than anything I faced before; it extends into the heart of the agency. I need to know where he's headed and what's in play."

"Then you're already in over your head," Maria warned, her voice low. "This isn't a game anymore. Trust has vanished—lines have blurred between allies and enemies. Do you know what you're walking into?"

"I can't afford to sit on the sidelines anymore, Maria," Jack insisted, a sense of urgency propelling him. "There's a chance Alex may be involved in something greater, and if we can expose it, we stop the larger threat. But I need your help."

"I'll see what I can do," she conceded, the supplemental threads of trust weaving through her words. "But if you're in, you'd better be ready for the fallout. I'll contact you later—be careful. The game has shifted beneath us."

Jack hung up, feeling both a sense of relief and impending dread. He turned to face the darkness of the room, the gauntlets of shadows wrapping around him. The true nature of the conspiracy had emerged, revealing connections that reached farther than Alex's fears.

The stakes had never been higher. With every step he took into the uncertainty, the fragility of alliances echoed in the back of his mind—a constant reminder of how dangerous espionage had always been.

The day slowly turned to night, and as the shadows began to envelop Jack's home, he felt the weight of betrayal looming. The choices before him were stark and immediate—a winding path riddled with danger where every misstep could lead to dire consequences, not only for him but for Anya and her family.

As he prepared to meet Anya again, he felt the icy fingers of doubt brush against his spine. But he steeled his resolve, knowing that this was not merely about uncovering the dark web twisting around Alex—it was a battle to wrest control from the hands of those who would manipulate for their gain.

They were teetering at the edge of something monumental, and within the gentle embrace of that impending doom, Jack found a strange sense of purpose. He was no longer a bystander but an active participant in a story woven with layers of deceit and revelation. And if Jack were to fight for truth, he would fight to the last breath.

The night deepened, holding secrets of its own as the two of them prepared to step forward into the unknown, poised on the precipice of a battle waged in shadows, their destinies irreversibly entwined.

Betrayal and Trust

Unveiling the Enemy

The morning light filtered through the kitchen window, casting soft shadows across the table where Jack and Anya sat. The remnants of breakfast lingered on their plates, but neither had much appetite. They were still grappling with the revelations from the previous day—Anya's discovery about the mole within the Ukrainian intelligence agency and the name that had surfaced in their discussions. The implications were as heavy as the weight of the sunlit silence that enveloped them.

Jack's mind raced as he tore his gaze away from the half-eaten toast before him. He studied Anya's face, which was tense with the pain of uncertainty and fear. She had confided in him, revealing the betrayal that lurked in the shadows of her husband's world, a world Jack had once known all too well and had tried so hard to leave behind. Now, it seemed those shadows were creeping back into both their lives.

"Do you really think Alex's fears are justified?" Anya finally asked, her voice barely above a whisper.

Jack leaned back in his chair, trying to muster a sense of authority despite the rising tide of doubt within him. "If Alex suspects there's a mole, we have to take it seriously," he said cautiously. "Even if it sounds far-fetched, it could be the truth. We can't afford to brush it aside."

Anya nodded, but her eyes betrayed her struggle with disbelief. "But who can we trust in his agency? If Alex's boss is truly a spy, then how deep does this go? How can we be sure he's not already aware of Alex's suspicions?"

Jack felt a pang in his chest at the thought. Trust was a high-stakes game, especially in espionage, where allegiances shifted like sand beneath one's feet. "We can't assume that everyone is against us," he replied, keeping his tone steady. "There are still allies out there, people who genuinely want to protect Ukraine. We just have to find them."

"How do we do that?" Anya's voice quivered, reflecting the anxiety bubbling just beneath the surface of her composure. "I don't want to put my children at risk. I can't do that. I can't lose anyone else."

Jack felt the tension radiating from her, a palpable fear that challenged his own resolve. He reached across the table, covering her trembling hands with his own, a gesture meant to offer solace. "We will find a way. I promise you that," he said, trying to inject strength into his words—strength he wasn't sure he possessed. "But we need to be smart about this. We must proceed carefully."

Anya pulled her hands away, her frustration evident. "You talk about being smart, Jack, but we're dealing with Russian spies! We're like pawns in a game far larger than ourselves, and I'm terrified of what might happen if we make one wrong move."

Jack hated to see her suffer, his heart aching for the torment that filled her eyes. He had spent years in the labyrinth of intelligence, and while he was no longer in the field, the skills he acquired had not diminished. Still, this felt different. The stakes had never been more personal, the consequences more devastating.

"We'll gather information, look for patterns," he urged, attempting to ground their conversation in a practical strategy. "If we can piece together what Alex knows, we can determine how big of a threat this really is."

Anya leaned back, crossing her arms defensively over her chest. "And what if the mole is closer than we think? What if we can't trust anyone within the agency? Do you really think it's just Alex's boss? What if he's merely one part of a larger network of spies embedded within the system?" Her voice trembled slightly, but her resolve remained clear.

Jack's mind raced with the implications of her words. "If that's the case, we need to tread carefully. Every step we take could be monitored. We need to establish a safe way to communicate with Alex."

"Easier said than done. How do we even reach him?"

A plan began to take shape in Jack's mind. "We can use a secure line," he offered. "I have former colleagues who can help set it up. We'll create a communication channel for him to get in touch if he needs to share something without raising suspicion."

Anya's eyes narrowed slightly, assessing his suggestion. "And what if they are watching you, too?"

"That's a risk we have to take. We need to find a way to protect Alex and ourselves at the same time." His voice was firm, but the truth was, he felt the pressure and anxiety rising as the weight of their situation settled into his bones.

"I just wish I knew—" Anya began, her voice breaking as tears filled her eyes.

Jack could hardly bear the sight of her pain, and instinctively, he reached out again, enveloping her hand in his. "We'll figure this out together," he whispered soothingly, as if his confidence could somehow infuse her with courage, if only for a moment.

"Together," Anya echoed, her voice teetering at the edge of despair. "But what if… what if I end up putting my children in danger by even talking to you?"

"We'll take every precaution necessary. No one goes near your children, I promise you that."

Silence enveloped them as Anya withdrew slightly into herself, shifting her attention to the window where the day was unfolding outside—life continuing on unperturbed while their world spiraled into chaos. Jack's heart sank at how helpless she felt. "Listen," he said gently, "I know this is overwhelming. But we have to stay focused."

"Well, we don't even know who the enemy is," Anya said sharply, a little fire igniting in her voice. "This isn't just Alex's boss; this could be anyone he associates with."

A tension crackled between them, the chasm of uncertainty and fear threatening to engulf them both. Jack leaned closer. "Then we need to start identifying those associations. Gather information, any intel that can help us draw a clearer picture—who is connected to whom, who might have motives, who might share Alex's concerns."

"And what if they catch wind of us investigating? When does it stop being about gathering information and start being about self-preservation?"

Jack's throat tightened at the thought. He hadn't faced this level of treachery in years, but he knew how relentless such adversaries could be. "Anya… if it comes to that, we will draw the line together. I won't let anything happen to you or your children."

"Easy to say for you, Jack," she responded with a slight edge in her voice. "You've faced enemies before, you're trained for this sort of thing. But what about me? I'm just a mother trying to protect her family."

Just a mother. The words stung because they echoed the insecurities lurking beneath her facade. "You're far more than that," Jack replied vehemently. "You're intelligent and strong, and most importantly, you're a survivor. You've faced unimaginable challenges already. This is just a continuation of that fight."

"But I didn't choose this fight," she countered, her voice quivering. "I wanted a normal life—a life away from all of this."

"I know," he said softly. "But we can't revert to that time. Not now. Think of your children. But think, too, of what you'd want for them in the long term. You'd want them to grow up free of fear and oppression."

With that, he saw a flicker of resolve return to Anya's eyes as she regarded him more intently. His conviction resonated somewhere deep within her. "Okay, then. Let's do it together," she said, a new sense of purpose igniting her voice. "But you must promise me we'll take it slow. I can't risk losing them, and I dread the thought of Alex being in danger."

"I promise," he said, feeling a sense of warmth swell in his chest—an acknowledgment of their shared vulnerability and the strength instilled in their alliance. "We'll be cautious."

"What do we do first?" Anya asked, her brow furrowed with determination.

Jack's mind raced as he considered their next steps. "Let's make a list of everyone Alex has been in contact with recently," he suggested. "We can cross-reference those connections with any known affiliations to Russian operatives."

A brief silence fell between them as they both contemplated the implications of their task.

"Okay," Anya agreed, taking a deep breath. "I can do that."

Jack watched her intently, observing the way her shoulders squared and her chin lifted, a sign of the resolve that dared to push through the layers of anxiety that had gripped her only moments before. This woman was capable of more than she realized, and he would help her see that.

As they began their brainstorming session, Anya jotted down names as Jack dictated potential contacts to consider. Each name felt like a thread in a tapestry they were beginning to weave—a tapestry of survival tied together by fear, courage, and perhaps something that could blossom into trust.

Jack spoke about Alex's colleagues—people he had summarily dismissed as allies back in the day. But now, the lingering remnants of his past seeped through the present. "What about Vasyl?" Jack suggested, as Anya's pen scratched across the page. "He's always had Alex's back. We can see if he can provide any insight that might corroborate Alex's claim."

"Vasyl," Anya repeated thoughtfully. "Yes, I trust him. He wouldn't betray Alex… or me."

Jack nodded approvingly. "That's good. And if there's a chance he's still on the inside, he could be our lifeline."

"Agreed." Anya added the name to the list. "But how do we contact him without raising too much suspicion?"

"That's where it gets tricky. We need a way to reach out to him that feels natural, something that won't alert anyone to our intentions."

"Like a casual check-in," Anya suggested. "Something innocent."

"Exactly. We'll have to find opportunities to bring that up in conversation. But in the meantime, we shouldn't lose sight of the bigger picture. We need to think about safety protocols."

Anya looked up, frowning. "Safety protocols?"

In response, Jack held her gaze, weighing how to convey the seriousness of what they were discussing without stoking her fears anew. "We need to ensure we have an exit strategy, especially as we start uncovering more. We can't just react; we need to anticipate."

Anya nodded slowly. "You mean if we're discovered."

"Right. If we start to notice anything suspicious—like being followed—then we need to have a safe place to go. I have some contacts I can reach out to, people who wouldn't mind offering some temporary shelter."

"Safe places?" Anya mused. "If all fails, we might consider fleeing. But where would we go?"

"London could be an option," Jack replied after a moment's consideration. "I have old colleagues there who have the means to help. We could lay low until the dust settles."

For a moment, they were lost in the weight of potential outcomes. Anya, her expression stricken, broke the silence. "It all sounds so extreme, Jack. But I realize now that if there's a mole in Alex's agency, we could be in real danger."

"We are in real danger," Jack confirmed gently, fighting to keep the fear from taking hold in his tone. "And we have to act as if our lives depend on it—because they do. I will not let anything happen to you or your children, Anya."

A look of uncertainty passed across her face. "If it gets to that point, what will we do about Alex?"

"We'll make that call when we have more information. But for now, let's invest our energy into figuring out who we can trust and what our next steps will be."

As they worked together to outline their action plan, a sense of solidarity began to emerge between them. Each name they listed, every strategy they discussed, forged a bond deeper than either had anticipated. In the crucible of shared adversity, vulnerability was eclipsed by determination, and they began to understand that they were not just two individuals lost in a tumultuous world but partners bound by hope and necessity.

The afternoon flowed into evening, and as the sky outside shifted to shades of dusky pink, they felt the weight of uncertainty press down upon them. Time was short, and every decision carried with it immeasurable risk.

Still, within the tumult of fear, Jack found solace in Anya's presence. Together, they could navigate the shadows that threatened to consume them. As the sun dipped below the horizon, they completed their list, taking a moment to lean back and pause, feeling the resolve swell between them.

The game was afoot, that much was certain. And as long as they had each other, there was a chance, however slim, that they could unveil the enemy lurking within the darkness and reclaim their futures.

Allies Turned Enemies

As the sun dipped below the horizon, painting the sky with hues of orange and purple, Jack Malaney stood by the window, his brow furrowed in concentration. The quiet of the countryside had offered him solace for years, but now, the peacefulness felt like a veneer stretched thin over the turbulent undercurrents beneath. Every creak of the floorboards, every rustle of leaves in the gentle breeze, seemed to echo with the ghosts of his past.

He turned to look at Anya, seated at the dining table, her hands restless as they fidgeted with the remnants of yet another meager meal. Despite her courage, Jack could see the underlying tension in her demeanor. The weight of their situation pressed down on them both, an invisible burden that often threatened to suffocate. He wished he could reassure her, ease her fears, but the truth was that every day they walked this perilous path, the stakes grew higher.

Anya had confided in him about her husband Alex's fears—about the whispers of a Russian operative within the upper echelons of the Ukrainian intelligence community. Every revelation felt like a thread unraveled from a tightly woven story, exposing the chaos lurking beneath the surface. Jack could feel the old habits of his MI6 days surfacing: analyzing, piecing together fragments of information to form a coherent picture. But this was different; this was personal. He was not just a detached observer in a game of espionage. He had become entwined in the fates of Anya and her children, and the thought made his heart race with both determination and dread.

As they sat in the dim light of the room, Jack's mind churned with thoughts of their former allies—contacts and colleagues in the intelligence community who now felt like ghosts haunting their every move. Tension simmered beneath the surface of their situation, each day spent searching for answers drawing them closer to danger. Jack felt the shadows closing in around them, a haunting reminder that trust was no longer an option. He hated the nagging feeling that loyalty could easily shift in the world they now inhabited.

It was not long before the phone rang, its shrill tone piercing the stillness. Jack instinctively reached for it, his heart pounding as though he had just received a death sentence. He exchanged a quick glance with Anya—her eyes wide, a mixture of hope and fear reflected in them. This had become the ritual: the call that would either bring them closer to the truth or thrust them deeper into peril.

"Jack," a familiar voice crackled through the line—Martin Shaw, a former colleague from MI6, one of the few people Jack had thought he could still rely on. "I think you need to be careful. Things are shifting fast. You aren't the only one looking for answers."

Jack's pulse quickened. "Martin, what are you saying? Is there something you know?"

"I've been hearing whispers," Martin replied, the gravity in his voice unmistakable. "Certain people in the agency have started to take a keen interest in your investigation. They're not your friends. They might even be watching you."

Jack's grip tightened around the phone. "What do you mean? Who?"

"I can't say over the phone. It's not safe. Meet me at The Raven's Nest in an hour. You and... Anya."

Jack's heart sank. The Raven's Nest was a pub known in their circles as a safe haven for clandestine meetings—an establishment that had stood the test of time, shrouded in its own history of secrets. But safe havens could quickly turn into traps.

"Do you trust him?" Anya's voice broke into his thoughts when he hung up. A small tremor ran through her body, an echo of the fear that danced in her eyes.

Jack hesitated, the weight of his past decisions and relationships loomed large. He had esteemed Martin; they had shared both triumphs and failures in their years at MI6. But could he truly trust someone whose allegiances were rooted in a world fraught with betrayal?

After a moment, he nodded, feeling the disquiet settle in his gut. "For now. We need to see what he knows."

The transportation to The Raven's Nest was a cacophony of anticipation and dread. Each passing car felt like a potential threat, a harbinger of danger. Anya's small frame beside him reminded Jack that every step they took was not just for him but for her and her children. His protective instincts flared anew, forcing him to compartmentalize his past while focusing on the immediate task at hand.

Upon entering the dimly lit pub, the smell of fried food and stale ale enveloped them like a comforting cocoon, but Jack knew better. The walls held countless stories, whispers exchanged in shadows, but in this context, it only heightened his senses. The bar was nearly empty except for a few familiar faces—those who had been drawn into the world of espionage and espionage-hunters. A tangled web of old loyalties sat woven into this space, but who held the knife, he had yet to determine.

Martin occupied a dim corner, his eyes scanning the room, calculating, discerning. Jack approached, Anya lingering a step behind him, her anxiety palpable. As they slid into the booth across from Martin, Jack noted the subtle rigidness in his posture, the calculated way he nursed his drink as though it were a lifeline.

"Thanks for meeting us," Jack said, keeping his tone steady. "What do you know?"

Martin leaned forward, lowering his voice. "There's a lot of movement within our ranks. Whispers of a mole—someone in a high position who's been feeding information to the Russians. And they're starting to suspect you might be looking into it."

Anya's hand gripping Jack's thigh tightened as if anchoring him to reality. He felt the weight of uncertainty sink deeper into his gut. "Who?"

"I would rather not discuss names here." Martin's gaze flicked to the entrance, the tension in his shoulders speaking volumes. "But there are people within MI6 who have been compromised. You, Jack, you seem to have stirred something that was better left dormant."

Jack's mind raced, each mention of potential betrayal igniting sparks of fear and anger. They sat on the precipice of a dangerous game, and in this moment, he felt the tightrope underfoot wobble perilously. "Is it possible to find out who? To get proof?"

"Not without risking your lives." Martin hesitated before adding, "You're no longer working in the shadows. You're a target—especially since Anya's situation is tied up in this mess."

Anya's demeanor shifted as she took a deep breath, her determination feeding into the building anxiety around them. She leaned into the conversation. "What do we do then? We can't just sit back and wait. That's how people die, Martin."

Martin looked at her, surprise and respect flickering in his eyes. "You've got more fire than most operatives I know. But dodging bullets in this line of work is a deadly gamble."

"Your words are great, but we need answers," Jack said. "We have to confront the enemy head-on—or we could lose everything."

Martin contemplated for a moment, swirling his drink. "It's all about layers. Before we confront anyone, we need to gather as much intel as possible. Find connections. Look for inconsistencies."

Jack nodded, feeling the plan formulate in his mind. This was a game he could play, a game where he could outmaneuver the pieces around him. "I'll reach out to the contacts I trust. I can get to Ben—he's in counterintelligence and has been looking at the same suspects."

"Good. I'll help you where I can, but tread carefully," Martin warned. "You have to remember, trust is fluid in our world. Old friendships can turn on you in an instant."

Something in Martin's demeanor shifted then; the subtle change in his posture spoke to a disquiet that resonated with Jack. The room felt stifling, shadows lengthened in the corners, and Jack's instincts screamed that this was not the safe enclave it once seemed.

Within moments of their conversation, a figure emerged from the entrance, a familiar silhouette that stopped Jack cold. It was Elena—a former MI6 analyst who had worked closely with Jack. They had shared lunch breaks filled with laughter, but as he locked eyes with her, suspicion rippled through him.

"Jack, Anya," she greeted, her voice smooth, too smooth. "Fancy seeing you here."

Martin straightened in his seat, his eyes narrowing in a way that did not escape Jack's notice.

"Elena," Jack replied, his tone deliberately neutral. There was an undertow to her presence that felt threatening, as if she held secrets that could shatter the fragile trust they had left.

"Interesting gathering," she continued, her gaze flitting between them. "I hope you're not planning anything reckless."

Jack's jaw tightened. "Just seeking answers."

"Be cautious, Jack. In times like these, even the best relationships can turn to ash," she warned, her smile bordering on condescending, her interest in Anya palpable. Jack felt a flare of protectiveness ignite inside him, realizing that their combined presence turned the table—suddenly, they were the ones being hunted.

As Elena left, her shadow lingered in the air, thickening the tension in the room.

Jack turned back to Martin, who was now clutching his drink with white knuckles. "We need to figure out who we can trust. If Elena is here, chances are she's not just passing by."

"You think she's connected to the mole?" Anya asked, her eyes darting toward the door in apprehension.

"I don't know," Jack admitted. "But I know our former allies—those who we thought could help—could be threats now. We can't afford to make mistakes."

The atmosphere grew heavier, the stakes escalating. Jack could sense the shadows closing around them, and he felt the remnants of safety slip away, replaced instead by a tangible sense of danger.

In the hours that followed, Jack and Anya worked in synchrony, a delicate dance amidst the rising tides. They combed through contacts, established layers of deception, and meticulously documented every clue. Yet, every lead seemed to either circle back on itself or lead to dead ends. It was a treacherous landscape they navigated, each moment weighed down by their growing paranoia.

Late into the night, a damp chill hung over their quiet home. Jack stood at the window, staring into the darkness, lost in thought. Outside, the world beyond was so beautifully mundane; the stars sparkled like diamonds in the vastness of the sky—a stark contrast to the chaos swirling through his mind.

Anya joined him, her hand softly touching his arm as she looked out too. "What's going on in there?"

"I'm trying to read the patterns," he admitted, rubbing the back of his neck where tension coiled. "It feels like we're racing time, but every moment that passes just makes the picture fuzzier."

"That doesn't help us, does it?" Anya replied, her voice steady but fatigue layering her tone. "We need to act. We can't allow them to take control of our fate."

Her defiance ignited something within him, a renewed conviction. Jack turned to face her, admiration surging through him. "You're right. But the question remains: how do we stay not only a step ahead but alive?"

"By outsmarting them," Anya countered. "We find a way to leverage their fears against them. If they think they're the hunters while we're the prey, we might just regain control."

Jack felt a flicker of hope, a glimmer of insight. Anya's fierce spirit reminded him that they were not powerless, that they still had agency in this fight.

"Let's take this to Martin tomorrow," Jack decided, resolve settling firmly in his chest. "If Elena is a threat, we need to anticipate her moves. She was always good at reading people's emotions—if she thinks she can play us, we have to turn that on its head."

As the night wore on, strategies formed. Their meticulously crafted plan ignited new energy, allowing Jack to shoulder the weight of his responsibilities once more. Together, they would navigate the minefield of deceit that lay ahead.

The next day unfolded with an air of cautious determination. Jack and Anya ventured to the MI6 safe house where Martin had agreed to meet them. As they pulled into the gravel driveway, a sense of unease washed over Jack.

"Remember, trust is fluid," he reminded her, the gravity of those words sinking in as they stepped inside. The familiar scent of worn leather and coffee filled the air, but Jack felt a chill running down his spine.

"Jack," Martin called, emerging from the back room. He motioned them into the small meeting space cluttered with old files and surveillance equipment. "You'll want to hear this."

Within moments, Martin laid out the information he had gathered. "I tracked some movements. It seems Elena has been in contact with a few names on our suspect list. She's digging into something she shouldn't."

Jack's stomach twisted. "She's part of it then? Has she been in contact with the mole?"

Martin nodded. "I suspect she's working to protect her own interests. You can't trust her."

As they spoke, Jack felt the weight of paranoia creep in, the familiar itch of distrust settling in his bones. "What do we do?"

"We need a way to uncover more details without alerting her first. If she's involved, confronting her head-on could trigger a response we can't anticipate," Martin warned.

Anya spoke up, her voice steady. "If she's building an alliance, perhaps we can create one of our own. We push for information, and while she thinks we're aligned, we dig deeper."

"Think you can handle that kind of deception?" Jack asked, his tone both urgent and admiring.

"I'm not one to shy away from risks," she smirked, determination radiating around her.

And just like that, Jack was reminded of why he knew he could trust her. They were bound together in a fight that had grown increasingly more desperate, yet their bond solidified amidst the growing tension.

Over the following days, they meticulously crafted their approach. Anya reached out to Elena, offering an olive branch in the form of a coffee meeting to discuss their shared concerns. Meanwhile, Jack utilized Martin's insights and the few remaining contacts he still trusted.

When the meeting day finally came, apprehension hung thick in the air. Jack and Anya took turns keeping watch, scanning for potential dangers as they approached a carefully chosen café.

As they sat down, Jack's instincts heightened. The air was electric with tension, and he wondered if Elena understood the precariousness they all faced—the risk she was taking by sitting down with them.

Elena arrived, her smile practiced as she slid into the chair opposite them. "Glad we could finally meet again. Things are very tense out there."

"Indeed." Jack studied her carefully, gauging her reactions. Anya leaned in, casting a sideways glance at him, as if urging him to speak.

"Anya was just telling me about some concerns regarding the recent developments in our agency. I've heard rumors that someone is trying to manipulate the information flow," Jack began, watching for her response.

Elena's eyes narrowed ever so slightly. "Well, there's always a shift, Jack. Intelligence is about power play."

Anya added, "We're just trying to know who we can trust. Since the rumors have started, we thought it best to come together."

For a moment, uncertainty swirled in the air as Elena weighed their intentions. She cast a glance around the café, her expression carved with suspicion. Jack barely breathed, the silence stretching like an elastic band threatening to snap.

"Let's be candid," Elena replied. "I've heard you've been poking around, gathering information. If you're looking into the mole, you need to be careful. There are consequences at play here."

"Elena, we're all in this together. If we can combine our efforts…" Anya pressed, the urgency in her voice palpable.

"Elena, why do I get the feeling you're not entirely on our side?" Jack demanded, leaning forward. "There's more at stake here than just your precious alliances."

At that moment, tension shattered the fragile façade of camaraderie. Elena's smile slipped momentarily; her eyes flashing with something darker. "Loyalty is fluid, Jack. You of all people should know that."

In that moment, clarity washed over him. Jack's instincts peaked, the realization that they had set off an alarm within Elena. He could almost see the gears turning in her mind, calculating the odds now stacked against them.

Before he could articulate another word, Elena abruptly stood, her chair scraping against the floor as she turned to leave. "Think wisely, Jack. The shadows aren't as vacant as you think."

Jack's heart raced as he glanced at Anya, who mirrored his own alarm. "What now?"

"We prepare," Anya said, her voice firm despite the tremor of urgency. "You were right. The past doesn't stay buried. If Elena is tied into the mole, we need to be smarter than ever."

In the days that followed, unease clung to their surroundings like a heavy fog. The boundaries of trust blurred as Jack wrestled with the deception swirling around them. He could no longer shake the feeling of being watched; paranoia lingered at the edge of his consciousness like an avalanche, waiting to bury him if he let his guard down.

The stakes started to escalate quickly. Each passing day brought new uncertainties, a creeping sense of danger replacing the relative calm they had established. Jack's mind began to spiral, combing through every detail, every interaction.

And then it happened—the confrontation they had both feared.

One evening, Jack came home after an exhausting day filled with uncertainty. Anya was sitting in the living room with the television muted, her expression unreadable. The air felt thick and charged.

"Anything wrong?" he asked, setting his bag down, instinctively reaching for the gun tucked beneath his shirt.

She looked up, uncertainty flickering in her eyes. "There were men outside. Two of them."

His pulse quickened. "What do you mean? Were they watching?"

"I don't know." Anya swallowed hard, her resolve wavering. "They were just... there. Watching the house. I felt it."

Jack felt a rush of adrenaline, igniting his instincts. "Did you see their faces?"

"No, but I could feel that they were here for us," Anya said, her voice barely above a whisper.

As the gravity of the situation settled in, Jack faced the reality—the safety they had sought to navigate had become another battleground. "We need to be ready."

They spent the night preparing, a newfound urgency fueling their actions. Every sound outside felt amplified, each passing car or distant voice a potential signal of danger. Jack was aware that the time for games had long passed—now was a matter of survival.

It wasn't long before the moment they feared most became a reality.

In the dead of night, Jack's phone buzzed violently, its harsh tone shattering the heavy silence in their home.

"Jack," Martin's urgent voice came through. "They're coming for you. You need to get out now."

"Who?" Jack shouted, his heart racing.

"I don't know, but there's a team moving in on your location. I can stall for time, but you have to move fast."

"Anya!" Jack yelled, turning to her. "We have to go—now!"

They were thrust into action, a rush of adrenaline pushing them forward as they grabbed the essentials and slipped into the dark night. The world beyond the threshold felt both familiar and foreign—a strange paradox where every leaf rustled with the potential of a threat.

As they moved stealthily through the shadows of their yard and into the embrace of the night, Jack couldn't shake the feeling of paranoia that clung to him like a second skin. He had to keep Anya and the children safe—nothing else mattered.

"Where do we go?" Anya quivered beside him.

"Anywhere but here. Martin should be able to lead us—there's an old safe house a few miles from here," Jack admitted, even as uncertainty gnawed at his resolve.

They continued moving stealthily, a dance of survival that had become instinctual. As they reached the street, headlights illuminated the darkness, casting elongated shadows and igniting their instincts. Jack tightened his grip on Anya's hand; they had to be quick.

But then the shadows shifted.

Without warning, a vehicle screeched to a halt nearby, tires gripping the asphalt as figures spilled out. Jack's heart raced as dark silhouettes pulled weapons and moved with purpose. The night shimmered with dread as he realized they had been cornered.

"Run!" he shouted, adrenaline surging through him as he shoved Anya forward. They sprinted down the street, the echo of footfalls behind them like a haunting refrain.

The chase unfurled with a brutal urgency, but Jack pushed Anya ahead, urging speed, their lives hanging in the balance. Every brush against danger ignited a feeling far more potent than fear—it was the roaring need to protect.

"Over here!" Anya shouted, suddenly veering into an alleyway, a dim path lined with shadows casting a treacherous veil over their escape.

But just as they slipped into the narrow passage, a heavy thud resonated against the bricks surrounding them, dragging at the edges of Jack's focus. The darkness loomed like a specter, taunting them with every hurried breath they took.

The night felt poised to crush them, and as they pressed on, the weight of betrayal and trust hung heavy in the air. The uncertainty of motives and intentions gnawed relentlessly.

They finally reached the safe house—a nondescript building hidden within an unlit street, void of the chaos that had been their lives. Jack threw the door open, urgency flooding every minute action.

As they slipped inside, Jack bolted the door, his chest heaving with panic and determination. He turned to Anya, their gazes meeting as fear and resolve intermingled.

"We'll stay here until we figure out our next move," he said, his voice steady despite the chaos swirling inside.

"Do we trust Martin?" Anya asked, worry etching her brow.

"Right now, we have no choice," Jack replied, attempting to soothe both Anya and himself. "Just keep your eyes open. We'll keep each other safe."

Days in hiding turned into an agonizing cycle of tension, each minute heavy with uncertainty as they waited for Martin.

With limited communication, they stayed within their self-imposed isolation, making it even more challenging to determine who among their past acquaintances had joined the treachery. Each moment of silence felt like the calm before an impending storm, and Jack's mind continued to churn with paranoia.

Finally, Martin arrived—his expression a mix of urgency and anxiety. "We have to move again."

As they gathered their belongings, Jack glanced at Anya, her resolve unshaken even in the face of mounting danger. She had become a beacon of strength, a reminder that together they could navigate the storm.

Outside, the tension was almost palpable. A heightened awareness cloaked them; Jack's instincts screamed warnings as they picked their way through the shadows.

"Where are we headed?" Anya asked pocketing what little comfort she could carry.

"There's a convoy we can use," Martin replied, his voice low and urgent. "But we need to be quick. They're getting closer."

Jack felt the weight of responsibility once again—each step they took pinned with hope and vulnerability. Their tapestries of trust had frayed, and as they moved together through the alleys, he wondered who might betray them next.

Just when they thought they had reached safety, shadows danced from the rooftop, and chaos erupted.

Gunshots rang through the air—sharp and violent. Jack thrust Anya down, instinctively shielding her as the world dissolved into chaos.

"Go!" he shouted, trying to reach the others as the grim realization of betrayal pressed into their reality. "Run, now! I'll hold them off!"

But Anya wouldn't budge, defiance sculpted into determination. "No! We stay together."

The gunfire intensified, carving into the night, and Jack's mind raced. He had to protect her; that was his sole focus, but now their allegiances were all put into question. Were any of them allies?

In that storm of fire and chaos, everything felt surreal, every instinct overflowed with dread, but amidst the shadows emerged a single thought: trust was a double-edged sword, cutting both ways.

As bullets ricocheted off the brick walls, Jack pushed Anya again. "Move!"

In that moment, their battle for survival intertwined with the labyrinth of betrayal, and with every second passing, they were forced to confront the reality of their choices. In a world of shadows, where one misstep could cost them everything, Jack leaned into the truth that whispered insistently against their odds: sometimes, the most dangerous alliances were born from the simplest of desires—trust and protection.

Nicholas P. Clark

And as the fight unfolded around them, they had to cling to the hope that, beneath the facade of shattered loyalties, they might yet find a light shining through the darkness.

A Moment of Decision

Jack stood by the window, the dim light of the setting sun casting long shadows across the room. Outside, the world continued in its oblivious rhythm, while inside, a tempest raged within him. Anya had gone quiet, her breath shallow as she huddled on the couch, her eyes searching his face for answers, for assurance that somehow everything would be alright. He felt the weight of her gaze deeply, as if it were pressing against his chest, constricting his breath and slowing his thoughts.

He turned away from the window. The sprawling fields of the English countryside, with their endless horizons, contrasted sharply with the suffocating conviction he felt inside. The lines of his past, once clearly drawn by duty and allegiance, had blurred, and the stakes had never been higher. In this moment, he was no longer just a retired MI6 officer; he was a man on the precipice, tasked with decisions that could alter the lives of those he cared about most.

There was a knock at the door—hard and abrupt. Jack's heart raced. It could be a harmless neighbor, or it could be someone sent to silence him for good. The thought sent a jolt of adrenaline coursing through him. He glanced at Anya; her face had gone pale, and the children were playing quietly at the far end of the room, unaware of the darkness brewing around them. They had become a sanctuary for each other—he, a weary soul seeking redemption; she, a fierce mother desperate to protect her little ones amid chaos.

"Stay here," he whispered to Anya. His voice was steady, but he saw the flicker of fear in her eyes. She nodded, her expression a silent reminder of why he couldn't turn back now.

Jack approached the door with measured steps, his instincts sharpening. He opened it a crack, peering through the narrow slit. A familiar figure stood there, one he recognized but hadn't seen in years. It was Simon Parkes, an MI6 contact who had once been both a mentor and a friend. Simon's expression was grave, his eyes scanning the surroundings with an urgency that set Jack on edge.

"Jack, we need to talk," Simon said, pushing the door wider as though he were being pursued. Jack stepped aside, letting Simon in. The moment the door closed, the weight of their shared history hung in the air like an ominous omen.

"What's happened?" Jack asked, keeping his voice low, conscious of the children's proximity. He gestured toward the kitchen, where they could speak away from prying ears.

Simon wasted no time. "Word's gotten around about your investigation. People are uneasy. There are whispers of a mole inside our agency, possibly linked to the same conspiracy Anya's husband is caught up in."

The blood drained from Jack's face. He had feared this moment, the intersection of personal and professional would collide in the most dangerous way. "And what are you suggesting? That we back off?"

"No, not at all. I'm saying we need to escalate our actions." Simon's intensity surged. "You need to confront this head-on, Jack. We're in too deep, and your connection with Anya complicates things. It's not just about Alex anymore—it's about national security."

Jack felt a sharp jab of anger at Simon's words. "You think I care about the job? You think I care about that when Anya's family is at risk?" His voice had risen, bitterness seeping through the cracks of his carefully constructed façade.

Simon matched his tone. "This is exactly why I'm here, Jack! You're playing with fire. If you get too close to the truth without the right support, you put everyone at risk—especially her."

The word "her" echoed in Jack's mind, a stark reminder of the living, breathing person who depended on him. He turned away, furious not only at Simon's admonishment but at the unyielding reality that his choices had repercussions beyond personal feelings.

"What do you want me to do?" Jack demanded, the frustration spilling over. "Do you want me to run for cover? To abandon Anya?"

"No." Simon paused, and Jack could see the weight of his responsibility etched on his features. "I want you to gather enough evidence to expose the mole and dismantle this operation. You must choose between protecting Anya's family and pursuing justice. The latter may destroy her in the process."

Jack clenched his jaw, a surging mix of emotions battling within him. Did he really have to choose? Was there any path that would allow him to protect Anya and the truth?

"I can't risk her life," he muttered, more to himself than to Simon.

Simon stepped closer, lowering his voice. "You might not have a choice, Jack. This is a dangerous game, and lives are at stake. Think of the children."

The mention of Anya's children struck a nerve. Jack's heart wrenched as he imagined their innocent faces, unaware of the storm surrounding them. The weight of their vulnerability crashed over him, a tidal wave of responsibility that pinned him in place.

"What if there's a way to do both?" Jack ventured, desperation creeping into his tone. "If I can gather evidence, make the necessary connections without putting them in immediate danger—"

"It's risky." Simon interrupted, his expression unsympathetic. "And the more you linger, the more dangerous it becomes for all of you."

Jack turned away from Simon, his mind racing through the possible scenarios. If he decided to pursue the truth, how could he ensure Anya's safety? Conversely, if he chose merely to protect them, would that mean turning a blind eye to a greater threat? The moral complexities twisted in his gut, and all he wanted was a moment of clarity amidst the confusion.

He felt Simon's eyes boring into the back of his head, a silent expectation hanging over him. "You need to make a choice, Jack,"

Simon finally said, the steel in his voice undeniable. "This is a moment of decision, and you can't walk away from it."

"Can I really trust you?" Jack threw back the question, indignation rising to meet Simon's intensity.

"Brotherhood doesn't die easily, Jack. But trust can fracture in the shadows. I'm offering you a lifeline, a chance to do something before it's too late. You know what's at stake."

Jack closed his eyes, running through every encounter he'd had since Anya and her children arrived at his door. Each conversation had drawn lines between past loyalties, memories lurking in the edges like ghosts reminding him of choices he'd made and consequences he'd avoided. Could he embrace the shadows of his old life?

"Time is not on our side," Simon pressed. "You need to decide now."

Slowly, Jack opened his eyes and met Simon's gaze, reading the urgency etched in his features. Then, he turned to the door, his heart pounding. This would be the fateful decision that could either save or doom Anya's family as well as himself.

Without thinking, Jack stepped toward the kitchen where Anya waited, a world of anxiety written across her face. As he looked at her, he was painfully aware of the exquisite fragility of their lives at that very moment. A single second might tip the balance, a fleeting decision could plunge them into darkness, and the shadows of the past loomed threateningly.

"What did he want?" Anya asked, her voice trembling. Jack knew she could sense something amiss in his demeanor.

"It's complicated," he replied slowly, mentally sifting through his thoughts. He could see the concern deepening in her eyes, and the instinct to shield her from the darkness curdled in his chest.

"Jack." Her voice grew firmer, settling the air around them. "You can't protect me without being honest. You need to trust me as much as I trust you."

Jack's breath caught in his throat. Those simple words pierced him like a blade. He had been so caught up in trying to balance protecting her and pursuing justice that he'd overlooked the very foundation of their connection—trust. "Anya, I want to protect you, but—"

She stepped forward, meeting him with unwavering resolve. "But what, Jack? Tell me. I deserve to know. We need to face this together."

It was an impossible choice, one that clawed at him, grappling with both the consequences against the backdrop of their shared history. Would he be able to go down a path that could destroy the foundations of their fragile bond?

"I have to confront this," he blurted out, the words escaping him before he could pull them back.

Anya's expression shifted, her eyes wide with fear. "What does that mean for us?"

Jack grappled with the answer, his heart heavy with the weight of his confession. "It means I need to investigate the mole. I need to find out who it is and bring them to light."

A myriad of emotions flickered across Anya's face, and he could almost see her weighing the possibilities. "And what about our safety?"

"I'll do everything I can to ensure your safety—"

"But that might not be enough!" she interrupted, her voice breaking. "Jack, do you understand what you're putting us all at risk of? You are considering throwing yourself back into danger!"

Tension filled the room like smoke, the air thick with unspoken fears. "It's not just about me anymore," he insisted, desperately trying to defend his course. "I can't stand by and allow this threat to linger; it endangers you just as much as it does me."

Jack could see the conflicting emotions whirl in her eyes—the fear, the anger, the fatigue of a woman who had fought too long for her family. Her impassioned gaze dropped to the ground momentarily, as though she were searching for ground beneath her very feet.

"I don't want you to lose yourself again, Jack," Anya said, the softness of her voice breaking through the tension like dawn breaking over a dark tunnel. "You cannot risk it all because of me."

"I might have to," he replied, his voice softer yet firm. "That's the reality of this situation."

"But what if this means you abandon me?" Anya's words quaked with vulnerability, and Jack felt something primal rise within him at the thought.

"I will not abandon you," he swore, though fear gripped him at what that commitment might entail. What if justice meant dragging her deeper into the mire, losing her in the process? The paradox tightened around his chest, and he found himself wishing desperately for a way out, for a clear decision he could wrap around like a lifeline.

"Then let's find a way together, just like before." Anya stepped closer, closing the distance between them. "We need to share everything, Jack. I can't lose you as well."

A sudden surge of clarity coursed through him—a realization that the decision could not reside solely in his hands. They had become allies bound by circumstance, drawing strength from each other's vulnerability and tenacity. If he could trust her to stand alongside him, perhaps they could find a path to navigate the minefield while keeping her family intact.

"Alright," he conceded, "we'll do this together. But it may mean taking risks we both dread. It might mean lies and betrayal before the truth emerges. Are you willing to face that?"

Her gaze sharpened. "I'll face whatever it takes if it means saving Alex and protecting my children."

Jack reached for her hand, squeezing it tightly. "Then together we'll find a way to expose this threat—whether it's the mole or the fear that's shackled us," he vowed quietly.

As Jack pulled her close, an unspoken agreement formed between them—the will to charge into the abyss together, bound by courage, shaped by the uncertainties ahead.

Just as he thought they had found their rhythm, an unexpected hammering jolted them from the moment. The knocking grew faster, more frenetic this time—urgent, and insistent. Jack instinctively turned toward the door, heart racing once more as adrenaline surged.

Anya's eyes widened, fear etching itself across her features. Jack pulled her back behind him protectively, heart pounding as he approached the door cautiously.

"Stay behind me," he commanded quietly, his voice steady despite the storm brewing inside him.

His hand trembled on the doorknob as he took a deep breath and pulled the door open wide.

A figure rushed in, breathless and frantic. It was Alex, haggard and disheveled, with fear blending into desperation on his face. Behind him trailed two men, cold and calculating, a palpable threat burdening their presence.

"Jack!" Alex yelled, an edge of panic to his voice. "They're after me! We have to move now!"

In that moment, the weight of Jack's decision crashed over him. He had been faced with an impossible moment—a fragile choice of loyalty stretched between familial love, duty to justice, and looming chaos.

As the door swung wider, the darkness of betrayal that he'd feared came flooding in, crashing down around them with all the ferocity of a winter storm.

And in that heart-stopping second, Jack realized his life had changed forever. The moment of decision had transcended into action—a choice made not just for himself but for Anya and the family they were bound to protect.

Now, as shadows merged into a whirlwind of uncertainty and danger, the true battle began. But whether it led to redemption or despair, he didn't know. All he could do was plunge forward, hand in hand with the woman whose future now intertwined irrevocably with his own, ready to face the tempest together.

A Light in the Darkness

Finding Strength

The soft morning light filtered through the kitchen window, casting slants of gold across the dark wood table where Jack and Anya sat. The remnants of their chaotic week lay behind them, yet the weight of their shared trauma lingered in the air like an uninvited guest. Jack watched Anya, her brow furrowed in thought as she stirred her tea absentmindedly, the steam curling upward, twisting and dancing—a fleeting whisper of grace amidst their harsh reality.

"Do you remember the first time we met?" Jack asked, breaking the silence that felt both comforting and heavy. His voice was gentle, almost hesitant, as if stepping carefully over fragile ground.

Anya looked up, the shadows in her eyes brightening slightly with the hint of a smile. "You were just this grumpy old man with a garden," she replied with a playful spark. "I thought, where is this poor woman and her children going to find comfort?"

Jack chuckled softly, the sound easing some of the tension between them. "Hardly grumpy. Just lacking purpose." He paused, reminiscing about how simple things had felt back then. The green of the garden, the smell of freshly cut grass, and the bird songs that had seemed like a balm to his soul. All of that had felt so distant now, overshadowed by the intense demands and dangers of the past months.

"Life was easier, no?" Anya said, her tone reflective. "Before this storm came and broke everything apart."

Jack nodded, swallowing hard. The stark realities of their lives were stark contrasts to the calm moments they often reminisced about. "It was," he agreed, but he knew that those days were also shadowed by his internal struggles. He felt a mix of regret and relief at the thought that, perhaps, those days had been comfortably mundane to the outsider but emotionally hollow for him. "But you've brought some light back into my life. I don't think I could have navigated the chaos without you."

Anya's gaze softened. She leaned forward, placing her hands around her mug, desperately seeking warmth. "And you have kept me strong, Jack. I don't think I would have had the courage to keep moving forward without your presence."

The truth of her words struck him. She had fought against all odds to protect her children, to preserve their family, and to make sense of the world crashing down around them. Anya's resilience had become a source of inspiration for him, a reminder of the strength of the human spirit amidst suffering. Together, they had created a bond forged in adversity, one that was not just about survival but about hope.

"Together, we've done something incredible," Jack stated, his sincerity emerging from the depths of his heart. "With everything stacked against us, we've held on. Those nights we spent planning, strategizing, even just sitting in silence, have brought us closer."

Their shared experiences, from the fleeting moments of joy to the haunting memories of fear they had endured together, created an unbreakable tie. They were not alone in this fight anymore; they had each other.

Anya took a deep breath, centering herself. "What are we going to do next? I feel like we've covered so much ground, but the shadows are still there, waiting for their chance."

Jack leaned back in his chair, considering their position with a deeper sense of strategic clarity. The threat wasn't just a distant specter; it was a gnawing reality that echoed in every knock at the door and every rustle in the bushes outside. Their investigation had pieced together bits and pieces that were troubling and had raised more questions than answers.

"We need to establish clearer lines of communication," he finally said, picturing their options like maps in his mind. "We can't rely solely on what we have discovered. We must dig deeper, find allies we can trust, and understand who stands with us and who stands against us."

"Trust," Anya echoed, a subtle frown crossing her features. "But how can we trust anyone? Who can we really believe?"

Jack held her gaze firm. "That's the dilemma we face. Trust is a fragile commodity in our world, especially now. But we need to start somewhere. Let's work on gaining the confidence of those we know can support us—our old contacts, and maybe even see if there are avenues within the Ukrainian network that can provide us with more information."

The determination in his voice flowed into Anya, igniting her spirit. "Yes," she agreed, her resolve strengthening. "But we also need to keep the children's safety as our priority. Every move we make has to be thought through."

"Of course," Jack replied, nodding solemnly, aware that the stakes were rising at every turn. "They deserve the world, Anya. We must fight for them, not just for ourselves."

A fleeting comfort wrapped around Anya at his words, reminding her of the vibrant dreams she once held for her children. She envisioned them playing and laughing, unburdened by the shadows that now loomed over them. Jack's unwavering commitment to their safety cemented the gravity of their alliance.

"Then let's create a plan," Anya said, feeling the sparks of hope flicker back to life. "We can outline our next steps, take it one day at a time. There has to be a way through this."

She grabbed a nearby notepad and pen, her fingers trembling slightly with adrenaline. Jack watched her, the quiet fire in her determination reaching out and around him, pulling him in. Together, they made a formidable team, crafting a tapestry of courage and resolve in the aftermath of chaos.

Their conversation flowed seamlessly into the creation of a more detailed plan. With every note she took, Anya's belief in their capability to reclaim control deepened. The initial shock of their circumstances faded with purpose, replaced by a stark realism that both invigorated and frightened her.

The sun settled higher overhead, casting bold shadows across the paper as if the universe itself was both challenging and urging them forward. The dialogue about strategies shifted towards options for gathering intelligence while keeping the children in mind—because safeguarding their innocence remained paramount.

"We need a way to monitor our surroundings," Jack suggested, contemplating their vulnerabilities. "If we can ensure our home remains undetected, we can give ourselves the time we need to plan properly."

Anya nodded, enthusiasm brewing anew. "Perhaps we can set up a system of signals? Something discreet, but effective. If something seems off, we'll immediately know."

"Great idea. I can rig up some sort of alarm at the back of the property. And we can talk to the kids about being aware of strangers or anything unusual around them," Jack added. "It's all about being proactive."

"Communication is essential. We have to ensure they know how to alert us, too," Anya emphasized. Despite the gravity of the situation, a sense of warmth enveloped her heart. This man, once a stranger, had become her anchor.

Together, they charted out a map of action. They sketched ideas, drew lines connecting potential allies, highlighted key neighborhoods, and discussed possible routes for exits should trouble arise again. Laughter mingled with serious discussions, a surprising blend of energy that pulled them forward. The more they collaborated, the more hopeful they began to feel.

"Do you always have to be so good at planning?" Anya teased, her smile teasing the corners of her lips.

"Years of practice," he replied, feigning an air of nonchalance, though his heart raced with excitement. "Or perhaps, just fighting my own shadows."

She glanced at him sharply, the reality of his past swirling in the space between them. "We're stronger together, you know. You don't have to bear this burden alone."

Jack met her gaze, feeling the weight lift slightly off his chest. The vulnerability and accountability shared between them created a sacred bond that transcended their individual struggles. "Sometimes I forget that it's okay to lean on someone else. Thank you for that reminder."

In the stillness, an understanding passed between them. They were evolving, their relationship shifting from mere survival to one built on trust and shared goals. This was not just about the threats they faced together; it was about finding strength in each other's presence amid the shadows that loomed large.

The kitchen filled with a comfortable silence while they continued to work on their plan, the warmth of the sun wrapping around them like a soft blanket. Every scribbled note, every idea exchanged, became a thread that wove their lives together more intricately. They were more than two people coping with chaos; they were partners driven by hope, united in purpose.

As they crafted the framework for their next moves, Anya suddenly placed her pen down, feeling the gravity of this new endeavor. "Jack, do you think we'll ever find peace?"

The moment hung thick in the air, the question both profound and haunting. The uncertainty lingered, poking at the edges of their newfound determination. Jack leaned forward, seeking words that could encapsulate their fears and aspirations.

"Peace is a journey," he finally said, choosing his words carefully. "It's not always something you find; sometimes, it's something you create. We've already taken steps toward that goal by standing our ground, by planning for a better future."

"But it's the unknown that frightens me," she confessed, her voice barely above a whisper. "What if we fail? What if it all comes crashing down again?"

Jack took a moment to respond, allowing the weight of her worries to settle within him. "Then we will pick ourselves up and start again. We will not break, Anya. We will bend, flex, even sway with the wind…but we will always stand together."

The steadfastness in his words wrapped around her like a shield. It ignited a flicker of belief deep within her, fueling her spirit as she pondered the countless possibilities ahead. They were each other's safety net, a refuge they hadn't known they needed until chaos had driven them toward it.

"I want to believe that," Anya said, her voice gaining strength. "I want to believe we can find a way through this darkness."

"You will see," Jack assured her, resolute as ever. "We will emerge from this stronger, side by side. It won't be easy, but this bond we share will guide us through unimaginable challenges. We will fight for our futures, together."

The intensity of his promise resonated within her. Anya felt the shadows receding ever so slightly, making room for the light that had begun to seep back into their lives. She could feel it in her bones, the slow resurgence of hope replacing despair.

"You're right, Jack," she spoke, determination unfurling in her heart. "Together, we can weather any storm. We will find our peace."

Their laughter mingled again, an effervescent quality breaking through the heaviness that had clouded the room. For the first time in what felt like an eternity, it was a sound filled with sincerity. Hope blossomed between them, intricate and rich, as they turned their thoughts to practicalities blending in with dreams.

They returned to the planning, each note and idea weaving a story of resilience authorized by the belief in their strength drawn from one another. A sense of clarity washed over them, igniting resolve in their hearts. With every passing moment, the shadows surrounding them began to acquire less power, as the light of possibility reclaimed its position.

"Let's do this," Anya said, settled into a new rhythm. "The future awaits us."

"It does," Jack replied, his heart lighter than it had been for what felt like an eternity. "And as long as we have this bond—this light—none of that darkness can extinguish our courage to move forward."

As they strategized and planned, they ignited something deeper than mere survival. They cultivated an abiding belief in one another, root-deep, promising a brighter future that beckoned just beyond the horizon. Together, they ventured into this chapter of their story, emboldened and united—ready to face the next challenge, shadows be damned.

A Plan in Motion

The window of Jack's home was barely illuminated by the weak morning light, filtered through the persistent mist enveloping the English countryside. Inside, the atmosphere was thick with tension as Jack and Anya huddled around the kitchen table, papers strewn across the surface like a battlefield of ideas and information. A weathered map of Ukraine lay open, peppered with hastily scribbled notes in Anya's beautiful, looping handwriting. Each mark represented a potential ally, suspect, or safe house—a constellation of strategy formed from desperation and hope.

"Jack, we need to act quickly," Anya said, her voice steady yet strained. Despite her poised demeanor, the shadows under her eyes betrayed the sleepless nights spent worrying about her husband Alex's fate. "The longer we wait, the more dangerous this becomes—for Alex, for us."

Jack nodded, his heart heavy with the weight of their shared understanding. "I agree. We have to be precise with our actions. We can't leave any room for errors."

He leaned over the map, tracing the lines that marked Alex's known associates within the intelligence community. As a former MI6 officer, Jack felt the familiar rush of adrenaline mixed with a dread he thought he had left behind, a sensation he had counted on finding extinct in his retirement. It felt bittersweet and uncomfortably familiar—the thrill of chasing the truth, of piecing together the puzzle, and the horrors that it could bring.

"We should start with Mikhail," Anya proposed, her finger resting where the eastern border of Ukraine met the vastness of Russia. "He's connected to Alex and knows the intricacies of the department. If anyone is aware of the threat from within, it's him."

Jack's brow furrowed as he considered her suggestion. "Mikhail is a risk, though. He has a reputation for shifting allegiances. If he suspects we're onto something, he could just as easily relay that information to those we're trying to expose."

Anya, catching the doubt in Jack's voice, leaned in closer, her earnestness resonating in the quiet space between them. "But he also knows the stakes. If he believes Alex is in danger, he might help us. We can be discreet."

The desperation in her voice was palpable, stirring something within Jack that hadn't surged in years. The mission to protect this family—and Anya in particular—drew him from his self-imposed exile, igniting a flicker of purpose. But alongside that warmth came the sharp pangs of loyalty—loyalty to a system he had served, and loyalty to the truth they now sought, a balance that felt precariously delicate.

"Okay. Let's assume he's our best starting point," Jack conceded, dialing back his reservations. "But we need a solid plan. We can't simply reach out and hope he responds positively. We need a way to approach him that ensures his cooperation."

Anya nodded, a hint of determination creeping into her expression. "We can leverage Alex's information to convince him. If we provide Mikhail with evidence of the Russian infiltration that Alex has unearthed, he might come to see it as a threat worth confronting. If he believes Alex's life is at stake... he'll have no choice but to help."

"Right. We need a secure channel to convey this information without arousing suspicion. With the scrutiny on every member of the intelligence community, any hint of impropriety could lead to grave consequences—not just for us, but for Alex."

Jack sat back, folding his arms across his chest. He admired Anya's resolve; it ignited a sense of shared responsibility. "Then we'll need a cover story. Something that makes our motives seem more benign. Maybe an inquiry into Alex's dig concerning the Russian agent that Mikhail might find intriguing."

As they discussed the finer points of their approach, Jack could feel the gears of strategy turning. This was no longer just about Alex; it was about more than saving lives; it was a battle of ideologies. Jack had spent his life operating within a web of lies and half-truths, but now he stood at a crossroads. The decisions he made for Anya and her children blurred the lines between right and wrong, loyalty to the institution, and loyalty to those who needed him most.

"Additionally, we need to create a safe escape route once we get the information we need from Mikhail," he said. "If he gets nervous or senses danger, we can't risk any confrontation. We need to plan to get out before the situation escalates."

Anya leaned back in her chair, considering his words. "I can reach out to some friends I trust, ones who belong to our former network. They could provide safe houses. We might need to keep moving until we can navigate this storm—if Mikhail's information leads us to confirm the Russian spy's identity, we can't risk being caught."

Jack admired her foresight. She was stepping back into the role of a strategist—exactly what they needed in this world of uncertainty. "And we should also gather intelligence on Mikhail. We need to know whom he associates with now, how to approach him without alarming him or compromising ourselves."

Anya picked up her cellphone, sketching a half-hearted smile as she braced herself. "I can tap into my old contacts. We might be able to twist a few arms to gather intel on him without raising eyebrows. We need to know his recent connections—who he's been in contact with and any intel he may be privy to himself."

"Do you think your contacts in Ukraine will cooperate? Given the current climate, everyone is on high alert."

She hesitated, briefly biting her lip as if weighing her past frustrations against the urgency of the now. "If I can communicate securely—using encrypted messages—then they might." Her confidence hung in the air, tinged with the heaviness of uncertainty. "These connections run deep; they know our situation. Some may have reason to distrust the bureaucracy; they too could be hungry for the truth."

Jack admired Anya's determination and grit in this chaotic moment. It reminded him of the initial sparks of a clandestine operation that masked the urgency of survival. Their partnership was blooming, forged in adversity—not of choice, but necessity.

"Good, then we'll base our next steps on that," Jack agreed. "Let's get this plan in motion, and once we hear back from Mikhail, we'll make a decision from there."

"Right," Anya said, a new spark lighting within her eyes. "Let me make a few calls."

Jack watched as she rose from the table, the weight of the world seemingly lifted from her shoulders, even if only for a moment. Her determination grew as she stepped into the fray, energizing their joint venture with newfound possibility. His own spirit stirred, echoing a mission that felt both thrilling and formidable.

As Anya stepped into the next room, Jack took a moment to collect his thoughts, staring blankly at the walls plastered in mundane country decor, decorations reflecting a life he had chosen away from chaos. The drumming of his heart echoed in the silence, reminding him of just how fragile their situation was. The peace he sought in retirement was, it seemed, a mere illusion; the shadows of his past were ever-present.

As the kettle began to whistle, Jack took a deep breath, digging into his internal thoughts about loyalty. In his years with MI6, he had always felt loyalty like a dual-edged sword. It was both the compass guiding him through the fog and the anchor holding him in place when knowing what was right became an overwhelming burden. His sorrow for the lives left behind, the secrets carried, and the impact of every decision weighed heavily. Yet at this moment, his loyalty felt renewed—anchored to Anya and her children. This was the loyalty that had begun to redefine him.

The familiar echo of footsteps brought him from the depths of reflection. Anya returned with her phone in hand, her expression fierce and focused. "I have connections who might provide intel on Mikhail."

"Excellent. Tell me everything," Jack urged, excitement threaded with caution.

"He's been more involved with new recruits lately," Anya reported. "He's taken on a mentorship role. There's word of increased surveillance on the intelligence sector, especially after the assassination of the deputy director last month. This could make him cautious, but if we're clever… we could catch him at a vulnerable moment."

"Good. We'll need to tread carefully. Let's arrange to meet discreetly in a public place—a café or park. That way, if anything goes wrong, we can slip away into the crowd," Jack suggested, his brow furrowing as he considered every angle.

Anya smiled, the lingering worry in her gaze softening as they began to visualize the prospective meeting. "We could meet during the morning rush. That way, I can introduce the conversation casually. If we can get him talking about Alex, we might uncover details that can direct our inquiry."

Jack found comfort in their dialogue. The seamless way their strategies built upon one another reminded him of the old days when he worked alongside seasoned agents who sought an edge in every interaction. Each word exchanged felt purposeful, as if they were weaving a lifeline together.

"And once we have Mikhail's cooperation, we'll leverage his connections," Jack continued, keys to intelligence slipping naturally back into his mind. "We'll look into Alex's network too—see if anyone else might have information about the Russian spy. It's crucial to widen our scope."

Jack stood abruptly, a sense of urgency overtaking him. "We'll need a way to document everything we find without drawing attention. I can't get too heavily involved, Anya. If word gets out I'm back in the field, it could be the end of this operation. I'll help, but you're going to have to lead this."

Anya's brow furrowed slightly. "But you're the experience we need. I can't—"

Jack raised a hand to stop her, the determination in his voice resolute. "You're more than capable of this, Anya. Your instincts are sharp. But we need to be smart about our roles. You're the person they'll trust—the dedicated wife of Alex seeking answers. I'm just a retired agent trying to stay no longer in the game. That dichotomy works for us."

"Okay," Anya said, her voice steadier than before. "I understand. We'll approach this from different angles, but I won't hesitate to ask for your help when I need it."

"Good," Jack replied, feeling a surge of confidence yet not forgetting the very real dangers lurking on the horizon.

They set about their work: Anya drafting messages and Jack looking for contact records while sharing bits of history from his agency days. The hours rolled by in a productive flurry, a collage of determination and stubborn hope painted against the canvas of uncertainty. Each detail meticulously threaded their plan together into something larger than themselves—akin to two spies creating a new world amidst the chaos.

Yet, as evening fell, an unsettling thought gripped him. Jack couldn't shake the feeling that time was running short, that the adversaries they faced were always one step ahead. The urgency of the situation gnawed at him.

At that moment, he decided they needed backup—not just in terms of information, but in the form of trust. "Anya, let's bring in someone we can both rely on, just in case."

"Who do you have in mind?" she asked, intrigued yet cautious.

"There's a contact from MI6 I trust. A Hollis—Rebecca Hollis. She was my partner during one of my last assignments, and I know she's still in touch with some networks. If we can pull her in, she'll be a valuable asset."

Anya considered his proposal, her brow furrowed in thought. "If we reach out, it could either help or backfire. She could alert the wrong people and put us in jeopardy."

Jack leaned forward, his eyes steady on hers. "I understand the risks, but Rebecca is someone I know I can trust. The bond we formed in our years together runs deep. If anybody understands what we're up against, it's her."

A moment of silence hung between them, both calculating the stakes of their decision. "Alright, let's reach out to her cautiously, then," Anya relented. "But we should be prepared for any reaction. We need to tread carefully."

Jack could see the wheels turning in Anya's mind, her careful nature balancing his more instinct-driven inclinations. "We will. Let's get started. I'll send her an encrypted message and wait for a response."

As the night slinked on, the darkened windows of Jack's home stood as a backdrop to their collaboration. Jack felt a surge of gratitude for the woman across from him; for the first time in a long while, he felt a sense of belonging sprouting in a world otherwise marred by deception and shadows.

They spent the remainder of the evening sketching out ideas, fueled by determination and the hum of their shared existence. Jack's path had shifted unexpectedly, yet he felt a sense of contentment in this rekindled purpose, the blend of chaos and camaraderie setting a new tone in his life.

With the plan laid out, hope blossomed between them—a fragile light illuminating their fight amidst the shadows they sought to unravel. The clock ticked ominously in the background, each passing second a reminder that time was not on their side. Facing the unknown together, they forged ahead, thrilling in the transformation brought about by trust and shared conviction.

A Symbol of Hope

As dawn broke over the quiet English countryside, the soft light filtered through the window of Jack Malaney's modest home, painting the room in shades of gold and amber. The tranquility of the morning was a stark contrast to the turmoil swirling in Jack's mind. He stood at the kitchen counter, absentmindedly stirring a pot of coffee, his thoughts a chaotic mix of past regrets and present dangers. Yet, beneath the turmoil lay a budding sense of hope, one that had grown roots through the bond he had forged with Anya.

Anya walked into the kitchen, a shadow of exhaustion crossing her face as she tried to mask her weariness with a bright smile. Her two children, Lena and Max, were still asleep, a temporary relief from the horrors they had left behind—fleeing their war-torn homeland, leaving behind cherished memories and, most heartbreakingly, their father, Alex. Jack noticed the flicker of fragility in Anya's eyes, the burden of her desperation often hidden behind her fierce resolve. As they prepared to confront the unknown adversaries together, Jack felt a shift in their relationship, one that had deepened through shared fears and collective aspirations for a future free of shadows.

"Coffee?" Jack offered, his tone warm yet tinged with concern. Anya nodded, accepting the mug he handed her, her hands cradling the ceramic as if it were a fragile lifeline. She took a sip, savoring the warmth, feeling the caffeine kick start her morning, but more significantly, she felt a momentary connection to stability.

"Thank you, Jack. I don't know what I would do without you," she admitted, her voice barely above a whisper but rich with sincerity. Jack's heart swelled with emotion—a mixed bundle of protectiveness, admiration, and an undeniable desire to shield her from the mounting uncertainties that were creeping closer, like shadows inching across their lives.

"You've been so strong, Anya," Jack replied, filling the silence that hung between them with praise. "You've navigated so much, and yet here you are—still standing."

His words stirred a flicker in Anya's soul. The road had been long and arduous, and she could feel the weight of everything pressing against her chest—a grieving wife, a mother protector, and a woman searching for justice. Now, they stood on the precipice of danger, balancing hope against fear.

The two exchanged glances, understanding passing between them without the need for words. In that brief moment, the realities of their respective pasts converged. Jack, with his MI6 past littered with decisions that haunted him, and Anya, with her memories steeped in love and loss, both trod paths of regret yet faced them with brave hearts ignited by the desire for a better tomorrow.

Anya set her mug down and took a deep breath. "We need to organize everything for today. There's a meeting…the potential for information," she murmured, her brow furrowed, determination creeping into every syllable. The gravity of the moment pressed heavily against her resolute exterior, but Jack could see the fire burning beneath.

"Let's make a list," Jack suggested, feeling the momentum shift even as they were still battling the whispers of their burdened hearts. They knocked ideas between them like a game of ping-pong, their shared practicalities helping to weave tighter the ties of collaboration and camaraderie.

As they strategized, Jack felt the weight of their initial meeting, that fateful night when Anya had turned to him in desperation seeking help. At that moment, she had been a ghost, haunted by the specter of her husband's fears, driven by love and survival. Yet, now, she stood beside him with strength not only of purpose but a growing clarity that galvanized his own resolve.

After an intense brainstorming session and lists made, the coffee pot emptied and stale remnants of breakfast cleared away, a subtle silence fell over them. Their eyes locked momentarily, a moment pregnant with unspoken words—the understanding that the confrontation they were gearing up for wasn't just a fight against the Russian spy threatening Alex's life, but a battle for their very being, for a future unmarred by fear. Jack felt a swell of responsibility birth within him, an urge to protect those who seemed to need him most.

"Whatever happens today," he said finally, his voice steady, "I'll be by your side, Anya. No matter what."

The sincerity in his words wrapped around Anya like a warm embrace. She nodded, lips trembling slightly before she spoke. "I know. And you give me strength, Jack. We will face this together."

The sentiment hung in the air, charged and electric, a declaration that transcended the mere exchange of promises. It solidified the essence of what they had begun to forge—a partnership born from adversity, dependent on trust, and fortified by the resilience of their spirits.

As they traveled through the winding roads towards their appointed rendezvous, the morning mist clung to the world around them, shrouding their path in mystery. Anya sat in the passenger seat, clenching her hands in her lap, the tremors of fear wrought against her skin. Jack stole glances at her profile, at her solemn expression, and the way her brow creased in contemplation. She was a mother who needed strength, and as he gripped the steering wheel tighter, he vowed to provide her that unwavering support.

"Do you remember the first time you talked about Alex's fears?" Jack ventured, trying to ease the tension while offering an anchor to their shared memories. "You said you felt he was watching shadows."

Anya's eyes flickered to him, and a rush of emotions played across her face—a cocktail of sorrow and steely determination. She nodded, the memory rekindling feelings of both worry and purpose. "Yes…

but the shadows were more than just ominous figures. They were a reminder of my fears, of losing my family, of…" Her voice trailed off, and for a heartbeat, Jack felt the chasm of vulnerability that lay just beneath the surface.

"Of fighting for them, for Alex," he finished gently, not wanting her to dwell on the ache that had nestled inside her heart. "But today, we reclaim that power. We're not alone in this fight."

As they neared their destination, Anya's breath quickened. The thought of confronting the unknown made her stomach twist into knots. Jack could sense her hesitation, the almost palpable fear that had begun to tangle itself within her. "What if… what if they recognize us? What if…"

"Anya, listen to me." He turned to her, catching her anxious gaze. "We are prepared. You are stronger than you realize. Trust in that. If we hold on to each other through this, we will not just face them—we will emerge from it. Together."

Anya nodded slowly, each beat of her heart murmuring her need for belief—belief in herself, in Jack, and in their cause. She took a deep breath, letting the air fill her lungs as she focused on the newfound determination that had been woven into the fabric of her spirit. "Together," she echoed, emphasizing the word as if summoning its power.

The rendezvous was tucked behind the façade of a dilapidated warehouse, an unassuming place for the bearing of secrets and unshackled truths. Jack parked the car, and they stepped out, the cool air wrapping around them like a cloak, awakening their senses. Anya felt each step resonate in the ground, turning the fear into fuel for resilience as they approached the shadowed entrance.

Inside, tension hung thick in the air. Jack's instincts flared to alertness as their eyes adjusted to the dim light spilling from flickering bulbs overhead. The weight of deception pressed down, but it coalesced with a surge of purpose that pushed them forward. Anya's hand brushed against Jack's, and he felt the electricity pulsing between them—a tether of hope, binding them as one against the unknown.

As they navigated the room filled with ticking clocks and hushed voices, Jack's memories flickered like silhouettes against a haunted backdrop—the endless nights spent hunting for truth, working within the labyrinth of secrecy that had become his life. Yet now, it was no longer the thrill of espionage that drove him. It was the promise of safety for Anya and her family, the chance for a new beginning, a life beyond the shadows.

They reached their designated meeting spot, a table tucked in the far corner. A figure loomed in the shadows, his features obscured. Tension bled into the air; it was palpable, an entity of its own where fear and resolve collided.

Jack gestured for Anya to stay close, their proximity becoming a source of strength as they stood shoulder to shoulder. The figure stepped forward, and Jack's instincts kicked in, his heart racing. Trust had become a currency they could not afford lightly.

"I've come for information," Jack spoke, his voice steady despite the rattle of anxiety coursing through him. "We're looking for answers."

The man's eyes narrowed, observing them carefully before he allowed a slow nod. "You both know what you're getting into, yes?"

Anya felt the import of the question, her gaze unwavering as she interjected, "We've come too far to turn back. I need to know what's happening to Alex."

Silence settled, thickening with the weight of commitments yet to be made. Jack grasped Anya's hand slightly tighter, squeezing it as if to remind her of their shared strength. The figure before them faltered, and then, as if releasing a long-held breath, he spoke.

"There's a mess brewing within the Ukrainian intelligence. It's more complicated than you know, and not all allies are trustworthy."

In that moment, they became anchored to their purpose—the reality of their mission solidified among the chaos. The revelations rain down like heavy droplets falling from the sky, soaking through the earth, both threatening and life-giving. Yet even so, the specter of danger lingered just beyond their periphery.

With each passing conversation, Jack and Anya found themselves bound tighter by their resolve, and as the meeting concluded, they stepped back into the uncertain light. The weight of hope lay heavy in the air around them as they faced the road ahead, ready to confront the shadows that dared to encroach upon their lives.

Jack turned to Anya, meeting her determined gaze. "No matter what happens, we're in this together. We'll face whatever comes our way."

Tears glimmered in Anya's eyes yet her chin tilted up defiantly, the fire ignited anew. "Together," she affirmed, clarity flooding her heart, washing away the doubts that had once threatened to drown her spirit.

As they walked back towards the exit, the world opened up before them—a landscape veiled in both promise and peril. In that moment, amidst uncertainty, they forged ahead, bruised but unbroken, bonded by their shared experiences and anchored in the resilience of the human spirit.

With every step, they carried the weight of each other's stories, the transformation of pain into purpose illuminating their path. The dawn of a new chapter stretched against the horizon, a symbol of hope guiding them through the darkness—a light not easily extinguished. Together, they were prepared to confront what lay ahead, a testament to the strength of their alliance, the power of their hope, and the unwavering spirit to reclaim justice.

The Final Confrontation

The Calm Before the Storm

The rain began to fall in a steady drizzle, tapping softly against the windows of the small cottage that had been both refuge and a battleground in recent weeks. Inside, the atmosphere was charged with an intensity that felt almost tangible, a silent acknowledgment of the gravity of the situation that lay ahead. Jack Malaney and Anya sat across from each other at the wooden dining table that had seen its share of joyous laughter and dark conversations. Today, it was the latter that governed the air between them, thick and heavy as the impending storm outside.

Jack absently traced the grain of the table with his fingertips, lost in thoughts swirling within him like leaves caught in a gust of wind. This moment was unlike any other since Anya and her children had arrived on his doorstep months ago. They had come seeking refuge, unwittingly pulling Jack back into a world he had thought he'd left behind, a world brimming with secrets and shadows—and now, it was all about to erupt.

Glancing up, Jack studied Anya's face, noting the tense line of her jaw and the worry etched in her brow. She was a woman transformed. The quiet mother who had first walked into his life, clutching her children closely amidst the chaos of war, had been forged into a determined ally, a warrior willing to face the unknown for the sake of her husband, Alex. The woman before him now was fierce, but that fierceness came cloaked in fear—fear for her family, fear for what she knew they were about to confront.

"Jack," she whispered, breaking the silence, her voice unsteady but resolute, "what if we're wrong? What if this is all for nothing?"

The vulnerability in her question pierced through the weight of their shared resolve. He could feel the choices they had made together pressing down on him like a lead blanket. Their investigations had unearthed a series of lies, tracing the threads of a deception woven through the Ukrainian intelligence community. They had come too far to retreat now, yet doubt tugged at the corners of his mind like a shadow lurking at the edges of a lit room.

"Anya," he began softly, searching for the right words, "we've looked at the evidence. I've spoken to contacts, and everything points to the fact that there's an internal threat. We need to be certain, but we can't ignore the risks."

She met his gaze, searching for reassurance that her own heart craved. In that moment, Jack wished he could give it to her. He remembered the warmth of the summer sun, the way it used to bathe everything in amber light—a stark contrast to their current situation. Yet, as he looked into Anya's clear blue eyes, he felt a flicker of hope.

"We'll face it together," he continued, willing himself to convey the strength he couldn't fully feel. "Whatever happens, you and the children are safe with me. I promise."

But even as he spoke the words, Jack felt the gnawing doubt within himself. Inside the vast network of spies and shadows, his experience told him no promise was binding. Still, it was the sincerity in Anya's eyes that kept him grounded. He noticed the way she clenched her hands on the table, her knuckles going white as she toyed with the edge of a worn napkin.

"Alex is counting on us," Anya replied, letting out a shaky breath. "I just… I keep imagining what will happen if we fail."

The unease crept into the corners of his mind, swirling with the tension that filled the air. Jack pushed his chair back and stood, pacing the length of the small room, the silence in the cottage amplifying the echoes of his fevered thoughts. Each step took him deeper into the labyrinth of his past, where choices loomed large, and outcomes had never been guaranteed.

"Failure isn't an option," he murmured under his breath, half to Anya and half to himself. The mantra had become his shield, yet he knew its fallibility. He was casting shadows over everything they had worked towards, along with a specter of his own failures—a long legacy of missions gone wrong.

"Jack," Anya's voice broke through the fog of his thoughts, a lifeline tethering him to the present. "What are you thinking about?"

He turned to face her, the anticipation of the upcoming confrontation weighing heavily upon them both. "All the times I've been in similar situations, planning everything down to the last detail—only to watch it unravel."

Anya nodded, understanding threading through her expression. "And now you're afraid it might happen again."

He was caught, unable to deny the truth that she had struck upon. It felt like a weight pressing down on him, the specter of his old life rearing its head, taunting him with memories of failed missions and lost relationships—the lives he had touched and sometimes ruined in the name of duty. It echoed the conflicts now at play as they prepared to dive into the murky waters of espionage together.

"Those were different times," he finally said, forcing himself to remain steady. "We have the advantage of knowledge, of being able to prepare. We know more than they think we do."

Anya leaned forward, her expression intense. "And what will we do when we finally confront them? If the evidence is true, it won't be enough to simply have their names."

Jack knew she was right. They would need to gather more than just whispers and suspicions—they needed proof that could withstand the scrutiny and vile machinations of a conspiracy that threatened their very lives. The stakes were high, and the tension rose like a rising tide.

The clock on the wall ticked monotonously, each second echoing in the stillness, as if marking the time until their confrontation. A distant rumble of thunder rolled, punctuating the uncertainty that lingered between them. Jack's heart raced, charging adrenaline through his veins as he concocted plans in his mind—formulating contingencies, assigning roles, considering every possible outcome.

"How much time do you think we have?" Anya asked, her voice low, breaking the silence that had settled like dust.

"Not long," Jack replied, glancing at the window where the rain had intensified, smattering against the glass like small missiles. "They'll know we're closing in."

Anya nodded, the gravity of their situation settling like a stone in their stomachs. "We need to be ready. I can't bear the thought of returning to that darkness without knowing the truth."

Jack stepped closer, feeling the need to bridge the emotional distance between them. "You have to trust me. We'll cover each other's backs. I won't let anything happen to you or the kids."

Something shifted in Anya's expression, her fierce determination transforming into a flicker of vulnerability. "I trust you, Jack. It's everything else that scares me."

"I know. But fear can be a catalyst. Let's use it."

Taking a deep breath, he wondered if it was possible to funnel the dread—the fear—into something tangible, something that could sharpen their focus. If fear could become fuel, they might harness it into the action they so desperately needed.

"Do you think Alex is okay?" she asked, her voice barely above a whisper.

Jack felt a pang of anguish for the man who had painted much of Anya's world. Alex was a voice of love and laughter, now shrouded in uncertainty and peril. He tapped into his feelings of empathy but knew the harsh realities loomed in the backdrop—a man trapped in a political game that transcended his personal safety.

"I have to believe he is," Jack replied, "but we need to act quickly. If he's still in danger, every second counts."

As the minutes passed, each tick of the clock punctuated their silence. Jack and Anya dove deeper into conversation, contemplating strategies for their meeting with the conspirators. Each plan felt heavy with consequence, the weight of their decisions palpable. Jack sketched possibilities in the air with his hands, illustrating scenarios that fluctuated between cautious optimism and daunting odds.

"Timing is everything," he murmured, half to himself. "We need to be at the right place at the right time. We can't show our cards too early."

"And what if we're ambushed?" Anya interjected, her voice tense. "What if they know we're coming?"

Jack could see the spark of fear flickering in her eyes, and he knew that fear, while destructive, could also be transformed into a powerful ally—pushing them to think creatively, nudging them into action.

"Then we adapt," he answered, letting his resolve seep into every word. "We've seen this before; we know how these operatives think."

A momentary silence fell, punctuated by another fat drop of rain splattering against the window, and Jack felt an overwhelming urge to reach out, to touch her hand as a gesture of solidarity. They were partners now—bound not only by the mission but by shared vulnerabilities. He stepped forward, allowing his palm to rest lightly on hers.

"We're not alone in this," Jack reassured her, his heart swelling with conviction. "We'll find the truth, and we'll save Alex."

Slowly, the tension between them eased ever so slightly, a flicker of shared understanding passing in that small action. Anya breathed deeply, her fingers curling around his as the storm continued to rage outside, reflecting the turmoil within.

Just then, the sudden blare of a siren echoed in the distance, jolting them both upright. Jack felt the adrenaline surge once more through his body, flooding his senses like ice water. His heart pounded in rhythm with the sirens as the reality of their precarious situation crashed upon him.

They had to get moving.

"Anya, we need to prepare," he said abruptly, releasing her hand and pushing aside the remnants of calm that had lingered in the air. "Gather everything we have—the documents, the recordings, anything that can prove our case. We can't let our guard down."

Anya's eyes widened at the urgency in his voice as she nodded resolutely, moving with a newfound purpose. The storm outside had intensified, rain lashing against the cottage, but it was the storm brewing within them that shook the very core of their composure. The moment to act had come; the calm before the storm had quieted, giving way to the tempest that loomed ominously on their horizons.

As Anya dived into gathering their belongings, Jack's mind raced, strategizing their next steps, envisioning the confrontation that awaited them. Whatever darkness lay ahead, they would face it together—an alliance forged in desperation and resolve.

The air hummed with impending action, thickening as they steeled themselves for the confrontation that could upend everything they had fought for. And as the sirens howled in the distance, the world around them came alive with purpose, a quiet fury ready to break into a storm.

The Showdown

The dim light of dusk settled over the desolate warehouse, casting elongated shadows that danced eerily against the cold, concrete walls. Jack Malaney and Anya stood side by side, their breaths shallow yet resolute, the air thick with anticipation and an undercurrent of peril. A lone flickering bulb illuminated a patch of the floor, highlighting the dust and grime that had accumulated over the years—a dismal reflection of the secrets hidden within these walls. They had arrived at the rendezvous point, ready to confront the unknown adversaries threatening not only Anya's husband Alex but their lives as well.

Jack's pulse quickened as he scanned the area, his instincts honed from years of training now tinged with a protective urgency. He felt Anya's presence beside him, a comforting weight amidst the uncertainty. They had come a long way since their paths had crossed, and the bond they had forged in shared vulnerability had transformed into an unbreakable alliance. He could see the determination in her eyes, a fierce light that reminded him of everything they were fighting for—family, safety, and justice.

"Stay close to me," Jack whispered, his voice low yet firm. His hands tightened around the grip of the concealed weapon at his side, a steady reminder of the stakes at hand.

Anya nodded, her expression a mix of fear and resolve. Her heart raced, but she was no longer the timid mother seeking refuge; she was a woman prepared to confront the dangers that threatened her family. "I'm ready," she replied, her voice steady despite the turmoil within. The moments shared during their investigation had infused her with an inner strength she had never known. She was fighting not just for Alex, but for her children's future as well.

They approached the entrance cautiously. The door creaked ominously as they pushed it open, revealing a vast, darkened expanse within. An unsettling silence enveloped them as they stepped inside, the only sound being the echo of their footsteps on the concrete floor. Jack's eyes adjusted quickly to the dim light, revealing rows of crates stacked haphazardly, their contents unknown.

Suddenly, a low voice interrupted the silence. "I knew you would come, Jack." The speaker stepped into the flickering light, a familiar figure that sent a jolt of recognition through Jack's veins. Viktor, a former MI6 colleague turned double agent, stood before them, a smirk playing on his lips. "You always were drawn to danger like a moth to a flame."

Jack's heart sank, the betrayal cutting deeper than he had anticipated. Viktor had once been a trusted ally, a friend whose camaraderie had helped navigate the murky waters of espionage. "What are you doing here, Viktor?" Jack demanded, trying to keep his voice measured despite the whirlpool of emotions surging within him.

"I'm here for the same reason you are," Viktor replied, his tone dismissive. "To see how far this little charade of yours will go. You think you can save her husband? You're fooling yourself."

Anya stepped forward, her voice clear and strong. "This isn't a game, Viktor. People's lives are at stake, including my children's. You're playing with fire."

Viktor chuckled darkly, his gaze flicking between them. "You don't know the half of it, do you? The things happening in the shadows of your precious intelligence community are far more dangerous than you can imagine. Alex is merely a pawn in this game."

Jack felt the anger boil within him, a mix of protective instinct and guilt for not recognizing Viktor's treachery sooner. "What do you want, Viktor? Money? Power? What has this operation cost you?"

Viktor's smile widened. "Oh, it's not about money or power. It's about control. The chaos unfolding isn't a coincidence; it's all part of a larger scheme. And right now, you and Anya are in my way. You should have stayed in your quiet little life, Jack."

With that, Viktor signaled, and from the shadows emerged two burly men, armed and ready. Jack felt a surge of urgency. Each moment was thick with tension, time stretching as he assessed their options. He turned to Anya, their eyes locking in a shared understanding. They couldn't lose this opportunity; they had to fight for everything they had.

"Now!" Jack shouted, lunging forward as chaos erupted around them.

The warehouse ignited with movement, the once eerie silence shattered by the sounds of scuffling feet and shouted orders. Jack and Anya moved instinctively, sidestepping the first two attackers as Jack sprang into action. His body moved with a fluidity borne from years of training, his instincts honed by countless encounters similar to this. He ducked a swinging fist, retaliating with a swift kick that sent one assailant sprawling against a stack of crates.

Anya, empowered by Jack's resolve, fought with a determination she didn't know she possessed. She grabbed a metal pipe from the ground, wielding it like a weapon with surprising precision. In that moment, she was not just a mother but a warrior, defending her family against the encroaching shadows.

"Watch your back!" Jack shouted, feeling a surge of adrenaline as he disarmed another attacker, their weapon clattering to the ground. They moved in sync, a rhythm forged under the pressure of uncertainty and fear. Jack's mind raced with strategies and counterattacks, but always with a singular focus—keep Anya safe.

The fight was fast-paced and chaotic, adrenaline coursing through their veins as they grappled with their opponents. Just as Jack took down a third assailant, he saw Viktor retreating, his sinister smirk fading into the shadows. Jack's heart raced; he couldn't let Viktor escape. He knew the man held the key to unraveling the conspiracy that threatened not only Anya and her children but countless others as well.

"Anya, keep them back!" he yelled, his voice raw with urgency.

She nodded, her eyes fierce as she swung the pipe again, catching an attacker off guard. Jack pursued Viktor, navigating through the chaos, determination driving him forward. The warehouse felt like a maze, but he could feel Viktor's presence lingering just ahead.

As Jack rounded a corner, he spotted Viktor pacing toward a side exit, a flicker of fear glinting in his eyes. "You think you can run?" Jack called out, his voice echoing in the empty space. "This isn't over!"

Viktor turned, surprise flickering across his face. "Ah, Jack. Always the hero," he taunted. "But you're out of your depth."

With a sudden movement, Viktor pulled out a small device, and Jack felt the hairs on the back of his neck stand on end. "No!" he shouted, instinctively rushing forward to close the distance. It was a detonator, a whisper of danger that sent waves of anxiety coursing through him.

Jack couldn't let Viktor have the upper hand; he had to act quickly. With a swift lunge, he tackled Viktor, grabbing for the device. Their bodies crashed to the ground, the detonator slipping from Viktor's fingers. It skidded across the concrete, sliding beneath a nearby crate.

The two men struggled, grappling against the floor, the air around them thick with desperation. Jack's mind raced as he landed a punch against Viktor's jaw, fighting through the haze of anger and fear. "You're going to tell me everything," Jack hissed, his voice low and menacing. "You're not walking away this time."

Just then, Anya's voice rang out behind them. "Jack! I need you!"

Jack whipped around, uncertainty flooding his thoughts. Anya was locked in a fierce fight of her own, grappling with one of the burly men who had flanked them. In that instant, his heart wrenched; he couldn't abandon her. However, the growing tension between him and Viktor held him in a precarious balance.

"Leave her!" Jack shouted, letting go of his hold on Viktor. With a surge of adrenaline, he dashed towards Anya, his instincts overpowering every instinct to keep Viktor subdued. He launched himself at her attacker, delivering a sharp blow that sent the man crashing to the ground.

"Are you okay?" he asked, breathless, turning to Anya, her eyes wide with a mix of fear and strength.

"I'm fine! We need to get out of here!" she insisted, her gaze shifting back to Viktor, who had scrambled to his feet.

Jack's focus sharpened on Viktor again, who was now lined up against the wall, a look of defeat etched across his features. "This isn't over, Jack. You can't stop what's coming," Viktor spat, his voice wavering.

Jack took a step closer, fueled by a mix of anger and responsibility. "You don't get to dictate anything anymore. We're going to expose you," he replied, his voice firm. "You underestimated us."

Viktor made a desperate lunge for the detonator, but Jack was quicker. In a calculated motion, Jack kicked the device deep into the shadows, ensuring it was lost among the crates. "You've lost control," Jack hissed, his eyes intense.

With that, Anya moved forward, a fierce glimmer in her eyes. "You've harmed my family for the last time. We know everything." Her voice trembled with emotion but resonated with strength, and it was enough to unnerve Viktor.

"Your husband is not who you think he is!" Viktor shrieked in a last-ditch attempt to salvage his position. "He's deep in this with the Russians, and you're just a pawn in a much larger game!"

Jack and Anya exchanged a glance, unshaken by Viktor's desperate words. The emotional connection they had forged through this journey had erased any doubts—trust and loyalty were forged in the fires of adversity.

"Enough!" Jack shouted, his patience wearing thin. "You're nothing but a coward. We're bringing you to justice."

Before Viktor could respond, Jack lunged forward to restrain him, but Viktor, fueled by fear, managed to pull a knife from his belt. As the blade glinted in the waning light, Jack felt the weight of their confrontation press upon him like a vice.

"Jack, watch out!" Anya cried, a warning that echoed in Jack's mind just before Viktor lunged.

Time slowed as Jack's instincts took over. He sidestepped, feeling the rush of air as the knife grazed by him. In that heartbeat, he retaliated, grabbing Viktor by the wrist, twisting until the knife fell from his grasp. The moment felt suspended in time, a collision of choices and fate.

The two men fought fiercely, Jack pinning Viktor against the wall, the tension crackling like electricity. "You're finished, Viktor!" Jack growled, his voice a low rumble.

But Viktor's survival instincts kicked in. With a sudden surge of energy, he elbowed Jack hard in the gut, stumbling him backward. Jack's breath came out in a gasp as he struggled to regain his footing. Yet before he could fully recover, Anya intervened, stepping forward as Viktor attempted to back away.

"Enough of this!" Anya shouted, her eyes glinting with defiance. She grabbed a piece of broken glass from the ground, a shard with a sharp edge that caught the light. "You will not hurt my family anymore."

Viktor halted, assessing the fierce determination on her face, realization dawning upon him. Jack felt a swell of pride at her bravery, their bond fortified in the heat of the moment. "You've underestimated us for the last time," Jack echoed, mirroring Anya's resolve.

With a sudden rush, Viktor made one last try for freedom, darting for the exit as he glanced back at them, desperation driving his movements. Jack reached out in a reflex, grabbing a length of rope that lay coiled nearby. With a swift motion, he threw it in Viktor's direction, the loop catching around his ankles in a well-practiced motion.

"Gotcha!" Jack grinned, the corners of his mouth lifting with triumph. As Viktor stumbled to the ground, Anya was beside him in an instant, the glass shard still poised at his throat.

"Now you will listen," Anya said, her voice firm, holding the power of a mother's fury. "Tell us everything, Viktor, or this will be the last moment you ever have to make a choice."

The adrenaline surged through Jack, both exhilaration and relief washing over him as they held their ground against their adversary. It was a moment that encapsulated their journey together—two people united by a shared cause, willing to protect each other at all costs.

Defeated, Viktor's smirk faded, his bravado crumbling as he realized they had turned the tide. "You think you've won… but the game is far from over. There are others who will come for you," he warned, his voice filled with venom.

Jack leaned closer, steady and unwavering. "Let them come. We will be ready."

As they secured Viktor, Anya breathed heavily, her gaze darting around the warehouse, apprehension still gripping her. "What do we do now?" she asked, her voice softer, the weight of their struggle evident in her eyes.

"We regroup," Jack replied, feeling a sense of clarity. "We gather the evidence, expose the truth, and unravel this web of lies before anyone else gets hurt."

In that moment, they both knew there was much more work ahead, but for the first time in what felt like an eternity, they had taken a stand together. The shadows that had long enveloped them were beginning to lift, casting light on the path forward. As they prepared for what lay ahead, Jack felt an abiding sense of connection between them—a bond forged in the fires of conflict and tempered by newfound trust.

Together, they would face whatever challenges awaited them, side by side, united against the darkness.

Aftermath and Reflection

The chaos of the confrontation seemed to echo in the air long after the dust had settled. Jack Malaney stood outside the small, rustic cottage he had called home for several years, the scent of earth mingling with the faint trace of smoke still lingering from the confrontation. The late afternoon light cast a golden hue over the landscape, but the beautiful scenery did little to ease the weight heavy upon his heart.

Anya's figure crossed his line of sight as she slowly emerged from the cottage, her children following closely behind. The once lively laughter of Sasha and Igor was now replaced with an anxious silence that hung in the air like a storm cloud. Jack's heart ached for them, for the innocence that had been so cruelly snatched away. The remnants of fear and uncertainty lingered in their eyes, reflecting their struggle to comprehend the reality they had faced and survived.

"Jack?" Anya's voice was tentative, breaking the heavy silence that enveloped them. She approached him cautiously, her features etched with fatigue and sorrow, yet there remained a flicker of resilience deep within her gaze. "Are you alright?"

He turned to face her fully, his chest tightening at the sight of her disheveled hair and the smudges of dirt on her cheeks. "I'm fine," he replied softly, though the truth was more complex. He felt like a fractured version of himself, still processing the adrenaline of the confrontation, the pain of loss, and the weight of all that had transpired. "I just…" he hesitated, searching for the right words, "I need a moment to think."

Anya nodded, understanding etched across her features. She gestured towards the horizon, where the sky shifted from hues of orange to deep indigo. "The sunset is beautiful. We should watch it together."

The suggestion brought back memories of quieter times—moments spent admiring nature, not knowing that darkness would one day cast a long shadow over their lives. With weary legs, they moved toward the small wooden bench overlooking the valley, the children finding a spot at their feet, seemingly drawn to the comforting presence of their mother and their new protector.

As they settled, a profound silence enveloped them, punctuated only by the rustling leaves of the trees surrounding the property. Jack's gaze remained fixed on the horizon, but his thoughts drifted to the battle they had fought, to the sacrifices made to shield Anya and her children from the very danger that had haunted them for so long.

"You were incredible today," Anya's voice broke through his reverie, her eyes reflecting gratitude and admiration. "I don't think I could have faced them without you."

Jack felt the warmth of her words wrap around him like a soft blanket, but even that warmth was tinged with guilt. "I wish it hadn't come to that," he said, his voice a mere whisper. "The things we had to do…" He trailed off, the weight of those actions bearing down on him. "They'll haunt me forever."

Anya turned to him fully, her brow furrowing with concern. "You saved us, Jack. You protected us when no one else could. That's what matters." She took a deep breath, steadying herself as she continued. "I can't pretend it's easy. I still feel the shock of everything we endured—everything we lost."

Jack nodded in agreement, remembering the betrayal they had unveiled, the trust shattered by appearances. "And we'll carry those scars. They remind us of what we've faced, of how fragile our sense of safety can be." His voice wavered, revealing the emotional turmoil that had swelled within him since the confrontation—the memories of lives torn apart and trust eroded.

Sasha nestled into Anya's side, her small frame trembling slightly as she sought comfort amid uncertainty. Igor picked at the grass, his face scrunched up in concentration, as if channeling every ounce of his energy into finding some semblance of normalcy. It was a heartbreaking image, one that would forever etch itself into Jack's mind. The laughter of childhood had been all but extinguished, replaced by the lingering shadow of fear.

"Do you think we'll ever feel safe again?" Anya's question hung in the air, laden with vulnerability.

Jack took a deep breath, the evening air heavy with unshed tears. "I hope so," he murmured, "but it may take time. We can't rush healing."

Time. A resource that had both dragged and accelerated through the course of their ordeal. Jack reflected on the days that had stretched endlessly and those fleeting moments that seemed to dissolve in an instant. In the wake of all they had faced, he felt as if they stood on the precipice of a new beginning—a chance to define what safety meant, to reclaim joy amidst the remnants of darkness.

"It may be some time before we find our footing again," Anya continued softly, "but we'll do it together." She met his gaze, her resolve solidifying with the last rays of sunlight. "You and me, Jack, and the children. We'll make a new life from the ashes of the old one."

Her strength ignited something within Jack—a flicker of hope that dared to rise above the grief. "You're right," he replied, his voice steadying. "We're not alone in this. Together, we can face whatever comes next."

They sat in companionable silence, embracing the burgeoning light of hope as the sun sank below the horizon, leaving in its wake shades of indigo and violet. Jack watched as the last remnants of daylight surrendered to night, and he felt the warmth of Anya's hand slip into his own—a gesture both simple and profound.

As dusk settled around them, memories surged—both joyful and painful. He recalled the laughter of the children during their first weeks together, the warmth of their smiles, the rising bond they had forged amidst uncertainty and fear.

He could still feel the frozen winter of his own existence seep into those memories, a creeping ice that had surrounded him like a thick fog after retirement from MI6. He had coveted the downtime, the silence, where the echoes of espionage faded from haunting to a distant memory. Yet, as he gazed into Anya's eyes, he recognized that those days had forged a part of him—a part that had long craved connection, purpose, and the chance to be something more than a ghost of the past.

Nightfall brought with it an unexpected tranquility, allowing thoughts of healing to replace echoes of turmoil. Jack turned his gaze to Anya and the children, a soft smile breaking through the heaviness that had lingered for too long. Their resilience was inspiring, lighting a spark within him that urged him to rise above the shadows that lingered in his own soul.

"Hey," he said, his tone shifting to something more lighthearted, "I think the stars have come out to join us. Do you see them?"

Anya's expression softened, a flicker of surprise crossing her face as she followed his gaze. "They're beautiful," she whispered, the children now looking up in wonder, their small fingers pointing at the scattered constellations.

"Every one of those stars has a story," Jack said, feeling his enthusiasm rise. "Some of them have been through storms and darkness, just like us. But they still shine, and so will we."

"And some are still forming and yet to find their light," Anya added, her voice infused with hope. "We're finding our way, too. One step at a time."

He nodded, feeling a renewed sense of purpose surge within him. "Yes, one step at a time."

Their breaths came out in soft clouds, mingling with the crisp evening air, creating something new amidst the remnants of their pasts. Every shared glance, every hushed conversation painted a vivid picture of resilience. Jack recognized the path they now walked together, one he had longed for but never realized until Anya had entered his life like a gentle breeze through an explosive storm.

As the sky darkened, a feeling of serenity settled over the group. With nothing but the stars to bear witness, Jack expelled a breath laden with the fractured memories of their ordeal. They had survived the storm, and though healing lay ahead, they would navigate the journey together.

Hours passed, their ongoing discussion filled the air with the flavor of quiet conversations punctuated by laughter, joyful yet tempered with the depth of understanding gained from their harrowing experiences. They spoke of dreams, hopes, and plans—a future crafted from the ashes of their trials.

Jack thought of rebuilding, of teaching the children new skills and helping them cultivate a sense of belonging, a sense of family. The shadows they created together would not only shield them from the past but also forge a new path ahead.

"I want to show you both how to garden," he said to Sasha and Igor, the eagerness bubbling beneath the surface. "We can plant vegetables and flowers—once they bloom, it'll remind us that there is beauty in regrowth, even after the darkest storms."

"Can we plant sunflowers?" Sasha piped up, her eyes gleaming with excitement, the fear of the earlier hours nearly erased by the possibility of new beginnings.

Jack chuckled, the sound resonating within him—a melody misplaced, now finding harmony. "Sunflowers it is."

He glanced at Anya, who beamed with pride, and he felt a comforting warmth blooming in the depths of his heart. This was not just about survival; it was about reimagining life in the aftermath of turmoil, embracing every scar left behind as part of a story waiting to be rewritten.

With renewed determination, Jack vowed to help them create a safe haven, where memories of loss transformed into respect for resilience. Their journey would not be easy, but as long as they held on to each other, they would rise—not just as victors over the darkness they had faced but as individuals molded by hope and love.

As the stars twinkled above them, a gentle breeze rustled through the trees, whispering promises of brighter days ahead. Jack knew there would be work to do—building trust, healing wounds, and facing the past—but they were ready to confront it all together.

Both Jack and Anya caught each other's gaze, sharing a moment of understanding beyond words, a silent agreement. They had emerged from the shadows as partners, friends, and perhaps something more.

The scars would remain, reminders of their journey, but they were determined to stand against whatever storm might come next with strength and unity.

With hearts full of hope, they returned to their cottage, not as mere survivors but as architects of their own futures—ready to embrace every sunrise, every challenge, and every laugh that awaited them in the days to come. And as they settled into their new reality, Jack couldn't help but think that even in the darkest nights, the stars would always shine brighter in the wake of a fierce storm.

A New Dawn

Healing Wounds

Anya stood by the window, the morning sunlight pouring through the glass and casting a warm glow across the modest kitchen. For the first time in months, the air felt charged with a sense of possibility, the remnants of yesterday's storms slowly clearing. She watched as her children, Daryna and little Oleg, played in the garden outside, their laughter ringing out like music. It was a sound she had almost forgotten—joy unfettered by fear.

"Look, Mama! I can jump higher!" Daryna shouted, her dark hair flaring out behind her as she leaped, arms outstretched. Oleg, not to be outdone, clapped his hands and giggled, mimicking his sister with all the enthusiasm a five-year-old could muster. Anya couldn't help but smile; their resilience was a balm to her aching heart.

The scars from their past were still fresh, the memories of chaos and uncertainty lurking just beneath the surface. But as Anya embarked on this new chapter of their lives, she remained determined to cultivate an environment filled with safety and love. The small cottage nestled in the heart of the English countryside had become a sanctuary for her—an oasis where healing could begin.

Each morning, Anya prepared breakfast with newfound zeal. The kitchen, once bare and uninviting, now brimmed with the aroma of freshly baked bread. She had spent hours experimenting with recipes, hoping to infuse her children's lives with the flavors of home. Today, she had made pancakes sprinkled with cinnamon and topped with sweet berry compote. Daryna had always adored pancakes, and Anya was eager to see her little girl's smile when she seen the breakfast spread.

"Time for breakfast!" Anya called, her voice carving through the gentle morning stillness. The children hurried inside, their cheeks flushed with excitement, and settled at the table.

"Did you see me jump, Mama?" Daryna asked, her blue eyes sparkling.

"I did, my sunshine! You were brilliant!" Anya replied, her heart swelling with pride as she watched her daughter devour the pancakes with delight.

As they sat together, the cottage filled with laughter and the warmth of togetherness. It was a world far removed from the uncertainty of their previous life. Anya found comfort in these moments, grasping at the normalcy they had been stripped of for so long. She watched as Daryna animatedly described the games they would play later that afternoon, her voice imbued with a joy that melted away the echoes of their past hardships.

After breakfast, Anya decided it was time to venture into the nearby village—a small but vibrant community that felt welcoming and alive. Jack had encouraged her to explore, insisting it would help her find a sense of belonging in this new land. The thought both thrilled and terrified her. Stepping outside of the security Jack's presence provided felt monumental, yet she yearned to experience the world beyond their garden.

"We can visit the market!" Anya announced, feeling her heart race. Oleg squealed with delight, while Daryna expressed her enthusiasm for discovering new places.

"Will we find strawberries, Mama? I want to make a pie!" she exclaimed, her excitement contagious.

"Yes, strawberries! And maybe we'll find some flowers to bring home as well," Anya replied, her confidence growing. She picked up her coat and ushered the children outside, feeling the cool breeze against her skin.

The village was a short walk from their cottage, framed by rolling hills and lush greenery. As they made their way along the winding path, Anya took in the sights—the quaint houses with colorful flowerboxes, the scent of freshly cut grass mingling in the air, and the distant sound of laughter spilling from a nearby playground. It filled her with hope, a soothing balm for the ache deep within her heart.

Upon arriving at the village square, Anya was greeted by the vibrant pulse of life. Market stalls lined the cobblestone streets, each one bursting with fresh produce, handmade crafts, and delightful scents that wafted from nearby cafés. Anya felt as if she had stepped into a new world, one filled with the potential to create special memories.

"Look, Mama!" Daryna tugged at her sleeve, pointing excitedly at a stall overflowing with strawberries. "Can we get some?"

"Yes, let's!" Anya replied, filled with a sense of purpose as they approached the vendor. The elderly woman behind the stall greeted them with a warm smile, and Anya felt a flicker of comfort at the warmth emanating from this kind stranger.

"Freshly picked this morning," the woman said, her voice full of cheer. "Best in the village, I assure you."

Anya picked up a basket, inspecting the bright red strawberries. They looked plump and juicy, the kind of fruit that beckoned promises of sweetness. She exchanged a few coins for the berries and watched as Daryna clutched the container to her chest, her face radiant with delight.

As they meandered through the market, Oleg was drawn to an artist creating whimsical paintings on an easel. The vibrant colors and playful strokes fascinated him; he tugged at Anya's arm, urging her to stop.

"Mama, can I have a picture like that?" He pointed, eyes wide with wonder.

Anya approached the artist, who grinned and invited Oleg to try his hand at painting. She felt a surge of warmth as she watched her son pick up a brush, his focus unwavering as he mimicked the brushstrokes of the artist. It was a moment of pure joy—a glimpse of the carefree childhood Anya had yearned to protect.

"Bravo, Oleg!" she cheered as he stepped back, proud of his colorful masterpiece, capturing the essence of their day—a world that was brightening, piece by piece.

After exploring the market, they returned home, the weight of their purchases shifted into the joy that filled the small cottage. Daryna insisted on making a pie with the strawberries, her excitement palpable. Anya's heart swelled as she watched her daughter deftly mixing the ingredients, Oleg bouncing around, stacked up with flour—his face dusted white like a little chef.

In the midst of the chaos, Anya took a step back, allowing herself to breathe deeply. This was healing; this was life. They were creating memories that would flourish in a place that was beginning to feel like home.

That evening, as they sat around the table enjoying the warm strawberry pie, Anya reflected on the journey that had led them here. It had been fraught with fear, loss, and uncertainty, yet amidst that chaos, they had found snippets of joy. Memories of fleeing their home in Ukraine, the panic of escaping, had begun to ebb. She was learning to let the past exist without allowing it to consume her present.

"Tell me a story, Mama!" Daryna chimed, her eyes wide with anticipation.

Anya's heart fluttered. She began to tell them tales from her own childhood, stories of adventure and laughter that echoed through the years. Bit by bit, she shared fragments of her life before the war, painting pictures of sunlit days filled with laughter and friendship.

Daryna listened intently, absorbing every word, while Oleg fought exhaustion, his eyelids fluttering as he tried to stay awake.

With each recollection, Anya felt as though she was weaving a safety net for her children—a framework of love that would help them heal. She saw in her daughters' eyes the spark of imagination ignited by her stories, a testament to the resilience of their spirits.

Later that night, after tucking her children into bed, Anya sat at the kitchen table watching the candles flicker softly. The gentle glow held a promise of peace, a respite from the madness of the world outside. She felt a profound transformation within herself, the slow unfurling of her heart from the tight grip of fear.

Her thoughts turned to Jack. He had become a constant in their lives, a steadfast presence who supported them unconditionally. She was grateful for his quiet strength, the way he encouraged her to be brave and step outside her comfort zone. He had opened doors they never knew could exist, guiding them toward a brighter future.

In the mornings, she would catch glimpses of him tending to the garden, his hands working the earth, planting seeds of hope. The flowers that bloomed were a reflection of their journey—a path toward healing that unfolded slowly, petal by petal.

As the days turned into weeks, their routine became a balm—taking weekend outings to explore the surrounding countryside and visiting parks where laughter echoed. Anya noticed her children beginning to flourish in this new environment, their spirits rising with each passing day.

The colors seemed brighter, the air fresher; the lives of those in the village intertwined with theirs, and they felt the genuine warmth of belonging wash over them.

One sunny afternoon, Anya gathered her children and took them to the local playground. Daryna and Oleg rushed off to make friends, leaving Anya sitting under a sprawling oak tree, her heart full. She watched the children playing, their laughter intermingling with the joyful shouts of others around her. It felt surreal; this small slice of normalcy felt vital.

With a book nestled in her lap, Anya gazed around, absorbing the scene—parents chatting, children laughing, communities thriving. It was a world thriving with life, one that filled her with hope.

Slowly, she began to connect with other parents, discussing everything from gardening to children's games, finding solidarity in shared experiences. She never imagined she would forge bonds outside her own culture, yet here she was—opening her heart to friendship, acknowledging that she was no longer an outsider looking in.

Every day was a new opportunity—she began volunteering at the local school, assisting with language classes for new arrivals like herself. She understood the weight of being displaced and the fortitude it took to rebuild. In helping others find their footing, Anya found her own.

The weight of trauma still weighed on her, a ghost lurking in the corners of her mind, but it had lessened. She learned to navigate those feelings with grace, understanding that healing was not linear; it was a tapestry woven with moments of joy and sorrow.

In next few weeks, Daryna suddenly excitedly suggested that they host a small gathering for their new friends in the village—a potluck where everyone could bring their favorite dish. Anya hesitated at first, her insecurities creeping in, but then she saw the sparkle in Daryna's eyes, the hope that blossomed there.

"Okay, sweetheart, we'll do it," Anya finally relented, feeling a surge of joy as she kissed Daryna's forehead.

The preparations began with an air of excitement, Daryna crafting invitations and Oleg helping by decorating them with crayons. The kitchen buzzed with activity as Anya prepared the dishes that marked her heritage, drawing from flavors familiar yet woven anew into every dish.

On the day of the gathering, Anya watched as the cottage filled with laughter and warmth, as neighbors brought their contributions, each dish telling a story—spicy stews, freshly baked bread, sweet desserts—and they shared recipes and anecdotes, laughter filling every corner of the room.

In that moment, Anya reveled not only in the celebration of cultural exchange but in the warmth of connections being forged. Together they were building a community, and the barriers that had once felt insurmountable were slowly dissolving.

Serving her potato pancakes, Anya reflected on the significance of that evening. Each smile exchanged, every shared experience—a mark of healing, a step toward belonging. For every kind word, every joyful moment, the wounds of the past began to close, replaced by a scar of resilience.

In the weeks that followed, the healing unfolded, finding form each day in small gestures of love, in shared laughter, and forgiveness toward themselves for the burdens they carried. The children thrived, painting new colors in their lives, and Anya found not just solace but a deeper strength bolstered by the connections that blossomed around them.

As the cottage garden bloomed under the sun, so too did Anya's spirit. Each petal that unfurled, each leaf that danced in the wind echoed with promise—a reminder that even amidst the shadows they emerged from, there flowed the light of hope.

Reflections of what once was faded like echoes, allowing room for what was to come—an embrace of belonging, warmth of community, and above all, an unyielding love that would guide them onward in this journey of healing, together.

Jack's Redemption

Jack stood at the kitchen sink, warm sunlight pouring through the window, casting a golden hue upon the breakfast dishes he scrubbed with meticulous care. The rhythmic clink of plates and the gentle sound of water splashing seemed to echo the peaceful morning outside. Birds chirped merrily in the trees, and a light breeze rustled the leaves, reminding him of the simplicity he had long yearned for in his retirement. Yet, amidst the tranquility, Jack's heart brimmed with something new—purpose.

In the past, he had often found pride in his intelligence work, the thrill of the chase, and the satisfaction of unraveling threats to the nation. Yet, after his retirement from MI6, that sense of significance had waned, replaced by a creeping sense of losing his place in the world. He had buried himself in books, gardening, and solitary routines that had filled the emptiness left by a career filled with danger and choice. But now, as he stood washing dishes for Anya and her children, he began to understand the deep-rooted fulfillment that came from pouring his energy into others.

A soft voice snapped him from his thoughts. "Jack?" Anya entered the kitchen, her dark hair pulled back into a loose bun, and a flicker of uncertainty in her eyes. She held a large bowl filled with fresh fruit her children had helped pick from the garden.

"Good morning, Anya," he replied, turning to face her fully, feeling the warmth of a connection that had grown over the last several months. "That looks delightful."

"Thank you. They wanted to help this morning." Anya's eyes sparkled as she nodded toward the bowl. "They've been so excited about the strawberries."

Jack couldn't suppress a smile as he recalled how Misha and Katya, with their innocent laughter, had filled the house with energy. Their spirit reminded him of what it felt like to have a family. "Let's wash them up together, shall we?"

The sweetness of camaraderie enveloped them as the two worked side by side, washing the strawberries while the children played in the garden. Anya looked at Jack with a blend of gratitude and admiration that melted away the walls of formality he had built around himself. She had stepped into his life when he had been wandering through the shadows of his past, and now she illuminated his present with her unwavering strength and resilience.

"I wanted to thank you, really," she said softly, her voice almost a whisper, but with sincerity that rang clear in the air. "You've done so much for us, Jack. The kids... they're thriving here. I can see it in their smiles."

"It's nothing, really. Having you all here has reawakened something in me," Jack found himself saying. It surprised him just how true those words sounded. Initially, he had merely wanted to assist a family in distress, but now, it felt as though Anya and her children had breathed new life into him.

Anya paused, her expression shifting to one of curiosity. "What do you mean?"

Jack rinsed a few more strawberries, searching for the right words, a minor shift in the tide of his memories rushing to his forefront. "I spent years chasing after threats, dealing with shadows, living in a world of secrets and lies. I thought that was how I'd find meaning. But in doing so, I lost sight of the simple joys, the connections that matter."

Anya listened intently, nodding with understanding as she leaned against the counter, her eyes never leaving his. "It's easy to lose ourselves," she affirmed. "I lost so much back in Ukraine. My life... my home—it feels like it was taken from me, piece by piece. But here, with you, I feel like I am rebuilding. Every image of normalcy gives me hope."

Jack's heart thudded a little harder as he grasped the threads of companionship binding them together. She wasn't merely a refugee in his home; she was a co-architect of their shared humanity, echoing the very understandings he had buried in the depths of his experience. "Maybe it's a chance for both of us," he replied, his resolve deepening.

"But what can we do? Just surviving seems challenging enough," Anya said, a flicker of vulnerability appearing. Jack recognized that phrase. It was similar to sentiments he heard when he was deep in espionage. It revealed the very real struggles people discuss in hushed tones, the whispered fears that claw at their hearts.

"We survive, and then we inspire," Jack answered, his voice firm, surprising even himself with the conviction behind it. "I know from my past that there are always shadows where there's light. And occasionally, one finds a way to take those shadows and turn them into something... something meaningful."

Anya raised an eyebrow, intrigue glimmering in her gaze. "You mean to help others combat their own shadows?"

"Yes, exactly that. People like you, who have been through the unthinkable, can be a guiding light for others facing despair. You have already made such an incredible impact with the children. Your love and nurturing spirit are the foundations they will stand on as they grow up."

A moment of silence passed, and Jack could almost see the wheels turning in Anya's mind. "Perhaps we should start with those in our community. Most of them don't know much about our situation. They don't understand what it means to leave everything behind in search of hope."

Jack nodded, picturing small community gatherings, informal meet-ups, and perhaps informal classes. Discussions on culture, sharing food, weaving stories that provided insights for those still grappling with the stigma of refugees, and those who simply desired to open their hearts.

"Yes, we could host some evenings. Share food, stories, crafts." Anya said, excitement bubbling in her words. "There are so many

Ukrainians in the area—families just like ours. They are trying to find normalcy too."

"And perhaps we welcome the locals to learn alongside us," Jack added. "Encouraging them to ask questions, to understand your culture and your history."

Anya was staring at him now, a soft smile slowly forming. "You make it sound so easy."

"It might not be easy, but it has potential—an opportunity for a genuine exchange," Jack replied with a grin. "The very essence of survival and hope."

As the conversation flowed, Jack discovered that the walls he had unknowingly erected began to crumble. He celebrated Anya's ideas and the resolve etched across her face—a flicker of fire igniting within her, something he had once identified solely through the lens of espionage and national duty. But this was different; it was personal, it was real, and it was born from loss and love.

Over the next weeks, they collaborated on organizing their first gathering: a Ukrainian themed evening dedicated to sharing culture and food. Jack diligently assisted in gathering resources and disseminating the flyers throughout the village, determined to break free from the inertia that had once restricted him.

As the day approached, he could feel the butterflies flitting in his stomach, a stark reminder of the uncertainty that had characterized so many operations in his past. But this endeavor pulled at something deeper within him, something raw and magnificent—an instinct to battle against despair and forge meaningful connections.

On the evening of their first gathering, the gentle smell of borscht wafted through Jack's home, mingling with the aroma of fresh bread and pastries prepared by Anya and her children. The dining table was beautifully set, adorned with vibrant flowers and a colorful array of dishes that told stories from their homeland.

Jack stood near the door, peering out into the twilight, anticipation thrumming in his veins. He could see groups beginning to form on the street, some uncertain, others filled with curiosity. The mix of locals and Ukrainian families arriving brought with it a sense of camaraderie akin to a mission briefing before a high-stakes operation.

"Jack!" Anya's voice pulled him from his reverie as she approached him, her face alight with excitement. "Look at everyone! They're coming to see."

"They are," Jack replied, the warmth in his chest swelling. "And this is just the first step."

As the evening unfolded, Jack felt his initial apprehension vanish amidst laughter, chatter, and the sound of chairs scraping against the floor. He and Anya shared stories and dishes, introducing their neighbors to various Ukrainian customs while simultaneously absorbing the joy that flooded into their home.

A resident named Martha, a retired teacher, voiced her surprise at the stories of resilience shared by Anya. "You've endured so much, yet your spirit shines through," Martha said, her voice laced with admiration. "This evening brings hope to those of us who have often forgotten how to look beyond our routines."

Jack watched as Anya responded to Martha's praise, grateful yet humble. "No one truly knows the strength within them until it is tested," she shared. "In these moments of darkness, we find a light in one another."

As the evening continued, something within Jack transformed. He watched as Anya blossomed, her laughter lighting up the room and her vulnerability encouraging the others to open up. He realized he had not just offered her a roof over her head—he had given her a platform from which to rebuild and reshape her identity. In turn, he was finding his own sense of purpose through her journey.

Before long, he felt himself drawn into conversations, sharing his past not with a cloak of secrecy, but as a testament to human connection. His eyes sparked with new fire, and he began to see the echoes of his former life not as burdens but as lessons from which to draw strength. He didn't shy away from acknowledging scars, knowing they were proof of survival and resistance.

As the gathering began to fade into spirited conversations and laughter, Jack found Anya standing by the window, looking outward. He joined her and handed her a glass of wine. "You did well tonight."

Anya glanced at him, and her eyes glimmered with unshed tears, but there was an undeniable resilience that shone through her frailty. "No, Jack. We did this together. I couldn't have imagined this without your support."

In that moment, Jack realized he had been seeking redemption in the lives he had saved and the secrets he had unraveled as a spy. But his true redemption lay within the very act of coming together—of allowing others to dictate their own narratives while contributing to their journey towards healing and hope.

"You have shown me the importance of showing up for one another," Jack acknowledged, emotion woven through his words. "I always believed the weight of my work defined me, but tonight, witnessing your spirit, I found new meaning. I understand more than ever now that sometimes, the simplest gestures—sharing a meal, a story, a listening ear—carry the greatest significance."

Anya turned to him, her heart visibly moved by the gravity of his realization. "You have found your way, Jack. We all have. It's about brave choices, leaving silver linings behind, and carrying one another through the darkness."

And in that instant, Jack knew the essence of their budding partnership had evolved from mere survival into a tumultuous journey of rebirth. They were no longer two disparate souls caught in an ocean of despair; they were allies pooling their strengths, echoes of resilience woven into the fabric of their everyday lives.

As they stood side by side, contemplating the journey ahead, Jack understood that the shadows that had haunted him were not insurmountable. They were merely stepping stones, guiding him toward the light—forged through compassion and connection, nurtured within the stronghold of shared humanity.

The following weeks saw their small gatherings grow, evolving into a community bond that flourished under the umbrella of shared experiences. Jack felt invigorated, filled with newfound energy that rose from the connecting spirits of myriad individuals, each threaded into their own tale of survival.

He marveled at the serendipity of it all: that a retired MI6 officer had found his footing through the strength of a Ukrainian mother and her children. Her bravery ignited something within him that had lain dormant, and in return, he provided an anchor and support system that she desperately sought.

Jack's redemption may not have come in the form of spectacular espionage victories but through the simple act of offering hope—a reminder that new chapters could emerge from even the most painful scenarios. Together, they crafted their stories filled with strength and love, drawing courage from one another.

As the sun set on yet another day, wrapping the world in a warm glow, Jack felt a sense of peace wrap around him. He was no longer merely a caretaker respiting from a lifetime of shadows. He was a mentor, a friend, and perhaps most importantly, a family to Anya and her children.

In their laughter, in their shared meals, in the stories woven between their lives, Jack discovered that redemption was not a destination—it was a journey. And on that journey, together, he and Anya could navigate the unknown. Together, he and Anya would continue to conquer darkness.

A Brighter Future

Anya stood by the window, the morning sun casting a golden light across the room. It was a new day, and for the first time in what felt like an eternity, she felt as if she could breathe without the weight of fear pressing on her chest. The children were still asleep, their peaceful faces betraying none of the turmoil they had endured. She smiled softly, a warmth blossoming in her chest, and turned her gaze to the garden that Jack had nurtured with such care.

The flowers were blooming vibrantly, the colors bright against the pale blue sky. Each petal seemed to tell a story—of endurance, of hope, of resilience in the face of hardships. Just like her. Just like Jack. Anya recalled the first few days after fleeing Ukraine, the uncertainty, the palpable fear that had accompanied her every thought. She had often wondered if they'd ever find solace again, if they could piece together a semblance of normalcy amidst the chaos and despair.

Jack had been an anomaly in her life, a stranger who opened his home and heart to her in her time of need. His quiet strength had been a steady presence, guiding her through each day. They had forged an unspoken bond, something powerful and raw, born from shared experiences and unwavering support. And now, standing in this sunlit room, she felt the first stirrings of hope.

"What will today bring?" she wondered aloud, her voice barely a whisper in the stillness.

As if in response, the sound of tiny feet pattered down the hallway, followed by the unmistakable giggles of her children waking up to a new day. Their laughter was like a salve, soothing the deep-seated worries within her heart. They were becoming accustomed to their new life in England, the strange yet beautiful land that had become their refuge. She had watched them soak in their surroundings, learning the language, making friends, and discovering joy in the little things.

"Мама!" Dmytro and Sofia rushed into the room, their hair tousled, eyes sparkling with excitement. Anya's heart swelled at the sight of them. Despite everything, they managed to find happiness.

"Good morning, my brave ones," she greeted them, pulling them into her embrace. "Are you ready for today's adventure?"

"Can we visit the park again?" Dmytro asked, his eyes wide with anticipation. "The one with the big swings!"

"Yes! And maybe we can bring a picnic," Sofia chimed in, her voice chiming with enthusiasm.

Anya exchanged a glance with Jack, who had just entered the room, leaning against the doorway with a warm smile. He was a constant, solid presence in her life, and she could already feel the promise of wonderful moments ahead. The shared experiences of the past months had tethered them together like threads woven into a fabric too strong to break.

"Why not?" Jack replied, his deep voice a comforting melody. "Let's make it a proper outing. I'll pack the sandwiches." He strode toward the kitchen with a purpose, calling back over his shoulder, "And I'll be sure to include your favorite, Dmytro."

The children erupted into cheers, and Anya felt a spark of gratitude bloom within her. The simple joys—picnics in the park, laughter swirling in the air—were treasures she had longed for during those dark days of uncertainty. Moments like this reminded her of the strength of the human spirit, the ability to find light even in the darkest corners of life.

With each passing day, Anya became more attuned to the nuances of her new life. She embraced the culture and the language, her accent slowly sharpening with practice. Conversations that had once seemed daunting became delightful exchanges, and each successful interaction amplified her confidence. The community that had welcomed her was supportive, and she often found herself sharing stories over tea with neighbors who had become friends. They listened intently to her tales, rendering her fears into mere shadows of the past.

As the day unfolded, they made their way to the park, picnic basket in hand, laughter echoing, love radiating from each step they took together. The sun danced on their faces, and Anya couldn't help but pause to observe the world around her. Children played on swings and slides, parents tuned in to their joy, while couples strolled hand in hand, basking in the warmth of community and companionship.

"Look, Mama! The swings!" Dmytro exclaimed, breaking Anya from her reverie. She watched as the children darted toward the playground, their laughter ringing like sweet chimes, filling the air with innocence and exuberance.

"Just be careful!" she called out, even as she began to set up their picnic spot beneath the sprawling branches of an oak tree. Jack joined her, unfolding the blanket thoughtfully laid out on the grass.

"You've taken on the role of a mother, a protector, and a warrior, Anya," Jack commented softly, observing her as she prepared the picnic. "But you need to remember—you're also allowed to enjoy this life."

Anya glanced at him, her heart swelling at the sincerity in his voice. "I'm trying," she admitted, her fingers brushing the edges of the fabric as she laid it flat. "I just don't want to take anything for granted. Not after everything we've been through."

"No one is asking you to," he replied, his blue eyes holding hers with a gentle intensity. "But life will not wait for us to let go of our burdens. We have to carve out joy, no matter how small, each day we have together."

Their eyes met, and in that moment, an understanding passed between them—a silent promise of shared strength, of fighting for this life they were creating together. The past would never truly fade, but it need not dictate the future.

As they settled down for lunch, the atmosphere around them felt imbued with possibility. The children gobbled their sandwiches, their laughter mingling with the distant sounds of playful squeals and joyful chatter. Anya watched them, a sense of warmth enveloping her as she recalled how far they had come from their life in Ukraine.

They had journeyed through the valley of despair and emerged into a new landscape filled with hope. The dreams she had nurtured as a girl began to take shape once more. She imagined a home filled with laughter, with warmth echoing through the halls—a place where her children would thrive, where they would feel safe.

"Jack," she said, breaking the comfortable silence that enveloped them, "I've been thinking. Maybe I should look for a job soon."

"That's a great idea," he encouraged, stuffing a piece of his sandwich into his mouth. "What do you have in mind?"

"I could help in a café or a restaurant. Something where I can interact with people," she said slowly, pondering her aspirations. "I want to contribute and be a part of this community, to give back in some way."

Jack nodded, pride evident in his expression. "You have so much to offer, Anya. You're resilient, warm, and you have a spirit that draws people in. Whatever path you decide to take, I have no doubt you'll succeed."

"Thank you," she breathed, the sincerity of his words filling her with determination. She pictured herself engaging with the local café patrons, continuing to build her language skills, and contributing to her new life in ways that would help her feel rooted.

Conversations flowed easily, filled with laughter, shared aspirations, and even dreams for the kids' futures—desires that had seemed unattainable just months before. The weight of their past experiences was still present, but it transformed, no longer an anchor but a foundation upon which they could build.

Later that afternoon, as the sun began its slow descent, painting the sky in hues of orange and pink, Anya and Jack strolled arm in arm, Dmytro and Sofia running ahead, their playful spirits a dazzling beacon of life in bloom.

"I never thought I could feel happy again," Anya confessed, her voice barely above a whisper. "There's still a part of me that holds onto fear and anxiety, but... I'm learning to let it go."

Jack turned to her, his expression unwavering, his hand squeezing hers gently. "It's okay to feel that way. Healing is not a straight line; it's filled with ups and downs. But just remember—clarity and joy will always return if we allow ourselves to embrace them."

She tilted her head to meet his gaze, the sincerity in his voice resonating within her. "You've been a constant source of support, Jack. I can't thank you enough for being there for me, for us."

An understanding passed between them, transcending the need for words. They walked in a comfortable silence, the weight of the world lifted, replaced with a sense of hope.

The days that followed were filled with simple joys—shopping at the local market where familiar sounds of laughter blended with the rich aromas of fresh produce. Anya picked up new words and phrases, the language becoming less foreign with every passing conversation. Each day, she felt more grounded in this new existence.

She sought out volunteer opportunities in the community, eager to engage and offer a helping hand. There was a local charity dedicated to helping immigrants settle into new lives, and it felt like a natural fit for her to share her experiences and connect with others undergoing similar transitions.

Slowly but surely, Anya began to see life from a new lens. It wasn't just about survival anymore; it was about creation. Crafting a home, forming new relationships, discovering joy in the little things—these became her aspirations, and each day she worked toward them with quiet determination.

One evening, as dusk settled outside and the golden light flickered through the window, Anya sat with the children at the kitchen table, working on their homework. Jack had insisted on making their favorite borscht for dinner, and the aroma wafted through the air, a comforting reminder of her roots.

"Mama, what's this word?" Dmytro asked, holding up a paper with an English word he struggled to pronounce.

It struck Anya how quickly her children were adapting and learning. "It's 'ocean,' my love. Can you say it with me?"

His small face scrunched up in concentration, but as he repeated it after her—"ocean"—a grin erupted across his face.

"Good job, Dmytro!" Sofia cheered, her clapping hands causing her brother to giggle, and Anya felt a wave of pride wash over her. They were learning, growing, becoming a part of their new world.

Finally, as the day ebbed into evening, Anya and Jack sat side by side in the dim light of the living room, the children tucked away in their beds. They shared stories, laughing softly, both reveling in the warmth of their newfound reality.

"We've come a long way," she said after a moment of silence, her voice thick with emotion.

Jack turned, a smile gracing his features. "We have. And I believe we're only just beginning."

The weight of their journeys, the highs and lows they had traversed together, lent their words a weightiness that was both comforting and profound. "I want to keep building. To keep evolving and finding new paths forward."

"Yes," he agreed, his gaze fixed on hers, full of understanding. "It's not just about you or me anymore; it's about all of us."

He reached for her hand and held it between them, both of them aware of the invisible string binding them together.

"In this new life, we can weave a tapestry of new beginnings," he said softly, "with every decision we make, every step we take. Let's make it colorful."

Anya smiled, the promise of the future blooming in her heart. The journey ahead would undoubtedly have its challenges, but together, they had forged a bond capable of weathering any storm. With newfound resilience, they would continue navigating the beautiful complexities of life, hand in hand, ready to embrace whatever came their way.

In every glance exchanged and every word spoken, it was clear: joy could be reclaimed, and a brighter future awaited. Together, they would write their story and carry the essence of hope forth, inspiring others to find their own light amidst the shadows. As Anya stood on the threshold of a new dawn, she felt alive, ready to open herself to the echoing laughter of life surrounding her.

And as the night deepened and stars twinkled overhead, a profound sense of peace settled in. They were here, together—and that was enough. Together, they would take on the world.

From the Author

Dear Readers

Thank you for joining me on this tumultuous ride through the intertwined lives of Jack, Anya, and the world of espionage that enveloped them. The story we've traversed together is not just an adventure; it's a heartfelt exploration of what it means to grapple with the complexities of exile, loyalty, and the shadows lurking just beyond our sight. I hope that you found yourself as captivated by their struggles as I was while writing their tale. Each character has a heartbeat that resonates with the real-world experiences of individuals caught in dire circumstances. The closing chapters shed light on the essence of hope and resilience, reminding us that even in our darkest moments, a flicker of courage can ignite a flame of possibility. As you turn the final pages, reflect on the richness of these narratives and the powerful motifs of trust and betrayal woven throughout. In a landscape riddled with uncertainty, I encourage you to take the message of resilience with you. Remember that we, like Jack and Anya, are all navigating our own complexities—each step filled with choices that can lead to healing or further heartache. It's my heartfelt wish that this story inspires conversations about the challenges of displacement and the intricacies of human connection. May it incite a sense of urgency to understand and support those who stand on the precipice, just as Anya did. It's time to remember that the line between trust and betrayal is often razor-thin, and we must cherish those moments of genuine connection when we find them. Now, as this chapter closes, I hope you feel invigorated, perhaps a little wiser, and certainly more attuned to the narratives surrounding us in the world today. Thank you for not just reading, but for embarking on this emotional journey alongside me. It has been a privilege to share these moments with you, and I hope that you carry the threads of Jack and Anya's stories in your heart, illuminating the shadows of the real world. Until we meet again in another tale filled with human experiences!

With all my best, my fellow explorers

Nick

Printed in Great Britain
by Amazon

455c1728-0b04-4a97-8fb3-79efa58d37a4R01